The Void

By Christine Bernard

Copyright 2019 Christine Bernard

ISBN 978-0-6399846-4-3 (ebook)
978-0-6399846-5-0 (print).

Cover Design by: Warren Bernard.
www.flatwhiteimages.com

Please note: This book is set in Australia, and, in order to retain authenticity, uses local spelling and slang. Words like colour, centre, and realise are therefore not spelling mistakes, but part of the language conventions of the country.

Dedication

This book is dedicated to Tyler.
Just like this book, he was made in South Africa, but born in Australia.
And to Warren, my soul mate, for moving to another country with me and for
always being up for an adventure. Here's to the next chapter in our lives.

Prologue

Two down, three to go. I always knew they wouldn't last, but some had already surprised me more than others. I zoomed in on pod one, and increased the volume. The pods were interesting to me, each one in their own way, but I had a strong suspicion there would be only one winner at the end. The difference between the contestants was glaringly obvious, and with each passing minute their inner strengths were showing signs of depletion. I wasn't surprised. I'd already tried this challenge myself and failed dismally. I hadn't had the motivation for money, so I knew they'd last a little longer. Watching them unravel had been interesting, and for someone who had always been so against reality TV, I was now glued to the screens. I had barely slept since they'd been in. I could watch the tapes back whenever I wanted, but there was something far more exciting about events unfolding in real time, especially since some of them seemed so close to their breaking point. The fresh faces that had gone in at the start had changed far quicker than I had thought they would. They seemed to have aged inside, the lack of sleep and activity aging them at triple speed. I was already an old codger, so it was good I was on the outside looking in. As I watched, I wondered what would happen if I prolonged their stay without them knowing. It would make for good telly, wouldn't it? To see how much further they would push themselves, and to see what the mind was capable of. It would be fascinating. Was it legal? Probably not. I was already pushing the boundaries with this idea. Sure, there was no actual show yet, but that didn't matter. It would get snapped up after they saw the footage. I already had some incredible moments on film. And hey, if the show didn't get picked up, I'd just pay the contestants myself. What could go wrong?

I peered in again, switching over to pod three. As I did, a sudden pain shot through my arm, and my chest tightened almost instantaneously. I was old enough to have experienced many medical issues, but this was unlike anything I'd felt before. It felt as if someone was squeezing me, and I couldn't get out of their grip. I shut my eyes and drew several deep breaths to calm myself. When I opened my eyes again, I felt moderately better. The squeezing had eased to a slight embrace, as if an invisible man was holding me. I tried to shake him off. What the hell was that all about?

1

Ryan

I tried to explain to my father what I did for a living for the hundredth time, although I wasn't sure why I bothered. We were sitting in his living room, a place I abhorred, while my mother made tea for us. My parents were great—they were—but they seemed years behind the rest of the world.

"Dad," I said through gritted teeth, "I've already told you what I do. Anyway, what do you tell people when they ask you?"

He shrugged. "I tell them you're into computers."

I chuckled. "Dad! That's completely wrong. Is that why Uncle Pete asked me to fix his laptop the other day? That's not what I do."

"I know. I know. It's only what I tell them. I know what you do. You work on the Tube. I just don't really know what you do there."

"It's called YouTube, and I don't work on it. I upload videos to it. I'm a social media influencer. I show people the best products on the market. My latest video reached over a million viewers. Pretty impressive for a guy who works in computers, huh?" I smiled and turned to my mother, who had come in with a tray of tea. The tray rattled as she walked, and as she put it down, I noticed not all the cups were clean. I wiped mine with the edge of my sleeve when she wasn't looking. She'd always been so particular about cleanliness. "Thank you," I said to her. "Mum, you know what I do, don't you?"

"Sure, you get free stuff sent to you for reviews."

I sighed. She made it seem so trivial. "Well, yes, but that's not all I do. I have access to a huge audience. Companies come to me because they can trust me. It's actually a pretty big deal."

"I wish I got free stuff. I can make videos, too," my father said. I decided not to tell him he'd probably do quite well if he were to try this. There was something about my father that people gravitated toward. The things that irritated me most about him were the things other people found endearing.

"Don't listen to your father. I think what you're doing is fantastic. I'm very proud of you."

I changed the subject before I got too annoyed and listened to my parents talk about their weekend plans. A spot of gardening for my father, and a trip to the hairdresser for my mother. One plan each, and yet we spent the next hour discussing it in detail. My father liked to talk about his endless pursuit of weed removal, while my mother discussed different hairstyle options despite her continuing with the same style she'd had for thirty years. It was riveting stuff. I listened, or, at least, I pretended to, because despite wondering if I was adopted every time I saw them, they were my parents. It often felt as if we were from different planets, but they weren't bad people.

"Well, I better get going. I have a meeting to get to," I said the moment my father finished what felt like the longest story in the world. Who knew there were that many ways to get rid of weeds? I stood up, and the three of us made our way to the front door.

"You have meetings at Yute Tube?" he asked, and I resisted the urge to correct him. I was starting to think he might be having me on.

"Yes, we have meetings. Like I said, it's an actual job."

He nodded. "Well, see if you can get me some free herbicides for the garden."

"Dad, that's not how it works." I groaned. "It's...oh, you know what, never mind. I better get going. Thanks for the tea, Mum. I'll see you both next week."

"Sure you don't want to stay for something to eat?"

"No, I have to head off."

There was no meeting to go to, and I felt a little bad at the deception, but I was tired of my parents thinking I didn't have a real job. I knew the word 'meeting' would resonate with my old-fashioned father. Perhaps I'd even throw in the word 'payday' next time. Not that I really knew what that was either. I'd never had a proper job, and I cringed as the thought crossed my mind. This *was* a proper job. I was falling into my father's ways. I couldn't help myself. It always happened when I spent too much time with him. It was why I only visited once a week for tea. I did quite well for myself, and for the most part I was generally proud I'd managed to snub the system my father had complained about his whole life. Was that why he pretended not to know what I did? Was he just jealous? Whatever the reason, I needed to go home and unwind. The visit had left me feeling strange, and I had no idea why.

Home was a fifty square meter apartment that the owner had advertised as *perfectly pocket-sized*. Despite this, the price tag was hefty, and my parents couldn't understand why anyone would choose to pay so much for a place so small. They had a grand home, but growing up in Waratah was enough time for me to know for sure it was *not* where I wanted to live forever. No matter how many times my parents stood up for their area with words like *safe, relaxing, quiet*, all I heard was *boring, boring, boring*. I might pay too much for my miniature apartment, but Newton was right in the heart of the city I loved so much. Better yet, I lived on top of a thriving café, where I was served free coffee every day. My father said it wasn't right I didn't pay for it, but he didn't know the effort I put in for these guys. I was almost certain my Instagram photos of their coffee had doubled their clientele.

It took me just over an hour and a half to get home, but I would wait before letting Mum know I had arrived. It should take me two hours, and she'd complain I was going too fast, which I probably was. I couldn't help myself. The roads were quiet on Sundays, and the urge to get home as fast as possible had surged me forward. I flopped onto, or more like *into,* my red beanbag and sighed in contentment. The beanbags were one of the reasons my parents rarely visited, and why I drove out to them once a week instead. My mother had barely been able to get off it the first time she'd visited, much to my father's amusement. For me they were the most comfortable faux-sofas in the world. They were also cheaper and took up less space than regular furniture would. However, when my phone rang, I was admittedly grateful it was still in my pocket. Getting off these things was a little time-consuming.

"Yo," I said once I saw the name of the person calling. Jon and I were worlds apart in personality, and I was sure we wouldn't hang out if our families weren't such good friends.

"You want to make some money?"

I chuckled. "Who doesn't?"

2

Jon

A torrent of rain came down, and I jumped up to close the sliding door of the balcony before rain poured in all over my cables. Every day I told myself to sort it out, but I never seemed to get around to it. Who had time for cable management anyway? I wished we could move our TV cabinet to another part of the room, but there wasn't space for it. Everything looked different before Keri moved in. Now we played a constant game of real-life Tetris, trying to see which items best fit in which space. She was always trying to get rid of stuff, or begging me to move further from the city, but I wasn't going to give in. I liked it here. Anyway, in a year or two I planned on having enough money to move somewhere nicer. As I closed the sliding door, I heard the front door open and breathed a sigh of relief that I was no longer on the phone to Ryan. Keri was going to freak when she found out what I had done.

"What the hell? Where did this rain come from?" she said as she closed the door behind her. As she approached me, she left a trail of water with every step. I decided not to say anything as I needed her on my good side at the moment, but it was hard not to bite. Keri's hair was the one thing I both loved and loathed about her. The big afro style suited her, and it turned heads whenever we went out. Hell, it had turned *my* head all those years ago. Now, I wasn't so sure about it. She had no idea she was dripping rain, mostly because it was coming from her hair, and for some reason this annoyed me.

I forced a smile. "From the sky perhaps?"

She groaned. "Ah, I didn't think of that. You're a pain, you know that? You should be nicer considering I came bearing gifts," she said as she held up a bag.

I wiggled my nose like a dog as she got nearer. "Chinese? I *am* lucky to have you." Thank goodness she wasn't going to cook again. She'd gotten it into her head recently that she wanted to learn how to cook *wholesome, happy and hearty* meals—her words—and most nights have consisted of me wolfing down toast after throwing away yet another failed attempt.

She leaned in to kiss me. "Good day?"

"Not bad. I had Ray the x-ray today," I said as I sat back down in the living room. She took a seat and rummaged through her bag for her comb. I'd once stuck it in her hair and spent an amusing hour watching her while she tried to find it.

"Don't call him that," she said. "Oh, my hair is soaking wet."

"Well, it *is* raining. Your hair is like a natural umbrella. And I'm not being mean about Ray, but I've never seen a guy so skinny. I gave him an eating plan today but I'm not sure it's going to help. Poor guy. Guess what size dumbbells he used today?"

She sighed. "I don't know. Does it matter?"

"Of course it matters, I'm his trainer. It's my job to make sure he gets stronger. Four kilograms. *Four!* Can you believe it? I tried to get him to go up to five, but he couldn't lift his arms up. It took everything I had not to laugh."

"You're his trainer, which is exactly why you shouldn't be mean. It's not as easy for some people as it is for others."

"It's not easy for me either. I work hard to get my body this way, and I'm sorry but dumbbells that light are not going to do much to the guy."

"Hey, *I* use the same size dumbbells," she said.

"First, *you* don't ever work out. Second, you're a girl."

She sighed, then got up and headed to the kitchen, where she poured us each a glass of wine without asking me if I wanted one. We'd had this argument before, but while I'd called it presumptuous, she'd called it being nice.

"He's trying. I think it's brave. Hell, now that I know how much you talk about your clients, I'll never go to a personal trainer ever again. I'd be mortified to know they talk about me when I'm not around. How are you going to cope without the gym for two weeks?" she asked as she handed me the glass.

"Do you seriously think I can't cope? Come on! It's two weeks."

"When last did you not go to the gym for two weeks?"

"Last year! When we went to Fiji."

She chuckled. "You used the gym at the hotel!"

"That doesn't count."

"Honestly, Jon, what are you going to do? You're going to go out of your mind."

"I don't need a gym to work out. I've got a whole plan of exercises to do that don't require gym equipment. Your boyfriend is not as daft as you seem to think he is. Anyway, I was thinking of maybe bringing in a kettlebell for my one item."

"You're joking, right?"

"No. Why not? It's a good idea. We're going to need something to do in there to keep us busy. I have the sickest workout based just on kettlebells."

"You want me to work out with you every day, that it?"

"Of course. It will be fun. We can time each other. See who does the best."

She stood up, then sat back down. In our small apartment that was the equivalent of pacing. "Jon, come on, that's not fair. We're only allowed one item between us. Why do you get to choose what it is?"

"Like you said, I'll go crazy without working out. Anyway, you know I only want to look good for you." I flashed her the old charmer, the nicknamed she'd fashioned for me when we'd first started dating. I'd lucked out in the genetic pool, and my smile was easily my best feature. We'd been dating for years already, but I was pretty sure I saw her face soften as I smiled at her.

"You're full of it," she said in a gentler tone.

"You love me, though," I teased.

"You drive me crazy."

"That's the same as love," I said.

She chuckled and shook her head. "Yes, I love you. Would you at least consider another item? It's only fair we discuss this."

"Yes, of course. It was only a suggestion." This wasn't entirely untrue. My other idea was the dumbbell. I couldn't figure out which one I'd want more. Anyway, Keri had been saying she wanted to start working out again, so I was only helping her. It was one of those things she'd probably hate me for at first, and thank me for later. Keri was one of those lucky people who didn't need to work out, but lately I'd noticed a bit of softness around her belly that could do with some tightening up.

"I was thinking more along the lines of a deck of cards," she said. "You know, it could be something we could do together."

I resisted the urge to laugh. It was what I had told Ryan to bring when he'd asked for ideas. I figured he'd end up listening to me, so I'd told him the most boring thing I could think of. I pretended to mull it over, then nodded. "Not a bad idea. Okay, let's give it some more thought before deciding. We'll make sure we bring something we both agree with." The trick with Keri was to always make it seem as if she was in control. Happy wife, happy life, and all that. Well, happy girlfriend, at least. Right now, we didn't discuss our future too much. I still felt too young to worry about it, and I was pretty sure Keri wasn't going anywhere.

She smiled. "Thank you."

"You see, I can be nice."

"You can. Okay, I'm starving. Let's eat. That smell is driving me crazy."

We sat in the living room, eating noodles straight out of the box, and watched some telly. I wasn't really watching, though. I kept thinking about the contract, and how crazy our life would be for a while. Keri was obviously thinking the same thing. She turned to me at the same moment that one of the main characters got shot in the chest, barely flinching as the actor she liked best fell to the ground.

"You nervous?" she asked me.

I smiled. Nervous wasn't the word I'd use. "No, I'm confident."

She laughed. "You always are."

<u>3</u>

Sarah

I hadn't been to the park in years. Quite strange really, considering there were so many around me. Although, some were more like green patches, too small to be considered parks. Must look pretty from above. Not that I would know. People often said I had my head in the clouds, but my feet have always been firmly on the ground. Literally, that is. I'd never left Victoria Point, and barely ever visited the city. "What was the *point?*" was what I always told other people. It was a funny joke, and how others reacted told me a lot about that person. Anyway, I was still young. I had plenty of time to see the world. Right now, I was happy where I was. My mom always told me I was an old soul. Perhaps she was right.

Going to the park was about as spontaneous as I got, and I was looking forward to it. I only worked the morning shift that day, so I had the whole afternoon to myself. I even packed a picnic, although my bag was mostly filled with things I ate every day. It was easy when you worked at a café, especially one known for their baked goods. I had packed an extra chocolate brownie today. Those were worth the extra calories. I'd walked here from work, which had taken much longer than I expected, and while the sunshine was nice, I wished I had remembered to bring a hat. I even had one sitting at the café, and I'd seen it in on my way out, but I'd thought a bit of sun would be good for me. I swear it had gotten hotter with each step I took. Now that I was here, the only thing I could think about was shade. I avoided the kids' play area completely. I liked kids, but only in small doses, and they went against the very reason I had come to the park. It was hard to find anywhere with shade that wasn't occupied, though—who knew the place was so popular—but I finally found a great wild fig tree to sit under. My mother said it was called a Moreton Bay fig tree—or some other fancy name I couldn't remember—but I never thought of it like that. Looking up at it now, I felt a longing to climb it. It was huge, and twisty, and it was hard to figure out where it stopped and started. Man alive, it was beautiful. Not only was I going to come to the park more often, but I would make sure to always visit this tree. I pulled out the blanket from my bag and sat down. I then spent the next few minutes arranging all my picnic goodies around me. I hadn't planned on coming here when I woke that morning, so everything I had was what I had grabbed from the café. Except for my book, which I always carried with me. I was currently making my way through all of Jane Austen's novels in the order she wrote them, and I was now on *Mansfield Park*. Seeing the title made me giggle. I was clearly meant to come to the park today. Gazing around at my little ensemble, I felt as if I was doing this picnic right. What had given me the idea to come here in the first place? Maybe it was Larry. I smiled as I thought of him.

I loved Larry. He was like a slightly off-beat, eccentric grandfather to me. I saw him most days, enough to have formed a slight bond with him. Our conversations didn't go much further than talking about the weather, or about the coffee and food he ordered, but he had been coming to the café for his breakfast for so long it was hard not to feel like I knew him well. He'd been there early this morning, and the two of us had spoken ever so briefly about things beyond our usual scope of chatter. It had happened straight after he'd ordered a second cup of coffee, and for a man who was so stuck on routine I'd been taken aback by the request. I had never been good at suppressing my feelings, so the surprise on my face must've been obvious.

"Am I that predictable I can't order another cup of coffee without rousing suspicion?" he'd asked.

"Yes." I couldn't help but be honest with him. I figured he was the sort of man who would appreciate that. "I've been serving you the same thing for years."

"Except that crazy day you didn't have eggs," he had pointed out.

"Don't remind me. Everything went wrong that day. So, another coffee, huh? Stepping out your comfort zone or somethin'? I was listenin' to a podcast on that just the other day. It's good to do that sometimes. They say life is all about finding that happy balance between routine and spontaneity." I'd become a podcast junkie these days, mostly to fill the time between customers at the café, and this one in particular had resonated with me, probably because I had a tendency to do the same thing all the time. Maybe that's why I had always felt such a kinship with Larry. He was the male version of me in fifty years. A stickler for routine.

"That's exactly right." He'd seemed delighted by my observation. "It's the sweet spot to the perfect life. Good for you for figuring it out at such a young age. Took me far too many years. So, today, I shall be spontaneous."

"That's great. I'm surprised you don't usually have two cups. The coffee here is great, don't you think?"

"I must agree. Did you know coffee releases neurotransmitters that are beneficial to the brain and the body? That's why you always feel so good after a cup."

I really did love Larry. His kookiness pleased me. "Neurotransmitters, huh? Wow, you've gone all Bill Nye on me. You know what, I'm going to have another cup too then. Hey, are you a scientist or something? I know you were a professor, but, I mean, on top of that." He sure *looked* like a scientist.

"I'm just a regular guy," He replied with genuine modesty. He was not an airs-and-graces sort of guy. Maybe that's why I liked him so much. Old souls didn't like people who spent too much time looking in the mirror.

"Nah, you're definitely better than regular."

I was so busy thinking about the conversation with Larry, that when I looked up and saw him walking with a group of people, I thought I had conjured him up. It didn't take me long to know it was really him, and not a wizardly figment of my imagination. His white hair glistened like a beacon, and I eagerly ran up to greet him.

4

Keri

Just before we got into the van, a woman came running up to us. She had pale skin, which made me wonder if she was from somewhere else, and small pink circles had appeared on her cheeks from the heat. You get two types of people in this world. You get those who look horrible when sweating, and those who shine from it. She glistened under the sun's rays, but she was so cute it was difficult to feel any bit of jealousy toward her. She may look of European descent, but the moment she spoke she was all Australian.

"Larry!" Her voice was as cheery as her demeanour. "I thought it was you. I see our talk about spontaneity wasn't in vain."

I looked to Larry, who seemed as if he'd seen a ghost. He pushed his glasses back up his nose and shuffled his feet as if he had been forced to do a solo dance in front of a crowd. "Oh, hi Sarah. Beaut of a day, hey?"

She beamed, and seemed completely unaware of his awkwardness. "It sure is. Fancy seeing you here on the one day I decide to go to the park." She looked around at all of us. "What's going on here?"

"Oh, well, it's…" Larry stumbled. The show was meant to be a secret. Some bureaucratic thing he'd explained to us that was out of his control. Apparently these sorts of shows could take up to a year to air, although he assured us we'd get our money much sooner.

"Ah, you're teachin' again, aren't ya?"

"A little," he replied.

"Well, I'll let you get on your way," she said. "Lovely meeting all of youse," she said even though Larry hadn't introduced us at all. There was nothing I hated more than the term youse, something I had desperately tried to get Jon to stop saying, but somehow, like the sweating, she made it look cute. By the way we were all hanging onto her every word, it was clear we all felt the same way. I'd been told I was likeable, but I was pretty sure I didn't stack up against this girl. Only Larry didn't seem to be as smitten. He was acting as if she was the last person in the world he wanted to see. "I'll see ya tomorrow, Larry," she said and frowned at him. She must've picked up on his attitude.

"Sure, Sarah. Uh, yes, tomorrow."

Jon raised his eyebrows at me and whispered, "That was weird," but I couldn't reply. If I did, I would end up saying something I shouldn't. I was still seething, and I couldn't imagine I'd looked all that friendly to the poor girl, but Jon had gripped my hand so tight I knew I couldn't say anything. We'd been sworn to secrecy, and there was no way Ryan just happened to find out about this thing, too. This meant that not only had Jon pushed him to apply, but he'd done so without my knowledge. Why? Just to see the surprise on my face? Just to avoid me arguing with him? If I didn't need the money so much I would've left and called the whole thing off, but I was desperate for it. My parents had already helped me so much, but it was time for me to make it on my own. It was just the sort of thing Jon would do, too. I wasn't sure if he had a reason, or if it was to prove once again that he could get poor Ryan to do whatever he wanted him to do. I loved Ryan, but he was always second guessing himself, and having Jon as his friend didn't help much. Jon said he was trying to toughen the guy up, and perhaps he was right, but I couldn't help but feel he should be a little gentler on him. Ryan was a sensitive soul, while Jon…I sighed…Jon was sensitive, too. Only nobody knew that but me, and even I had a hard time believing it at times. I tried to push everything aside, and concentrate on what was ahead. I still couldn't believe I was doing this.

We climbed into the van that had been waiting for us down the road, and Ryan gave me a wink. I rolled my eyes but chuckled despite my annoyance. Jon looked as if he was about to burst, like he always did when he was holding in a secret. I hoped he didn't say something and give the whole thing away. If we missed out on this opportunity because Jon couldn't keep his mouth shut, I'd never forgive him. Thankfully, Elton had opted to ride out in front with Larry and seemed to be keeping him entertained—not by choice—with a slew of jokes that seemed never ending. I could not understand how Jon found the guy funny. Then again, comedians had always annoyed more than they amused me.

I noticed the girl, Melanie she'd said her name was, gazing resolutely toward the front of the van, as if she didn't dare look at any of us and start a conversation. She was fascinating, and exactly the sort of person I'd want to photograph. People were my best subject matter, but I preferred ordinary people over the ones photographers usually went for. Not that Melanie wasn't pretty, because she was. The more I stared at her, the more beautiful she became. People like her always made the most interesting models. She sat so still now, so statue-like, and the complete opposite to the rest of the buffoons in the van. She seemed so at peace with herself, and didn't feel the need to fill the space with unnecessary chatter. If only I could be more like that.

"What's up with the black-out windows?" Jon said.

"For *secrecy*, I suppose." I directed the word to him.

"Or maybe," Jon continued, ignoring me. "Maybe *this* is the actual challenge. What if this is where we have to stay for two weeks. Together."

"Don't say that," Ryan gasped and wrinkled his nose. "Imagine how much this place would stink after two weeks."

"I'd rather not," I said. "Uh, so, uh, Ryan, you said your name was?" I inwardly groaned at my feeble attempts at acting.

Ryan sniggered. "Yeah. Ryan, and you're Keri?"

I nodded. "So, Ryan, are you nervous about this challenge? Think you're going to make the full two weeks?"

"Nah, I'll be fine. Two weeks is nothing. Told everyone I was going on a two-week retreat without signal so nobody worries when they don't hear from me. Imagine how much catching up I'm going to have to do when I get back."

"What are your poor followers going to do without you?" Jon smirked.

Ryan was about to retort but jumped when I gave them both a quick kick in the shins. Larry was driving, but I was pretty sure he could hear all of us speaking. These guys were going to ruin everything. I quickly turned my attention to Melanie.

"Melanie, are you excited? Nervous?"

She turned to me and smiled. Everything about her was slow and deliberate. She nodded. "A bit of both."

I thought about saying something more, but she didn't seem to be in the mood to talk. She didn't have to though, because the van came to a sudden halt causing all of us to shift quickly in our seats.

"Sorry about that," Larry called out. "I'm not used to driving this van. Good news, though. We're here."

When Larry opened up the door for us, and we all got out, I saw we were in a garage and that we were parked next to a beautiful blue vintage car. It was the sort of vehicle rich people kept but didn't drive, and I wondered if it was for another show being set here. The boys were swooning over it, and as Larry helped with the bags, he seemed proud, as if the car belonged to him. Perhaps it did. These TV guys probably earned a great deal. We stood a little too long while they spoke about the car, until Larry remembered we were there for another reason. He was a strange character, yet another type whom I'd want to photograph. His white hair would contrast beautifully against a dark background. He wasn't at all what I was expecting in a TV producer, although he'd mentioned something about being the creator of the show. Odd that he had come to fetch us, and not some crew member. Perhaps, as the creator, he wanted as much to do with the process as possible. He was strange, but interesting, and as we all followed him into the house, we exchanged amused glances at one another.

Once inside, Larry made us each sign documents, and once again I wondered where everyone was.

"Where's everyone?" Jon said.

"I'm preparing you for what's ahead," Larry said. Then he chuckled, as if he were remembering some old joke and shook his head. "Don't worry. The cameras are all set up inside. Okay, Elton, I'll take you in first."

Elton got up and bowed dramatically while we all clapped for him. It was Jon who had started the clapping, and we'd all dutifully followed suite. "See you all on the outside. Best of luck, hope you don't suck, and you two…" he said as he winked at Jon and I, "at least you've got each other to—" He stopped for effect, then wiggled his eyebrows up and down. "Oh, you know the rest."

Jon burst out laughing while I sat there dumbfounded. Did this guy really think he was funny? I could not believe Jon was laughing at something so revolting. I could still hear Elton chucking to himself as Larry led him away. Oh well, at least he'd keep himself entertained. If he was in there with me, I probably wouldn't have lasted half a day. When Larry came back, he looked like he felt the same as me.

"Right, Jon, Keri, if you'd like to follow me. I'll take you next."

I gulped. This was it. I turned to Ryan and Melanie, who both sat uncomfortably as they waited for their turn. Ryan looked as if he regretted his decision, while Melanie looked as she always did, calm and serene. She gave off the impression that she never looked anything else but this. Poor Ryan's face had scrunched up in distress, and he kept looking at the door as if he wanted to escape.

"Good luck you guys. Remember, it's only two weeks. We can do this," I said to them. Ryan simply nodded, his mind already elsewhere, and Melanie wished us luck, too. Then, with one last glance around, we followed Larry to the room.

"Larry," Ryan called out, and we all stopped to turn around. For a moment I thought that Ryan was going to tell him he couldn't go through with it. I tried to give him a look of encouragement. I hadn't expected him to be there but that didn't mean I wanted him to fail. I'd always had a soft spot for the guy. "What's the TV show going to be called?" he asked.

I breathed a sigh of relief. "Ooh, good question."

"Oh," Larry said in surprise. He seemed to have hit a blank as if he honestly had no idea what Ryan was talking about. Then he grinned. "*The Void*," he said.

The Void was an appropriate name for what we were about to experience, and as we stepped inside our new home for the next two weeks, I couldn't help but wonder why we had decided to do this. I wasn't sure what I had been expecting, but this small bit of space wasn't it. There wasn't much to it at all, and the walls seemed to close in on us the moment we were inside. I wondered if the low ceilings were on purpose.

"Holy shit. This is small." Jon had a knack of saying aloud whatever I was thinking, but in a way that made me wish I had said it first. He was honest to a fault at times. No matter how often I told him there were better ways of saying the same thing, he couldn't help himself. I hoped he hadn't offended Larry, but he seemed completely unfazed by the comment. Jon was right, after all. This place was tiny.

"Trust me, compared to jail, this is big," Larry said. "Which is where most people are when they're in solitary confinement. Don't worry. You'll be fine. At least you have each other."

I glanced at Jon and smiled. He smiled back. We were definitely on the same page with this one. I was grateful we were not doing this alone.

"There's not much to know other than what we already discussed over the phone. There's a camera there, and one over there," he said as he gestured to the cameras on the wall. "There's also one over here, which is your diary camera. I'd like you to use this whenever you want to talk to us and tell us how you're feeling. You can use it once a day, maybe before you go to sleep, or you can speak in it whenever you want. Remember, we are interested in the constant flux of your emotions so don't be afraid to speak into it. The only place we don't have a camera is in the bathroom area."

"Thank god for that," Jon said. "They're called private bits for a reason." Again, he'd spoken my truth. Again, he could do with a filter. I loved and loathed this part of his personality, depending on the situation. Larry didn't seem to be taking much notice of him. He looked like an excited child, desperate for this whole thing to start. I guess I didn't blame him. It would be way more fun sitting on his side of the wall.

"Lastly, even though you're here for two weeks, I've provided enough water for a month, so if you're thirsty you can definitely have more. There is also three weeks or so of food in the freezer in case you get hungrier on some days, but you can decide how to ration that yourselves. Once I close this door, the challenge will be begin. Please remember, if you want to leave at any time, all you have to do is press the buzzer. If you press it, your time is up, but you will not have completed the challenge." *And you will not get the money.* The rest of the sentence hung silently in the air.

"There's no clock," Jon pointed out.

"That's right. You'll be unaware of time while you're in here."

I frowned. "But how will we know when our two weeks is up?"

Larry smiled. "You won't. When you see the door open for the first time, *that's* when your time is up." He inhaled deeply. "And that's it, folks. Best of luck to both of you, and I hope you make the full challenge."

"Oh, we'll make it," Jon said. I smiled gratefully at him. If there was ever a time I needed his confidence, it was now.

The door closed, and I was surprised by the silence that engulfed us.

"Weirdo," Jon said and the sound bounced off the walls.

"Jon! There are cameras here," I said and hushed him.

He shrugged. "So what? What do you think of my cribs?" he said playfully. "How much time do you have? Let me give you the grand tour."

I laughed. "You are infuriating."

<u>5</u>

Ryan

The first thing I noticed was the silence. I had no idea it could be so loud. The next thing I noticed was the camera, then the other, and the other. I should be used to this considering the number of videos I posted each week, but this was different. This was…I struggled to think of the word. My brain felt hazy, as if a heavy fog had fallen on me. What *was* this feeling? *Think, dammit.* I shrugged, then went to sit on the bed yet again. I'd only been in the room a few hours. At least I *thought* it was a few hours, and already I seemed unable to figure out the simple task of sitting or standing. I sat, then felt an incredible urge to stand again. I lived on my own, so why was this so strange? I shifted back, so that I sat flush against the wall, and gazed around the room. Larry was calling this project, *The Void*, and I could easily understand why. It wasn't so much the boredom that was already getting to me, or the time confusion, but the silence. It screamed at me in a way that made me think I was going out of my mind. I had no idea silence could be so loud. I laughed, and the sound bounced off the walls. It didn't sound like it had come from me.

"You've got this," I whispered. "You've got this."

I would be fine. I was sure of it. I merely had to get used to the strangeness, that was all. Most things took at least a day or two to seem familiar, so all I needed to do was to get through it, bit by bit. I wondered how Jon and Keri were faring. A little unfair that the two of them got to do this thing together. Then again, Jon said if I didn't make the full two weeks, he'd give me a portion of his money, and I promised to do the same with him. So, it was nice to know we had some backup. This had been Jon's idea, and it seemed like a good one at the time. *I* was the stupid one to suggest we place a rule on it, that if someone gave up, they would only get the money if they lasted at least ten days. I'd only said that so Jon didn't give up after a day or two while I sat for two weeks alone to make us money. Maybe I'd been hasty with that rule. Considering I'd only been in here for a few hours, ten days suddenly seemed like a long time. Also, he had Keri. What did I have? I glanced around and caught sight of the small mirror by the bathroom. Myself, that's what I had. Right now, that wasn't comforting at all.

I was being silly. Everything was going to be fine. It was two weeks without having to worry about work. Without having to prove myself to my parents. Without wondering what I was doing with my life, something that happened far too often these days. Two weeks. I could do this. In fact, maybe it would be fun. I got up and fetched the pack of cards I'd chosen as my one item. There'd been a list of things we could not bring, but this was something Jon had suggested. He'd assured me he was bringing one too. I climbed back on the bed and played a game of Solitaire. It didn't take long, and I only won because I cheated. I played again, this time winning without fiddling with the cards. That's when I realised what a stupid move this had been. A pack of cards? What was I thinking? I wracked my brain for something other than Solitaire, but the only games I could think of were two-player games. Of course Jon was going to bring a deck of cards as his item. He had Keri to play with. He had hours of games to fill his day.

"Idiot!" I said out loud, then immediately regretted it. I glanced up at the camera, poised directly on the bed, and smiled. "I lost," I said and shrugged even though I had just won the game. Why was I lying to the camera? I doubted this would even get shown on the show. Then again, what *would* get shown? It wasn't like I was doing anything exciting. I moved the small desk, and built myself an impressively high house of cards. I looked into the camera again.

"More like a high riser, eh?" I forced a smile. What was I doing?

"Okay, time for something to eat. I'm starving." Shit, I was doing it again. Who was I talking to, and why did my voice sound so weird?

<u>6</u>

Elton

There were three reasons why anyone would do this to themselves. Either they desperately needed the cash, they needed the attention, or they wanted to get away from the world and thought this might be a walk in the not-so-proverbial park. A holiday sounded good to me, but I didn't want to escape. Nor did I think this would be easy. The money *would* be good. Hell, who was I kidding? The money would be fan-fucking-tastic. Still, it was the attention I craved. No, not craved, *needed.* I needed to get back into the limelight before I started fading into oblivion. I was already barely recognised these days. Which was what made Jon's reaction to me so damn enjoyable. It was the boost I needed in order to know I was doing this for all the right reasons. I was good at what I did. I was. I wasn't too old to be in comedy anymore no matter what some people might say to me. What did they know anyway? Jon was a youngster, and he found me hilarious. Sure, he had probably seen me on some rerun, but that didn't mean I still didn't have it. Someone didn't stop being funny all of a sudden. There was just a lot more competition these days. It was no longer a case of being good at what you did. The only way I was going to get ahead was to outsmart them. Like a self-published author pushing their way through an overcrowded market, the only way I would get ahead was by doing something different. I gazed around at the small pod and smiled. Now *this* was different. This was thinking out the box, while being in a box. I laughed at my own joke, then immediately rushed over to the diary camera as an idea for my first entry came to mind.

"Day one, and being in here is no joke," I started. "I'm Elton Rigby, and this is day one in the void. If this were Facebook, my status would be, 'Elton Rigby has checked into the void'. Tag friends?" I looked around for effect then laughed. "No, Elton Rigby is very much alone. Although, with an audience of one, I'm guaranteed to get a good reaction to my jokes. Hell, I'm even going to give myself a standing ovation." I stood up then sat back down. "Maybe this is the future of comics. Comedy for one. I'll throw in a few bad reviews, just to make the whole thing more authentic. Elton Rigby wasn't on form tonight. He was not interacting well with the crowd." I peered closer into the camera and winked as I pulled back again. "Man, you're a good-looking bunch. Right, I better get going. I'll be back a little later with another status update. Elton Rigby has signed out of Facebook. No, scratch that. VoidBook? FacePod? Elton Rigby has signed out of PodBook."

I was happy with that. Keeping it Facebook related would please the younger crowd. Wouldn't it? I'd been told that the younger people were moving away from that platform these days, but I wasn't sure how much I believed it. *PodBook*. I chuckled at my joke. Hey, maybe this would catch on. A sort of social media for one. Social media for introverts. I pondered on that for a while. Something like that could really take off. It didn't matter how it would work, that part I wasn't sure. What mattered was that people would find this funny. This was an angle I could use for my time in here. I had come here with many great ideas, but this one had occurred to me without me even trying. That's when I knew my comedy would do well. When things came to me without thought, they were always well received. Damn, I was good. I stood up and stretched, and felt almost as if I'd been up on stage again. I had even managed to throw in my name a good few times, which was something an old comic friend of mine had told me once when I was first starting out. A little bit of insider information that nobody thought of. The best way to stay on top of the game was all subliminal. You wanted your name to be engraved in people's minds. Thankfully, I had a good name for that.

Of course, Elton Rigby wasn't my real name. Of course not. My life would've been different if I had been born with such a stellar name. Unfortunately, my name was not the sort of name you'd associate with a famous comedian. Not the sort of name you'd see up with flashing lights. Bob Store. *Boring Bob Store!* I wasn't sure if I'd come across a name as dreary yet. Even Joe Bloggs or John Doe would've been better. Those placeholder names were so generic they now had a sort of coolness to them. But Bob Store? Horrible. Everything about it was bland, broad and non-specific. I'd come up with the new name at the start of my career. It was my agent who had suggested it, and I didn't bother fighting it. My parents weren't too happy, but I'd complained about my name heaps before to worry about offending them. They were the ones who had given me the dull name in the first place. Anyway, I'd probably done them a favour. Parental jokes featured often in my stand-up, and I doubted they would want to be associated with me after hearing some of the things I said. I had always planned on turning my name into a full-on comedy skit, but I didn't mind forgoing it at the chance of a new name. The moment I became Elton Rigby I felt reborn. The name gave me a new lease on life, and the opportunity to be the guy I had always known I could be. The name I was destined to be. I could still remember the day I walked up on stage with my new name. It was as if a light had been switched on. I had smiled out into the audience with confidence. I had arrived.

The name had been an easy one. "Eleanor Rigby" was my soul song, and I'd always wished I could have a name as creative as that. I'd simply changed Eleanor to Elton, only to keep the first letter the same, and probably because I'd been going through a bit of an Elton John phase at the time. I hadn't thought about the name in a while, mostly because it felt so normal to me now. I wasn't Bob Store acting as Elton Rigby. I *was* Elton Rigby. I whistled the tune now, a little mantra to keep me going. How applicable for where I was now. *All the lonely people.* I wasn't lonely. I was just alone in here. There was a difference. Lonely people didn't stand up in front of crowds. Lonely people didn't possess an endless book of jokes in their head. I was like a walking, talking joke book, an encyclopedia of wit. And now the world would finally see what I saw in the mirror every day.

I decided to take a shower, just to test the waters so to speak. I marked that little word twister away to use another time. The jokes were flowing faster than usual and I didn't want to forget them. They were no use in my head. Jokes were meant to be shared. Being away from the camera would also give me an opportunity to practice my next diary take. The first one had come naturally, but I wanted to make sure the people watching would get tidbits of perfection each time I spoke into the camera. I was going to be the funniest person they had ever seen, and by the time I came out of here everyone would wonder why they had never heard of Elton Rigby before. PodBook was going to shoot me to the sort of fame I deserved. As the water cascaded over me, I practiced my speech. I'd done research before coming in. I wasn't surprised to find that many comedians included loneliness in their gigs. It was a universal truth that everyone was lonely at some stage of their lives, so this was always guaranteed to reach someone. I'd gotten some good ideas and memorized some great one-liners. After all, dad jokes were making a comeback. With my next speech sorted, I felt ready to start my time in this pod. I walked out, singing softly to myself as I settled in. I loved "Eleanor Rigby", and I loved The Beatles, but it was time to make my own mark on this earth. I hummed the same tune, but found some new words. I was ready for greatness.

Elton Rigby, picks up his towel
In the shower where he got clean.
He's not what he seems.
Waits in the bedroom, wearing a shirt,
That he picked for the pod.
He's a comedian god.

7

Melanie

I lay on the floor, my stomach flush against the rug and my feet swaying from side to side. I used to lie like this as child, and the simple act brought me joy. My item was a book and pen combo, which thankfully Larry had deemed suitable as one item. I made sure the book was big enough to last me the full two weeks, and by my estimation would give me twelve pages a day to play around with. I had no idea what the time was, or how long I'd been holed up in this room. I figured I was on the second day, which would make it a Wednesday. I couldn't be sure of the time, but I decided on eleven as a rough estimate. Eleven on a Wednesday in my normal life would have me sitting at my desk, shifting my eyes from my computer to the clock repeatedly until lunch time came around. I had a game I would play with myself, where I would try not to look at the clock for a while, and then I'd guess what the new time was. I got quite good at it at the end, and I'd become attune to the sense of time. Sometimes I got it down to the exact minute. It was nice not having a clock to look at now, and to know how far removed I was from that routine. Since I worked as an accountant, it was assumed that routine was what I thrived on, and for a while I thought so too. The monotony of day-to-day living soothed me into a false sense of security. Being away from all of it completely stripped this away from me, but instead of feeling anxious, I felt relieved. I enjoyed my own company and, for the first time in ages, felt as if I could breathe. Now, instead of sitting at my desk with nothing but looming deadlines in front of me, I was lying on the floor and practicing my art, something I had not allowed myself to do in years. I used to love drawing, but it had been a long time since I'd made the time for it. I sat up and inspected my illustration. I had drawn a cat yesterday, curled up so tightly that his tail wound all the way round. I hadn't expected to draw him again today, but there he was. Maybe this was what I'd do. I'd just keep drawing the same cat until I perfected him. I'd move on to the dog after that. In my little sketchpad I planned on all my creatures living happily side by side. Big and small. Fat and thin. Old and young. Loud and quiet. I closed the book and scribbled a name for it on the front: *Together in The Void.*

Drawings done, I pulled out a piece of paper and scheduled a few activities for each day. I laughed at that. I'd just been thinking how good it was to not have routine, yet here I was about to create one again. I guess I was drawn to it, even when I actively moved away from it. The spontaneous drawing was fun, but the only way to survive this place was to have a few daily things put in place. I only knew this because I'd done some extensive research into solitary confinement, and the key to survival was simple: Keep busy. There was a fine balance between learning when to still your mind and knowing when to keep it active. I would do both, and I would walk out of this place a richer, happier person. I was sure of it. I hadn't been sure of many things in life, but this I could do. Anyway, I would find this easy. When you've already been through hell, not many things in life seem bad anymore.

I marked down the dates for the next two weeks, then created eight columns per day. I'd already started today off, so I would officially start on this tomorrow. Or, whenever I deemed tomorrow to be. Without the guiding light of the sun, it was hard to know for sure, but as long as I was close, I'd be fine. There would be nothing worse than thinking your two weeks was up when you still had a full week to go. I would not let that happen to me. Preparation was the key to success.

At the top of each of these I created an activity.

Exercise
Meditate
Draw
Alphabet game
Write
Yoga
Draw
Meditate

My goal was to spend roughly an hour to an hour and a half on each of these a day, and in between I'd eat, drink, shower, rest, and sleep. I would tick off each of these when they were done and move onto the next. Meditation had been a part of my life for the past six months, and during that time I'd gone from being able to meditate for two minutes at a time, to the occasional forty-five minute session. I'd never been able to do an hour, but hoped to do it here. Perhaps I'd stretch it to even longer without knowing the time. It was another game I used to play at home. I'd tell myself I wanted to meditate for thirty-five minutes, then see if I could get to it on the minute. I always got close. Meditation was by far one of the hardest things I'd ever done, but also the best. I had also memorized an hour-long yoga and exercise session which I could easily replicate without a watch. The alphabet game was something I came up with now, but it was something I had done since I was a child. I'd think of a topic and come up with something from every letter of the alphabet for it. Between this, writing, and drawing, my mind would stay active. I checked my list and grinned. I wished I could stick it up somewhere, but I had no means to do so. I placed it on the bedside table, ready to start on it the next day. Then I headed over to the fridge, and got myself a meal. It was lunch time. I was sure of it.

That night, as I lay in bed, an overwhelming sense of emotion gripped hold of me. I had been placed in a pod with Keri and Jon to my left, and Ryan to my right. Even though it made no difference, I was glad Elton wasn't next to me. The man was awful. I touched the right wall, wondering how Ryan was doing there all alone. He'd seemed so nervous before going in. The two of us had sat there in silence while Larry had shown the couple to their room first. Ryan was one of those people I sometimes wished I could be. He wore his emotions on his sleeve, and it was easy to tell exactly what he was feeling at all times. I liked people like him. I had a tendency to hide myself from people. I moved inward with ease and struggled to show my real self. The less people knew of me, the safer I felt. Ryan was my opposite, and yet in some ways I had a feeling we were very much the same. He'd reached inside his pocket endless times during the short time we were in the waiting room, and had punctuated it with a heavy sigh when his hand came out with nothing. What was he hoping to find in there each time? I pictured him lying in bed, his hair still perfectly in place, his hand on the wall. I tried to get a sense of where his hand was in relation to mine, and then I chuckled at the absurdity of it. I remembered the camera then. I thought I'd be far more aware of the ever-watching eyes on me, but I already paid it little thought. However, I couldn't help but wonder what moment the camera had caught. It had either captured a beautiful and surprising moment of kinship between two people who didn't even know each other: I imagined both Ryan and me touching the wall at the same place. It would make for wonderful TV. Or, and this was definitely the more likely version, the image would be of me touching the wall while everyone wondered if I was deranged or just lonely. The thought only made me laugh. I didn't need solitary confinement, or a TV show, to tell me what I already knew. I was both of those things.

The only thing I hated about the place was the inability to switch off the light. It was a strange light, a little bit yellow so that everything you looked at had a sort of weird mustard-like glow to it. If they were going for something homely, they'd missed the mark completely, although I had a strong suspicion they had chosen this sort of light because of the ugliness it gave the room. The last thing the producers wanted was for people to enjoy themselves in here. My eyes were used to it by now, but a moment of darkness would've been welcomed. I wouldn't let it get to me, though. I was one step ahead of them. I pulled out a long unused sock and fastened it around my head. It fit just perfectly, and the moment I put it around my eyes, the pod went black. The relief was instant, and it didn't take me long to fall asleep.

<u>8</u>

Keri

I stared at the mound in the corner of the room, where I'd pushed all the dust. I was disturbed by how much I'd managed to gather considering we'd only been in the room for what could only be a maximum of three days. At least, Jon thought it was three, but I was almost certain we were still lingering at the end of the second day. It was hard to know for sure, but I got the gnawing sensation that time was going a lot slower than we thought. Jon told me the dirt was mostly due to my hair, and unfortunately, he wasn't entirely wrong. My hair was hard to miss, and vastly different from the dark blonde of Jon's, but it wasn't the *only* thing I'd swept. I couldn't figure out where it had all come from. Other than the small vent at the top corner of the room, there wasn't much that could generate dust.

"Ke, just leave it," Jon said.

"Leave what?" I asked, surprised to find him awake. I thought he was sleeping.

"The dirt. It's driving you crazy. I can see it. It's only going to get worse, you know."

"But where is it coming from?"

"I don't know. The air. The room probably wasn't dust free when we came in. We more than likely brought some in when we arrived. Anyway, who cares?"

"You know what it is? It's probably our skin. Dead skin."

"That's gross."

"Yeah, that *is* gross," I agreed. "Sorry, I'm just bored," I said. "I thought you were sleeping?"

"Trust me, I tried, but your huffing kept waking me up. You're like a dragon."

I turned to him. He was lying without a shirt on, his elbow on his pillow as he propped his head up. He had his one leg up, turned slightly as if he were about to be photographed. He never lay this way at home.

"I wasn't huffing! And why are you lying that way? It's weird."

"You were huffing. It's what you always do when you're annoyed at something. You do it at home, too."

"Then why have you never mentioned it?" I challenged him.

"It sounds louder in here. It's annoying."

I huffed, then immediately stopped before he said anything. I didn't want to look at him, so I turned my head and found myself once again focused on the dirt mound. Annoyed, I jumped out of bed and went to the bathroom. I didn't need the toilet, but I found myself going there all the time. Without the cameras, or Jon, it was the one place that made me feel free. The day became littered with these tiny bursts of freedom, and I held onto each moment with a precious ferocity I couldn't comprehend. I knew this wasn't going to be easy, but I hadn't expected it to be quite so hard. A part of me even thought it might be fun, or a chance for us to reconnect again. A little honeymoon of sorts, where I could fall in love with the boyfriend of my past, the one I barely saw these days. Instead, I was getting more and more annoyed with him by the minute, which wasn't good in a place like this, considering every minute felt like an hour.

Suddenly, the tiny curtain—which I'd named 'the sanity line'—flew open, and Jon appeared in front of me.

"Jon! What are you doing? I'm on the toilet."

"So what? I've seen you naked, remember?"

"Yeah, but there are cameras. Get out. I'll be done soon."

He didn't leave. Instead, he stepped in, closed the curtain and looked down at me. "Are you even peeing right now?"

I groaned. "Jon, can't I have a moment's peace? I won't be long."

"Fine, but hurry up. I need to go, too."

I wasn't really using the toilet, so I made my way out, and let him in. The moment I crossed the sanity line, I felt the cameras on me, and my mind fogged over. I felt foolish at the thought of a TV crew on the other side watching our every move. I couldn't imagine we were coming across as the happiest couple in the world, and I hated the thought of all my friends and family seeing our small, pitiful fights. In the real world it was the one thing I always shielded from people. I was not a fan of public fighting, and our issues were not for anyone to see. If that meant sometimes fake smiling in front of people, then tearing into each other at home, that was fine. It was *our* life, and not theirs. I hadn't realised how much of a private person I was until now, and I so desperately wanted to fake some happiness for the viewers to see. Faking anything was hard in here, though. It was as if I'd left the happy part of my personality outside the door, and had brought only the bad parts with me. I tried to imagine what my parents would say if they saw the fights, or even worse, my sister. She wasn't a big fan of Jon in the first place, and I spent most of my time defending him to her. The look of 'I told you so' would be all over her face if she had to see this with me. I forced myself to smile, hoping that a happy exterior would force a happy interior. *I love you, Jon,* I practiced saying over and over again. I would tell him as soon as he came out. Maybe he wasn't the problem. Maybe it was me.

"Ooh boy, you do *not* want to go in there for a while," he said as he came out. "Let's just say, it's a good thing those cameras can't capture smell."

I love you. I love you. I... "I'm going to bed."

Hours passed (minutes?), and I could not sleep. Jon was acting strangely. I lay in bed watching him as he moved around the small room like a caged animal. I had no idea what he was doing, but as he circled the room I felt as if he may have truly lost his mind. Or maybe I was the one going crazy. Jon had always done things a little differently to most. It was why I had fallen for him in the first place.

"Are you doing laps or something?" I said.

He stopped, and it took a while for his eyes to focus back to me. He looked like he was riding high on some horrible acid trip, but then he blinked, laughed and morphed back into his normal self. "I'm exercising."

I chuckled. Hearing this made me feel better. I couldn't have Jon go all crazy on me. Not when I was feeling so strange myself. I figured we'd go a little stir crazy in here, but I didn't think it would happen this soon. If Jon was exercising, it meant that he was the normal one in all this. "Nice," I said. "Biggest circuit you've ever run, huh?"

"Sign me up for a marathon after this," he said. "Can't sleep?" he asked as he joined me on the bed.

I sighed. "It's hard with these lights always on."

"Just close your eyes. Then the lights are off."

I laughed. "I wish it was that easy. Anyway, you're not sleeping either. I'm sure we'll both feel better once we get some rest. Come on, join me. I need my snuggle bunny."

He groaned. "I hate that name." He climbed in next to me regardless and I wrapped my arms around him.

"How about we exercise together tomorrow?" I suggested. Seeing Jon do laps around the small room reminded me that it was the first time he'd done anything physical since being inside. No wonder I thought he was going mad. In the real world Jon never went a day without going to the gym. I thought he'd exercise so much in here that it would annoy me, but it was the other way around.

"You're going to exercise with me?"

"Of course, I'll have to clear my schedule first."

"Of course."

I chuckled. It was good to feel normal again. I nestled my head into Jon's back, desperate to block out the light. "Should we try to get some rest? I feel like all I do is lie around but I don't think I'm actually sleeping."

"Think it's night time?" he asked.

I shrugged. "Honestly? I have no idea, but I've never been averse to a bit of daytime napping anyway."

"Time is but an illusion," he said. "Okay, let's give this sleep thing a try."

"Goodnight, bunny."

"Goodnight, funny."

The old familiar saying wrapped around me, and I knew sleep was on its way.

2

Elton

"G'day Podsters, and welcome to another episode of PodBook. Status update: After a fascinating few hours of staring at the wall, Elton Rigby has warmed up a frozen dinner. He's still checked into The Void, and he still has no friends to tag. But thanks for asking. So, are you all ready for your joke of the day?" I asked as I waved my joke book in the air. "Tell me when to stop. Now? Okay. Ooh, a classic. A man is speaking to his gym instructor. 'Can you please teach me how to do the splits?' the man asks. 'Sure,' the instructor says, 'how flexible are you?' The man thinks about it, then says, 'Well, I can't make Tuesdays.' Ah, you can't beat these old jokes. Ya know, this is how I first started out in the business. Before I could even call it such. I was just a lad then, a little ankle biter really, and I found this old joke book in some secondhand shop. Yeah, this very one," I said and waved the book again. "Hell, that's probably why I didn't get many girls back then. All the rest of my friends were sneaking peaks at their dad's porno magazines, and here I was reading jokes. How do you catch a bra? With a booby trap!" I laughed. I couldn't help myself. That little joke was one I revealed whenever someone asked me to tell them a joke off the top of my head. People always laughed. Sometimes silly can be effective. "Porn. Joke books. Same-same. You know, next time I go up on stage I'm just going to bring this book and spend an hour running through these jokes. If you're anything like me, and by that I mean a teenage boy trapped in a forty-year-old's body, you'll laugh. What? You want one more. Okay, if I must. Gosh, you're a good crowd today." I peered into the camera with raised eyebrows. "And a great-looking bunch, too. I have just the one for you. Picture this, a young me, sitting at home alone with this book and coming across this joke. No wonder I ended up this way. What kind of bees produce milk? Boobees." I stood up and bowed. "Elton Rigby has signed out of PodBook."

A comedian god, I thought to myself with a grin. I needed to find a way to get those words into the minds of everyone watching without saying them myself. I was a few days in and already I was sure I was going to nail this. Bored out of my mind, sure, but worth it for the headlines I was going to make when leaving this place.

10

Jon

I stared at the wall, wondering, not for the first time, why the producers had chosen to make them cream. Why not white? It bothered me, and I had no idea why. I supposed white would've also bothered me. Everything about this place annoyed me. But cream? It was so bland. I'd managed a bit of sleep, but without the sense of time I had no idea if I'd slept too much or too little. I hoped it was too much. If I could spend most of my time here sleeping, I would definitely do it. Sadly, sleep didn't come to me as often as I wanted. I was trying to keep things positive, because if I admitted to Keri how strange I felt, it would also mean fully admitting it to myself. I wasn't ready for that yet, especially when I was the one who had begged her to do this show with me. She'd been sceptical from the start, but I'd assured her that it would be worth it. "We'll have each other," I had said to her over and over again until she'd finally given in. Anyway, it was normal to feel strange, wasn't it? I could hear Keri was still sleeping. She didn't snore, but she had a way of breathing when she slept that made it seem as if she was in the middle of a crazy dream. She let out small puffs of air, and every so often a little whirring sound would escape. I imagined her trying to propel herself out of the room. I clung onto the sound, wishing I could propel right out of here with her. I was annoyed at myself for struggling so soon. I thought it would be easy. People always said I was tough, and for the most part I thought I was too, but I felt strange in here. Before coming in I had imagined what it would be like to spend two weeks alone with Keri, with cameras watching our every move, and I had honestly believed it wouldn't be so bad. I figured we'd sleep a lot, work out a lot, and…well…laugh a lot. I wasn't sure if I'd really laughed since coming in. What was there to laugh at? Cream walls weren't funny.

"Is this legal?"

"What?" Keri said and turned to face me in confusion.

I stared at her. "Huh?"

"What did you say?"

Had I spoken out loud? "Uh, is this legal?"

She blinked a few times, waking herself. She looked older this morning (afternoon?), but I supposed the weird yellow light did nothing for our complexions. I just hoped we looked better on camera. Camera! I kept forgetting about it.

"Never mind."

She leaned over and kissed me. "Manage to get some sleep?"

"A little. How 'bout you?"

"A little."

"More like a lot. You were snoring like a tractor."

She punched me. "Liar. So, what were you talking about earlier? Asking about this being legal?"

I shrugged. "I don't know. This whole thing. Being locked up in here. Isn't it meant to make you go crazy or something?"

"Well, they're not *really* locking us in. We can hit the buzzer and leave at any time, remember? And we signed documents agreeing to this. Anyway, I guess the *point* is to see if we go crazy or not. We won't though," she said firmly. "We have each other." I could swear I saw a flicker of doubt pass over her. I hoped not. She'd always been the strong one in the relationship. I just liked to pretend I was. The thought surprised me. People had told us that before, and I'd always laughed it off.

"True. I wonder how the others are coping by themselves?"

She nodded thoughtfully. "I keep wondering about poor Ryan. I hope he's okay."

I laughed. "Bloody bludger. He's probably doing just fine. He's probably spending most of his time making sure his hair looks good. And did you see he was wearing those glasses again. They're so stupid. I know he doesn't need them. Since when is wearing glasses fashionable anyway? He looks ridiculous."

"You're so mean about Ryan! What the hell is he doing here anyway?" she said. Then she gasped. "Uh, he seems like a nice guy."

"Ah whatever, cat's out the bag now. Who cares? They should've done their research. Maybe they knew about the connection anyway. It's not like he wasn't allowed to apply."

"We were told not to tell anyone until we go out," she said. Then she sighed, resigning herself to the fact that the truth had come out. I was surprised we'd managed to last this long without talking about it to be honest. I thought she was going to kill me when she saw Ryan walking toward us. "Anyway, why did you tell him about it in the first place? I nearly died when I saw him at the park. You could've warned me. That Melanie girl probably thinks I'm a freak now."

"Sorry, Ke. I honestly thought it would be funny. Come on, it was, wasn't it?"

"It was very typical of you, that's for sure. Funny? Not so sure. Is he giving you some of the money or something?"

I grinned. "Ah, now you're getting it. In case one of us doesn't make it, we've promised to split the money."

She sat up and glared at me. Her eyes seemed darker in here. "Wait a second. So, if Ryan doesn't make it, then we have to give him some of *our* money? That doesn't seem fair. Also, you could've asked me about this, you know. It's not your decision to make."

"Fair point. Hear me out, though, Ke. If we *don't* make it, then he has to give us some of his money. Either way, we're guaranteed to have something when we get out of here, which, by my calculations, should be in ten days' time."

"More like eleven," she pointed out, but I was sure she was wrong. We must've been in here longer than that. "Are you telling me that Ryan could be sitting at home right now while we make him rich?"

"No, we only qualify if we make at least ten days here. See, I'm not such an idiot after all. I've thought this through. I did this for us. I know how much you want a new camera. I wanted to get you one for Christmas this year, but man those things are expensive. I really want this for you." A flash of the smile and Ol' Charmer returns. The camera she wanted really was ridiculously overpriced, and what I wanted to spend the money on was a new car, but this was definitely the right thing to say right now. I squeezed her hand and knew she wasn't upset with me anymore. Also, I figured this would gain me some brownie points for the audience. The man who would risk his sanity to give his girlfriend what she wanted. Hell, I was good at this.

"I guess. Next time, though, run it by me first. I would like a say in the matter. We're meant to be in this together, remember?"

"We are, and just think, *poor* Ryan is all by himself." I chuckled. Knowing Ryan was alone in a room next door felt a little like having a safety net to me. I may not be feeling great, but surely he was feeling worse. The camera was going to love him.

"He'll be fine," Keri said unconvincingly.

"What were your thoughts on Larry, by the way?" I asked. We'd kept our conversations quite superficial so far, but talking openly about Ryan suddenly made me want to say everything that was going on in my head. Well, not *everything*.

"Larry?" Keri asked. She'd climbed out of bed now. "Coffee?"

"Yes please." Thank god for coffee. "Yeah, what did you think of him?" I didn't get out of bed but watched as she scooped granules into a mug. I missed the ritual of grinding beans every morning, but this was better than nothing. It was amazing how much I enjoyed this purely because it gave the illusion of starting my day off right. A measure of normality among the crazy. Although, I didn't see why they couldn't have sprung a little on proper coffee for us.

"He seemed sweet. Interesting. I'd love to photograph him."

That gave me a laugh. "Oh yeah? I know what that means."

She turned to me. "What does that mean?"

"It means you don't find him attractive."

"What are you talking about?"

"Nice bum, by the way," I said and laughed when she wiggled it. I could tell she had been annoyed yesterday, so it was good to see her back to her normal self. Sleep seemed to be the key to surviving this. And coffee, I thought as she handed me the cup. I took a sip and smiled. "I mean, you only like taking photos of people you don't find attractive. The weirder someone looks the more interesting you seem to find them. That's why you don't take pictures of me."

"That doesn't mean I only like unattractive people. I just don't like typical models."

"Oh, he's definitely not model material."

"Jon!"

"Oh, come on, he's not. It's not an insult. It's truth. Anyway, I found the guy a bit weird to be honest. Like…I don't know… creepy. What if…What if there really is a camera in the bathroom? What if he's keeping those for his own personal collection? What if—

"Jon! Stop it. Come on," she pleaded. I knew Keri well enough to know what she was thinking. *Not now!* the look said. Keri spoke many truths, but only in private. She wouldn't want to hurt Larry's feelings.

"I'm *kidding*," I said even though I wasn't. I sat back against the cream wall, and sighed. Larry had been bugging me ever since I'd met him. I couldn't shake the thought out of my head. Something about the guy just didn't sit well with me. Why had he been the only guy we'd met? What if he was pumping some sort of weird hallucinogenic drugs through the vent to make us go crazy just to make good TV? And then the main thought, the one that kept playing over and over again in my head. What if there wasn't even a TV show?

"You know." Keri's voice boomed through the silent room. She must've realized it because her next words were close to a whisper. "It's sort of weird that Ryan got accepted, don't you think?"

"What do you mean? I told him to apply."

"Well, yeah, but what are the chances that they actually said yes to him? There must've been a million people trying to get on this show. Odd."

"Hmm." I couldn't reply. I could barely think due to the pounding of my heart, which seemed to resonate through my head. It felt as if someone was hitting my forehead with a hammer. I'd never thought of that before. *There is no TV show. Bang! There is no TV show. Bang! We're never getting out of here. Bang!*

"You okay?"

My head hurt, but as I turned, I caught sight of the camera. I sat a little taller and smiled. "I'm fine. Sorry, I'm just thinking of all the things I have to get done today. What to do first? What to do first?" *Bang!*

She giggled. "How about I whip you up a delicious breakfast?"

"Get to work young lady. Show the world your culinary skills." The banging eased to a soft knock, and I relaxed again. Of course there was a TV show. Everything was going to be fine.

Food was a dismal affair, not unlike Keri's cooking back home really, but despite this I looked forward to it each time. Every meal felt like an accomplishment, as if I was one step closer to the finish line. Our little fridge/freezer was packed to the brim with boxes, each one apparently delivering our quota in calories. I say *apparently* because I was sure I needed more. I was double Keri's size, after all, and back home I always ate more than her.

"Warm up two please," I asked her.

"I am."

"No. Not two in total. Two for me."

She groaned. "Are we really going to have this argument again? The food is supposed to last us two weeks. The last thing I want is to have no food for the last few days."

"He gave us extra remember. Come on, Ke. I'm starving."

"Yeah, he gave us extra, but we have no idea if we're even having three a day. What if we're having five a day without realizing it?"

"We're not. I don't know why you think we can't figure out time. It's the morning of the fourth day, and we're about to have breakfast," I said resolutely. I wasn't sure how much I believed that, but the more convinced I sounded the better for my state of mind. "How about I get an extra bit of food every few days at least? You know I need more than you. I'm always exercising."

"Okay fine," she said then mumbled something under her breath.

"What was that?"

"I said that's fine."

"Then you mumbled. What were you saying?"

"I said that's fine," she said again. "You can have two."

"What did you say?"

"Jon, does it matter?"

"Yes."

She sighed. A heavy sound that seemed to take forever to reach me. I imagined it pushing its way through the air, like someone swimming against a current. I could swear the air was heavier in here. Maybe that's why I was feeling so strange.

"I just said that you're not even exercising at the moment."

"What do you mean? I was doing laps remember."

"You call that exercising?"

This angered me more than it should, but I knew it was only

because I was ashamed at myself. I'd never gone this long without exercising, but since being in the pod I just couldn't muster the energy for anything.

"You should be happy. You're always saying that I exercise too much," I pointed out.

"Well, yes, but you're the one who brought those damn kettlebells in here. I said we should've bought a deck of cards, or a book, or something other than exercise equipment. I'm just annoyed that you made me give up something I wanted for something you haven't even bothered to use yet."

"You were supposed to exercise with me."

"Fine. Let's do a workout after breakfast."

"Fine."

Food was a weird egg mixture that made my stomach turn. I still wolfed down two boxes, even though I didn't feel like it. I couldn't exactly turn the second one down after I'd made such a big deal out of it. After, we sat around, doing little, and barely looking at each other. I kept expecting her to tell me that we should exercise, but she never said a word. Either she wasn't keen on it herself, or she could see that I wasn't and had taken pity on me. I didn't care. I was just glad she hadn't brought it up again. The more I *didn't* exercise, the more frustrated I felt at myself, but the more I felt like I couldn't do it. I felt heavy, and lethargic, yet I knew if I tried to sleep I wouldn't be able to. Instead, I sat with my back flush against the cream wall, and wondered if my cream shirt made me look like a floating head. Keri jumped up so suddenly I gasped.

"What's wrong?" I asked her.

"Nothing. Sorry. I thought I'd go for a shower. That's all."

"Didn't you have one earlier?"

"Did I? I'm losing track of time." She stood there for a while, and I swear I could hear her thoughts. Either that or she was talking and not thinking. Things were weird in here. "No." She shook her head decidedly. "It was yesterday. I showered yesterday. Anyway, it gives me something to do."

"Yeah, good idea," I murmured, then watched as she closed the sanity line. I shut my eyes the moment I heard the water and tried to picture myself back at home. I imagined myself at the gym, saw myself pushing weights, felt the feel of the treadmill under my feet. The warm room, the sweat dripping down my face. I stood up, pulled my shirt off, and sauntered to the bathroom. I yanked open the curtain, then blinked in surprise when I saw Keri standing there.

"Jon! Close the curtain. The cameras!" she yelled.

I stared. Blinked.

"Jon!"

"Sorry," I said, then closed the curtain and hurried back to the bed. *What the hell?* For a brief moment I could swear I was heading to the showers at the gym.

Get a grip! This was ridiculous. I found myself staring into the top right camera, which seemed to be focused right on me. The room felt hazy, and I pictured Larry sitting there, laughter spilling out of him as he pumped more strange gases into the room. I pushed the fumes away, stood up and moved to the camera.

"Don't mess with us, Larry. I swear, if I find out you're making us go crazy on purpose, I'll sue your ass. You hear me? I'll sue you."

"Jon? What are you doing, Jon? Who are you talking to?"

I stopped, and as I turned slowly, I noticed that the haze was just steam coming from the hot shower. I laughed, although the sound was strange.

"Ah, just chatting to the camera. Trying to freak them out." I turned back, offered the camera a huge grin. "Just kidding, Larry. Got ya good, didn't I?"

<u>11</u>

Ryan

"Uh, hi." I spoke nervously into the camera and wished I didn't worry so much about the way I was coming across. I should be used to things like this. I was always taking videos with my phone, uploading stories to social media, informing the world of where I was at all times. I tried to upload a photo or video once a day, once every two days at the least. If I didn't, I always felt as if I was failing my audience. The very fact they followed me made me feel like I owed them something. I kept a tally of exactly how many followers I had on each account and loved nothing more than watching that counter go up. Whenever it went down, I worried for days about what I could've done wrong. I thought I'd love this, but everything about it felt wrong. I kept imagining the camera as a real person, and once I swore I heard it laugh at me. Yet, at the same time, I liked having it there. It was like an emotional friend who mocked me all the time, but who I also knew I could rely on.

"So, it's Thursday today, and it's three in the afternoon." Then I laughed. "Who am I kidding? I've completely lost track of time. It feels like three, although most of my time here has felt the same. Who knew three pm had such a presence about it? In real life this is a time where I generally do nothing. It's that strange time of the day where it's too early to call it a day, and too late to start anything new. I used to call it *Limbo* time back home. Anyway, that's my thought for the day. I think I'm going to play some cards now. Cheers."

I cringed at the entry and wished I could do it all over. Why did I always sound so fake talking into the camera? At least at home I could redo the video endless times until I was sure it was right. I ran a hand through my hair, and pulled it back in surprise. What was that? Blood? I looked at my hand, expecting it to be red, but saw nothing. I jumped up and headed over to the small mirror to examine myself. I wondered why they had chosen to put the mirror out where the cameras could see me, rather than in the privacy of the bathroom. Was it the same for all the contestants? Or was each pod designed differently? If that was the case, was their design based on the people going in? What did that say about me? This bugged me. I felt a constant tugging to the mirror, and the desperation to know whether I looked okay was strong. I tried to resist it for as long as I could, just so I didn't come off too vain. The first few days I'd found myself at it far too often. Although, lately, I didn't feel the need as much as before. I didn't like the way I looked here. I wasn't sure if it was the odd lighting, the lack of beauty products, or the fact that I no longer had my camera's filter to smooth away the edges. My eyes seemed strange to me. The pupils were too big, and the red rim of my eyelid seemed more prominent. I averted my eyes whenever I looked in the mirror now. I stood there, examining my head. There was no blood, but my hair didn't look clean. I was sure I had washed it not so long ago. Had I? I tried to remember when last I'd showered. That morning? The day before? Why couldn't I remember the simplest things anymore? My gaze moved from my head to my eyes, and I flinched. I wanted so badly to move away, but I found myself peering closer. I'd always likened my eyes to the deepness of the ocean, the sort of mix of green and blue that changes depending on the light, but they seemed darker in here. Wait. I looked closer. Where was the ocean? Where was the blue or the green that was my trademark? It was gone. Did my pupils now take up the entire eye? I blinked. Holy shit. I looked away. It was just the weird lighting in here. That was all. My eyes didn't really look like that. When I played back the footage, I'd see that they looked normal. I…I…I ran my hand through my hair again, then gasped. *Blood!* I looked at my hand. No. No. Just dirty. I just need to take a shower, and then everything would be okay. A shower, a cup of tea, maybe a game of cards. A bit of normality. Everything was fine. I was fine. My eyes were fine. Fine.

I would never complain about my home shower again, which I'd always believed to *trickle* rather than gush the way a good shower should. I now knew the difference though, and the word would forever remind me of this place. Still, a shower was a shower, and I felt better just being there. Solitary confinement without this would've been a hell I might not have been able to stay in. I scrubbed at my hair, the part I was most concerned about. I missed my own shampoo, and my hair products, but they were luxuries we had not been allowed. Although, now that I was in here, I would swop my stupid pack of cards for some hair spray any day. I'd considered some sort of beauty product, but I was worried about the backlash I'd get when I returned. I was always going on about being happy with who you were, the whole inside is more important than the outside pitch. I'd get slaughtered if they knew just how much I really cared about my appearance. Right now, though, I'd give anything for—

What was that? A knock? Again! Someone was coming in. I was…could I be…was I…free?

"I'm coming. Hang on!"

I switched the tap off, wrapped a towel around my waist and threw a shirt over my head. I'd worry about getting dressed properly later. I was too excited. Either my time was up and I'd somehow gotten it all wrong, or they'd come to tell me something else. Was it bad? Excitement soon moved to panic, and I flung the curtain with an alacrity I hadn't had since being in here. I expected the door to be open, or for someone—maybe Larry—to be standing inside with a big grin. There was nobody there. I reached for the door handle and pulled, but it remained shut. I frowned. I'd heard someone come in. I was sure of it.

"La…Larry?" I called out tentatively. "Did you knock? I'm…uh, I'm out of the shower now."

Nothing.

I must've imagined it. Obviously. The place was too small for someone to be hiding in it. I stood for several seconds, trying to figure out whether I had really heard someone come in. The more I thought about it, the hazier the memory became, until I was sure I had simply conjured it up. Maybe the shower pipes were creaky. Perhaps my mind was creaky. I was still dripping water, and I hadn't yet rinsed off the shampoo. I headed back to the shower but waited for a while before turning the water on again. Creaky pipes. That was probably what had happened. Maybe Keri was showering too. Maybe Keri, Melanie and I had all turned on the shower at the same time. Perhaps all I had heard was some cross connection somewhere. I was not very 'hands-on' so I couldn't be sure if this was possible, but it seemed feasible. I waited, just to give the girls time to finish up. I counted to sixty, then tried to do it again and lost count. My mind was frazzled. When I was sure about five minutes had gone by, I continued with my shower, making sure to scrub off the rest of the sticky shampoo. The gooey mixture reminded me a bit of blood, and the thought brought me a sense of relief. Perhaps I hadn't rinsed my hair properly the last time, so my hair hadn't been dirty, just unfinished. I wish I knew what the hell this stuff was so I knew never to buy it again when I got out. Unfortunately, everything we had in here was in clear or white packaging, with simple handwritten labels. The water had mostly eroded the text of this bottle away, so that all was left of the word was the unfortunate end: Poo.

I chuckled and was grateful for the normal sound. If I could still laugh, then everything was going to be fine. I did one final rinse, and was about to turn off the water, when I heard the door open again. I reached slowly for the tap, turning until the water stopped. I leaned in for my towel, wrapping it slowly and quietly around me. As I did, I heard the creak of the bed. This time there was no dripping water to blame. This time I was certain someone had come in. I got changed as swiftly as possible, surprised at my ability to do something so normal in such a strange moment. I had not heard the door again, so whoever had come in was still waiting inside for me. I was now even surer that my time here was done, and that this was their 'fun' way of surprising me with the news. Had time really gone so fast? My excitement began to build as I imagined my time here to be over. Despite the slow unraveling of my sanity, which I figured was only normal, and the intense and excruciating boredom, it hadn't been too bad. If it was over, then all this would've been worthwhile. I stepped out the bathroom and gazed around.

Nobody.

I chuckled, looked directly into the camera, pointed to under the bed, then looked into the camera again. *I know he's there*, my look said. I thought of sitting on the bed, pretending as if I knew nothing, just to see how long they would take to show themselves, but I was too excited. I got down on my knees and peered beneath the bed. I was about to shout "Got ya!" but there was nobody there. "Got—" came out of my mouth, then turned to a gurgled gasp as I tried to fathom what was happening. I continued to look, as if someone might suddenly appear, then slowly got back up. I rushed to the bathroom, the only possible place someone could be, and looked inside. Of course there was nobody there. I'd just come from there in the first place. What was going on? Someone had been in here. I was sure of it. I checked under the bed again, for no other reason than not knowing what to do with myself. Nothing. Nobody. *Nothing, nobody, nothing, nobody.* The empty space mocked me. I got back up, and sat on the bed. I observed the room in quick darting spurts. The fridge, the bathroom curtain, the camera, the cream wall, the kettle, the water bottle, the mirror, the buzzer. The buzzer. The buzzer. The buzzer. I tried to look away, but my gaze kept returning to it. All I had to do was press it, and all of this could be over. I'd been convinced someone had come in to tell me it was over, but the sudden thought I was nowhere near the two weeks now loomed over me. I had fooled myself if I thought that my time in here been good. It hadn't. An intense desire to cry came over me. It reminded me of the many occasions I'd wanted to cry in the real world, and the amount of times I had. I always felt like a failure when the tears forced their way out of me. My father had told me on so many occasions that real men don't cry. My unmanliness was the one thing I was reminded of every time I saw him. I ran my hand through my hair, and gasped.

"What the—

My hair felt sticky again. Was it blood? I checked but my hand simply felt wet. Hadn't I just been through this? Or had I been sitting here all along? I pulled my feet up onto the bed, and wound myself into a tight ball.

"You're going to be fine." My head was down, squished by my legs, and my voice was muffled. The cameras wouldn't be able to make out the words, and this soothed me. "Fine. Fine. Fine."

12

Elton

"G'day Podsters. It's another beautiful day in PodBook. The sun is shining, but only out of my ass," I said with a laugh. I sometimes tried too hard to complicate things, but the simple jokes were often the best ones. I imagined Jon watching this once the show was finished, and laughing his own ass off. Maybe we'd even watch it together. I liked the guy. "The birds are singing, but there's only one in the band. Me." I sang my usual little Beatles tune, exaggerating the highs and the lows. "I've always wanted to be in a band, but I chose comedy instead, because, let's face it, I can't sing. At least in here I can pretend I'm good. That's what happens when you have nobody to compare yourself to. I'm as good as the guy next to me," I said and then turned my head to the empty space beside me. "Oh right, there's nobody here. Then I can honestly state that I'm the best singer in here. Oh, what's this," I said dramatically as I opened up my imaginary computer. "Ah, the emails are streaming through. Okay, we have this one that's just come through from a Mr. I.P. Freely," I grinned. That Simpsons joke had been a big hit when I was a kid. "Mr. Freely wants to know how big the pod is. Right, well, let's just put it this way, this place is so small that if a family of ants were to live here, they'd still call it a shack. Before coming in here, I was considering buying a new house, because the one I lived in was becoming a little too small for me. Yeah I'm only one person, but my personality needs a room of its own. In this place I barely have enough room for my ego." I grinned. I loved it when the jokes poured out of me without me trying. I was on a roll. I leaned in. "In here the only thing I have space for is my almost non-existent dignity. But in all seriousness, Mr. Freely, this place is tiny. But like they say, it's not the size of the thing that matters, but how you use it."

My jokes continued at a steady pace, and I only stopped because I found myself getting a little too crude for daytime television. Which I assumed is where *The Void* would be aired. If they cut me out because I was too shocking for their audience the whole thing would've been pointless. Also, my jokes seemed to move between being funny and being stupid, and I hated that I seemed to have no way of controlling them. Sometimes everything I said sounded so forced I had to add in my own one-man laughter track just to make up for it. Truth was, I was already getting a little bored of the place. And I had never been good with boredom. It reminded me of the last dinner party I had been to. The very concept of a dinner party eluded me. To me, the two things were so vastly different they didn't marry well. I preferred to eat at home, the sort of food I knew I would like. A party should be drinks and snacks, and a whole lot of laughter. This party had been typical of the friends who had invited me. They'd been married for like twenty years already, and they were now so similar that I struggled to tell the two apart. Perhaps mentioning this wasn't such a good idea. I mean, I didn't actually think that Angie *looked* like Tom, but their mannerisms were so alike it almost took over the physicality. Apparently, I was "rude" for saying so. Asking for better music – I mean, who even *liked* instrumental – and saying I didn't like the soup – broccoli, I mean, *come on!* – made me "obnoxious". I was only having a little fun with them. The cheese had been the last straw for them. They were vegans (don't get me started), and I had apparently made a massive faux pas when commenting on the not-so-stringy fake cheese that lay stiffly on the top of my pasta. They insisted it tasted like the real thing, but a few mouthfuls in and all I could taste was something akin to a spoonful of coconut oil – don't ask me how I knew what that tasted like. They hadn't been impressed, but quite frankly, I hadn't been impressed with them. Why lie? Why not tell me it doesn't taste like cheese but that they're trying to pretend it does to make themselves feel better? That's what being in this pod felt like now. It felt like a dinner party with fake cheese, where everyone was just pretending to be okay. *Far out!* I thought as the analogy swam to mind. Maybe I should be a writer and not a comedian. The thought should've pleased me, but somehow it left a funny taste in my mouth, just like that boring dinner party had done. I hadn't been invited back, but that was okay. They'd told me I should start acting my age, but if that meant spending my life pretending, then I wanted nothing to do with it. I smiled into the camera. This was a different sort of pretence. Wasn't it? Elton Rigby might have signed out of PodBook, but Bob Store has signed out of life. I wasn't pretending. I was being the me I was always meant to be.

Christine Bernard

13

Melanie

Either I was not ready to draw other animals, or I'd become too attached to this little cat I'd created, but so far I had not wanted to draw anything else. The little cat, or 'Todd in the Pod' as I'd named him, had become somewhat of a companion to me. I'd started with the whole art imitating life thing, where each drawing of him was based on my life in the pod. This was cute but grew tiring. After all, I did the same things over and over, and there was only so many ways I could draw the cat meditating or doing yoga. Somehow, the drawings had taken on a life of their own, and the cat had become my friend. Todd in the Pod was strolling in the park now, which I imagined to be a lot like the one where I'd first met Larry. I could almost smell the grass as his little paws touched the blades, and I chuckled as I made him lie down to rest under the shade of the tree. I spent some time with him there, drawing him over and over again, so that if I had drawn him on separate pages I could've flipped through the book and watched him move. I didn't need to create the illusion of movement, though. My mind did it for me. Todd in the Pod had become so real to me that I was almost sure he was waiting for me in the outside world. I didn't have a pet—I'd never dared to—but the thought of this little guy waiting for me to come out made me happy. I'd been drawing for a while already, and I still had the rest of my activities to get through, but I decided to draw a little more. I was happy with my new friend, and having him there with me made me feel like I wasn't so alone. I drew another one of him, and this time he had moved ever so slightly to the sun. Half of his body remained in the shade, with just his face and his two front paws getting his daily dose of vitamin D. I drew him again, exactly the same but included a small smile. This was his happy place. I got up and drew a window on the wall. The producers of the show might not be so happy, but I didn't care. What were they going to do with this place when the show was done anyway? The little window made me feel happy even though it wasn't real. What *was* real? What if everything in life was simply a figment of our own imaginations? If that was the case then I really needed to start thinking about more positive things. Then I lay back down, right next to Todd in the Pod, and imagined light shining through onto me. I closed my eyes and pictured myself at the park. I swear I could feel the sun warming my face, and I smiled. I imagined someone drawing me, just as I had drawn Todd.

I woke when a darkness loomed above, and I rubbed my eyes expecting to find clouds moving in front of the sun. I gasped when instead of clouds, I saw Andy. *He* was the dark cloud. Only, he didn't look the same. Hadn't I once described him to someone as having kind eyes? Who had I told that to? They seemed unkind now, scary even, and he was glaring down at me in a way that made my body shiver. Why was he so scary? Then I remembered. This was the Andy of the present, not the one from my past. He wore glasses, small tortoise-shell frames that did not suit him, and I wondered when he'd stopped wearing contacts. Was this why he looked so strange to me now? I couldn't remember his eyes looking that way. Maybe the contacts had made him look kind. Had they protected me from the truth? Why was he staring at me like that? And why was I still lying there? I opened my mouth to speak, but the only sound that came made it sound like I was trying to talk underwater.

"Thought you could run away, eh? Just lying here and catchin' some rays? Like you've got no worries in the world." *No worries, mate. No worries, mate.* Why did those words keep circling through my brain?

"How…how…"

"How did I find you? Do you think I'm a bloody fool?

"No. I…"

"Who the fuck is that?" he said. "Got a new friend, eh?" He laughed. Although, it was more of a jeer than a laugh. I hadn't heard the sound for a while, but it bounced through my very core with a sad familiarity.

"Who?" I asked. He moved slightly, and a bit of the light came shining back down on me. I shielded my eyes, then suddenly remembered who was next to me.

"Todd!" I cried, and then I jumped over the cat to save him.

I woke in a panic. I was on my haunches, clutching at my notebook. The sweat from my forehead had dripped onto the page, smudging the latest drawing of the cat. I looked at it in confusion, then sat up in surprise. It had only been a dream. Andy was not about to attack, and Todd in the Pod wasn't real. There was no real sunlight. Only a rough drawing of a window on the cream wall. It was a dream. A dream. Relief dawned on me when I saw the camera angled toward me. I stood, nodded into it, then made my way to the bathroom to splash water on my face. The dream had felt so real, but, even though I'd been slightly startled at first, it hadn't rattled me. If anything it showed me that I was here for a reason. I wasn't just here to prove my inner strength to myself. Perhaps one day Andy would see this, and he'd know he hadn't ruined me. And if *he* didn't ruin me, nothing would. That's what made me stand out from the others. Unlike them, I wanted to be here. Maybe I hadn't been chosen to be the thorn among the roses. Perhaps they had seen I was the sort of person who would survive a place like this when others wouldn't. Unlike them, I had been through so much worse.

It was drawing close to the end of the day or, at least, the end of the day in my new world. I couldn't wait to find out how close I was to real-world time. If my calculations were correct, then I'd been in here four and a quarter days. It was getting progressively more difficult, but I had no doubt in my mind I could do this. I used to be a strong person, back when I was in my teens. I was one of those characters everyone thought would go far in life. It had something to do with the way I presented myself, at least that's what someone told me once. I used to be laser focused, and my willingness to get ahead had always propelled me. It was something my father had taught me, and to this day he remained the strongest man I had ever known. Unfortunately, once he died, the men in my life seemed to get progressively worse. My mid-twenties to mid-thirties would forever remain a decade I would live to regret. Whether that was due to me or to circumstances, I was not sure. Probably a combination of both. I preferred to think I had no choice, that I didn't see the storm ahead, but I now knew I was only fooling myself. You know that stillness you feel just before the storm, *that's* what I had always felt with Andy. It took a long time to come, but when it did it knocked me right off my feet. I stood up, and stretched. It was time for my meditation, a warm meal, a cup of tea, and a sleep. The dream might have taken me by surprise, but I had my routine and I was going to stick to it. I set myself down in the circle I had drawn on the floor—apologies to the TV producers. I was about to start my meditation for the evening but something was bothering me. My smudged cat. I couldn't leave him like that. I reached for the paper, and drew him again. I made a little circle for him too and positioned him right in the middle of the page, with nothing around. I had a few extra pages to spare each day, and I felt he deserved his own space after what had happened. Once he was drawn, and ready to be left alone, I put away he book and shut my eyes.

***

I may have found strength in the void, but I had no control of my dreams. Seeing Andy again had awakened a slew of memories I had thought well and truly hidden. I'd shoved them at the back and deposited a whole heap of new memories on top of them. Still, I should've known that they would one day return. My subconscious mind was acting like a therapist, telling me I had to deal with what had happened. I was okay thinking about some of the things, but parts of my life were better left untouched. I had no intention of visiting them again. Hopefully my mind knew I was better off without remembering it all. Maybe I needed to up my meditation before bed to an extra half hour. I needed my mind to be as empty as possible before I fell asleep. I would have to try that tonight. For now, it seemed that being awake in the pod was where I was most comfortable at. Just me, my routines and my new little friend. It felt safe here.

"Safe." I whispered the word out loud and felt it dance in the air around me. The word hadn't been a part of my life for such a long time, and just saying it made me feel better. I said it again and smiled. The pod might not be the most riveting place in the world, but I liked it in here. The walls were arms wrapping around me. The mother I never knew. The father I missed so much. The friends I'd lost along the way. Tomorrow I'd make sure that little Todd got some walls, too.

<u>14</u>

Keri

A hand was moving up and down my arm. I smiled, happy by the comforting way it was making me feel. The hand moved to my stomach, circling my belly button, then slowly making its way down, down, down.

My eyes flew open, and the first thing I saw was the camera. I yanked up the duvet, turned around, and glared at Jon.

"What are you doing?" I hissed.

"Huh?" Unlike me, he had clearly been wide awake. I could tell by the crazed look in his eyes that he always got lately when he hadn't slept properly. I wasn't sleeping well either but I was definitely sleeping more than he was.

"Jon! You can't do that in here."

"Oh come on. You're my girlfriend. Anyway, you were obviously enjoying it."

"The duvet was down. The camera saw everything," I whispered.

He rolled his eyes. "They won't show that on the telly. Anyway, it's a normal thing for a couple to do. It would be weird if we *don't* do that in here."

"I don't care. I don't want footage of you doing *that* to me." I was mortified from what they had already seen. A thought came to me. "You didn't…you didn't touch my breasts did you?" I was *facing* the camera. I'd worn a bra in the beginning, but I'd started taking them off just to help me sleep better. At home I never slept with one on.

"Keri, calm down. I didn't do anything."

"You were going to though, and keep your voice down. Come on, Jon," I pleaded. He should know by now how much I hated anyone seeing us fight. That was *our* business.

"I can't help that you're so sexy."

I groaned. "Jon. Stop it."

He grinned, and I balked at the sight. Why did his teeth look so weird in here? He'd always had the whitest teeth out of anyone I'd ever known. Maybe that's why he looked so strange in here. The cream walls and the yellow light were playing tricks on my eyes. Nothing looked vibrant in here. There was a dullness to the room that was depressing. How Jon managed to even *think* about anything sexual was beyond me. Thankfully he didn't see my reaction. The last thing I wanted was for him to get all paranoid about his teeth. "I have an idea."

"Oh yeah?" I rolled my eyes. "What's that?"

"I happen to know of a place that has no cameras." He smiled in a way I supposed was meant to be seductive. This sort of thing might have worked for me in the outside world, but right now I just felt annoyed. I also had to look away because the only thing I seemed able to look at now were his teeth.

"Jon, we're still here for another nine or ten days—

"Eight."

"Whatever," I said with frustration. Jon insisted time was going by faster than it really was. I decided not to argue about it today. It was probably better if he thought that anyway. I was starting to see all facets of his personality in here, and if there was one thing I wanted more than anything it was to hold onto the happy moments. They were so fleeting. "Okay, so say we've only got eight days—

"We do." He nodded dramatically as if he were trying to convince himself more than me.

"Okay, then that's only eight days to wait until we're back home.

Eight days. That's nothing. Think about it, Jon. We'll have a much better time there. I'll be more relaxed, and we don't have to worry about anyone watching us." I reached out to touch his face, not because I wanted to but because I wanted to show him that I *was* looking forward to this.

His lips pulled back over his creamy teeth, and I wondered if I'd ever stop thinking of them like that. "Maybe people watching us could be part of the fun." He laughed when I gasped. "Ke, come on, stop taking everything so seriously."

I sighed. Why had I ever agreed to this stupid idea? I hated being on camera. It was why I had become a photographer in the first place. I liked watching other people. I didn't like other people watching me. I felt so tense in here. I hated that everything we said was being recorded. I'd also watched enough reality shows to know how things could get misconstrued. The producers would probably do anything to make sure they were getting good material to broadcast. Jon was right, the only way to get through this was to keep the mood light. "Okay, you're right, but no funny business until we're out of here mister," I said as cheerily as possible. "How about some coffee? I know a great little café."

He chuckled. "Now we're talking. Coffee would be great. I know that café. I hear the waitress is pretty cute there."

I hurried to the bathroom, where I'd left my bra ready to put on as soon as I woke. I felt immediately more camera ready the moment it was on me and a little more ready to start the day next day. I hurried, just in case Jon decided to try and seduce me again, but when I stepped over the sanity line I found him sitting up in bed, his face scrunched up in confusion.

"Everything okay?" I asked him.

He turned to look at me, his movements so slow he'd become robotic. His smile was just as slow to appear. I tried not to focus on his teeth. "Yeah, sorry, I zoned out. I keep..." He shook his head. "Nah, never mind."

"You keep what?"

"It's stupid. Don't worry."

"Ah, not this again. Don't start a conversation you cannot finish," I said. It was one of my biggest pet peeves, and something he did all the time. No matter how many times I had asked him not to, it always happened. "You keep what?"

He leaned back against the wall and pulled up his feet. He looked oddly small from where I was standing, and nothing like the strong man I had always known him to be. "I keep thinking that someone is missing. Like, when you came out the bathroom, I wondered where the other person was."

"Who?" I flipped the switch to the kettle and scooped the granules into the cup. I'd abhorred the coffee when we'd first made it, but I now looked forward to it. Even though I hadn't yet poured the water into the mug, I could smell the coffee fumes I knew were about to appear. It was these little things that were getting me through my time in here. I shuddered to think of what solitary in prison must be like without these distractions. No matter how hard this was for us, it could've been a whole lot worse. I gently reminded myself of that and promised to make more of an effort not to let this place get to me. We had food, water, coffee, a shower, a bed and a roof over our head. The place was tiny, but it was still a sort of heaven for those who didn't have any of these things.

"I don't know. Like I said, it's stupid. It makes no sense."

"Hmm. Maybe you're just tired. You're not getting much sleep, are you?"

"Not really."

"A good cup of coffee will sort you out," I said while I carried on with the coffee-making ritual. Sometimes just getting up and doing something normal made me feel better. There were times when the two of us would sit and do nothing, and the unease would grow stronger. I'd feel desperate to do something but would have no energy to do anything about it. It was strange. It wasn't like we were doing anything to make us tired in here. The kettle took forever to boil in here, and I wished I could time it. Was it really taking so long? Or did it just feel like it? Without a point of reference, it was hard to know for sure. My entire existence on earth felt shifted in this place, and I wondered if I would ever look at time the same way. Back home we were stuck in our ways. Jon always teased me because I liked to do certain things at certain times. Even if I was starving, I wouldn't eat until I saw the clock turn six-thirty. I was like that with a few things. I thought it gave me a sense of control over time, but I was starting to suspect that, all along, I was just letting time control me. I was not nearly as free-spirited as I liked to believe I was.

When I made my way back to the bed, I handed Jon the coffee, and realised he had never once made one for me. I'd so far been in charge of doing everything in here, bar go to the toilet for him. I'd never known Jon to lie around so much. At home he was always the most active. The stupid kettlebells mocked us every day now. For Jon they were probably a reminder of how little he was doing in here. For me, it was a constant reminder I'd let him get his way again. I had never wanted to bring them in, knowing full well we could exercise without them. I had so many other things I'd wanted to bring in, but I'd given in to him just to make him happy. I sat next to him on the bed now, the two of us not-so-silently drinking our coffee. You'd think drinking coffee didn't make much noise, but when it was the only sound in the room, it was deafening. No, not deafening. *Disgusting.* I heard every slurp and every gulp. We needed to talk to stop us from hearing it, but I could no longer think of anything to say to him without starting a fight.

"Hmm," he murmured and I shot him a look. "What's that look for?"

"Nothing. You're just making weird noises. That's all."

"I'm enjoying the coffee. *That's all.* What is with you today?" he asked.

"Nothing."

"Hope it's not that time of the month."

I clenched my jaw. *Breathe. Just breathe.* If we were already starting the day off this way then I dreaded to think what was coming. Was this what Jon would normally say to me back home? It felt like something I wouldn't put up with, but now I wasn't so sure. Had all of this become so normal to me that I now no longer regarded the things he said or did as wrong? I had a sudden image of being at home, and watching the show with other contestants in place of us. If there were two contestants on there like us, what would I think of his comment? I knew what I would think. I would think he was a jackass and I would wonder why anyone would put up with him. Was that why I never wanted the two of us to fight in front of people? Was it because I didn't want the rest of the world to see the things I saw at home? Because I didn't want to admit I was going out with a guy who would even say these things? Why *was* I even with him then? I shut my eyes, and tried to transport myself back to when we'd first met.

I was nineteen the first time I ever laid eyes on Jon. I was also lying on the floor with blood gushing down my leg, and tears rolling down my face. I'd often wondered what I must've looked like in that moment. My appearance had been terrible when I'd finally seen myself in the mirror, and by then the blood and tears had been washed clean. We weren't living in Newton then, but we were both at the age where we were thinking about leaving home. Staying with family had been easier though, but it also meant that we were stuck in Waratah. I sometimes wished I lived back there. The pull toward a more suburban lifestyle was a constant tugging at my heart. Back then though, the only thing I wanted was to get away. Who knew I'd find my way out on *that* day, a day that had started out so ordinary. I'd been out for a run, determined to get rid of some of the extra weight I'd put on during winter, when I saw a long stretch of road with nobody in sight. To this day I have no idea what compelled me to do it, especially because I was not much of a runner in the first place, but I had a sudden desire to sprint. A minute in and I tripped on who knew what. I launched into the air, and landed ungracefully on the uneven tar. I'd reached out to stop the fall, which hadn't helped, and ended up with a deep cut on my leg, a broken ankle, and a good few layers skimmed off my palms. I tried to get up, but the pain that shot through my foot was unbearable. So I did what I always did in situations I couldn't control. I cried.

That's when Jon appeared.

It was like an apparition, so Hollywood-like in his appearance I almost thought I was imagining him. Jon wasn't the sort of guy I usually went for, but there was no denying his looks. Of course, it was only after that I understood that the soft glow around him was only because the sun was shining right on him as I looked up. Still, at that moment he had been more like an angel than an ordinary boy. He got down on his knees, and told me everything was going to be okay. And, for a while, it *was* okay. Jon was different to anyone I'd met before. He was strong willed, and sure of himself. He was also the first white guy I'd ever dated, and he was always telling me how much he loved the way the two of us looked side by side. It was all very forward thinking and progressive, and I loved that about us. He looked after me that day, and when he asked me out on a date, I said yes. I said yes to the next one too, and soon the two of us were inseparable. I could still remember the day I took him home. My father didn't say much, but my mother asked me if I was sure about him. This had both thrilled me and upset me. I'd never been with anyone they had not liked before, and there was something about their disapproval that made me want to prove them wrong. I used to think it was because I wasn't going out with someone of the same race, but a deep conversation with my mother once revealed that she didn't think he was good enough for me. I put it down to a mother never truly finding anyone good enough for their child.

"Don't worry, Mum. He's a good guy."

"I don't like the way he acts, darling. He's…well, he can be a little disrespectful at times."

"Oh, Mum, that's just the way he is. He doesn't mean it."

"Since when is that any way to act?" she'd said. I thought she was old-fashioned, but maybe I hadn't wanted to see the truth.

I'm Jon without the h. Man with two N's. The sentence mocked me. I'd been saying it over and over in my head the past few days. Or was it a week? A day? Hours? Two weeks? I no longer knew. The only thing I knew for certain was that little things were starting to get to me. Things that might very well have annoyed me before, but had been easier to ignore without worldly distractions. A small puff squeezed through my lips.

"Why do you always tell people that your name has no h?" The words flew out before I could rein them in. I regretted them the moment I said them. They screamed 'I want to argue,' which I didn't. Did I?

"Why not? Better they get it right the first time, surely? Weird question."

"I don't tell everyone that I'm Keri with an i and not a y."

"You should. You're always complaining when people get it wrong."

"Hmm."

He had a point, which only annoyed me more. I had to snap out of these thoughts. These two weeks would've challenged even the strongest of couples. We were just tired. That's all. Tired, hungry, exhausted and bored. All the things we hated to be. I used to love these quirks of his. I had always loved that I saw something in him nobody else did. It was as if I were privy to a secret. For years I had stuck up for him, and I had believed we were good for each other. Why was that changing now? Tired. I was tired, I reminded myself.

The conversation had stopped and we were both sucked back into our thoughts. I was glad my question hadn't caused another big fight. I'd rather we look bored on the telly, than fight. Although, it did make me wonder about how we were coming across. It shouldn't bother me, but it did. Maybe I should do something romantic for him. Prepare a little picnic in the middle of the room. There was only so much I could do in here, but even a small gesture might help set us straight again. Jon had gone exceptionally quiet. I barely heard him next to me. Was he thinking about us, too? Was he remembering the first time we met? Was he thinking about whether he wanted to spend the rest of his life with me? Was he also—

A pillow flew across the room, and hit the kettlebells.

"What the hell was that for?" I asked with a hand to my heart. A flying pillow was the last thing I had expected.

"Sorry. I was just thinking about how much I want to exercise and how much I don't want to at the same time. Bloody kettlebells were just reminding me of how lazy I've become since being in here."

I sighed. No, he wasn't thinking of me.

"Jon, can I ask you a question?"

"Shoot."

"Did you really find that Elton guy funny?" I wasn't sure why, but it suddenly felt like everything was riding on his answer. That was another thing that had been on my mind ever since we'd met the guy. I couldn't believe that anyone would really find Elton funny. It said a lot about a person if they liked that sort of guy, and I really didn't want my boyfriend to be that person. Maybe Jon had just pretended out of politeness. *Say no. Say no. Say no.*

Jon laughed. "Strange question. He's hilarious. Ke, you should watch one of his performances. If you think he was funny when you met him, you're going to be rolling on the floor with laughter. Proper belly laugh sorta bloke. Oh my God! I just thought of something."

That you actually don't find him funny? "What's that?" I asked.

"I should totally do comedy with him when I'm out. He's Elton.

I'm Jon. The two of us were destined to meet."
Shit.

15

Ryan

I hadn't slept in a long time. I kept trying, but every time I closed my eyes, I would hear something that sounded like someone was in the room. Either the door was opening, or something would creak or squeak. Larry had told me the mission would be over when he opened that door, so either I was so close to it I could feel it, or I was losing my mind. I wanted to sleep more than anything. I wanted to get pulled into the darkness, and to not worry about anything for a few hours. I had never wanted anything more in my entire life. I'd never been the greatest sleeper back in the real world either, but I'd never battled as much as this. Now, it simply wouldn't come, and the more I tried to force it, the worse it got for me. I was sitting on the floor in front of the fridge now. I hated standing in this room for some reason, so I'd always walk somewhere and then sit down. Sitting made the room feel bigger somehow. It was odd, but I no longer cared about how I was coming across. I had no idea when I'd made the transition, but I'd gone from caring too much to not caring at all quite suddenly. I peered into the fridge and counted the boxes. Surely I could figure out how many days I would have left by the amount of food left over. There still seemed to be an alarming amount left though, but Larry *had* said he'd given us extra. Also, I hadn't eaten much since being in here. My appetite had all but vanished, and I seemed to be surviving more on coffee than anything else. I reached up for the coffee jar. I only had about a fifth of the granules left. I sighed. I'd made a deal with myself that I would consider leaving once the coffee was up, as by then my recommended stay would surely be beyond what Jon and I had decided on. Was that why I was drinking so much? Was I *that* desperate to get out of here? I was. Of course I was. I hadn't even showered that day. Or maybe even the day before. My hair was damp on my head. It felt awful, but at least I now knew it was either grease or the horrible shampoo making it feel that way, and not blood. I was a mess. I didn't look in the mirror at all anymore, but I didn't need the mirror to tell me what I looked like. I had never felt so low in my entire life. I ached for a sense of normality that never seemed to come. I lay on the floor and closed my eyes. Come on, sleep. Where are you?

I didn't fall asleep, but I did move into that strange place between sleeping and awake. In that place I imagined myself pressing the buzzer. I saw the door opening, and watched as I made my way out of the pod and into the real world. I saw the TV crew and smiled bashfully as they all clapped for me. Someone wrapped a towel around me, and they all told me that I had made it. I had made the full two weeks. No wonder I'd been so tired. A suitcase was waiting for me, with more money than I had ever seen in my life. As I took the case, I passed a mirror and I grinned at my reflection. My hair was messy, but it looked good. I looked even better than before. My eyes were the familiar ocean hues I had always thought them to be. Thank God. Thank God. *You did well, Ryan. You survived longer than everyone here.* I turned and saw the doors to the other pods were all open. I looked around, and there was Jon waiting for me outside. *You beat me,* he said, *you beat me fair and square, mate.* He smiled at me then, in a way he'd never smiled at me before. Like I was no longer the annoying kid his parents had forced him to be friends with. My father appeared, his smile as wide as my own. He too was looking at me in a whole new way. For the first time in my life, he was looking at me like I was someone he was proud of. I'd done it. I'd survived.

I jumped up! "Yes!" Only, when I opened my eyes I was still in the pod. I glanced around in confusion. No TV crew. No Jon. No proud father. No suitcase filled with money. I had imagined it all. I sank back down, but as I did my arm grazed the edge of the counter, and the jar of coffee fell to the floor. I must not have put the lid back on it, and I watched in horror as the granules scattered all over the floor. I tried to pick them up, but the area was wet from my sweat. I lay in the sticky mess, feeling hopeless and helpless. The coffee was finished. I was finished. I crawled over to the buzzer, and without giving it anymore thought, I pressed it.

***

I expected a great big beeping sound the moment I pressed the buzzer. I imagined the door would fly open almost instantaneously. Instead, nothing happened. I waited, but the only sound I could hear was the rasp of my own breath. I pressed it again, and waited. Panic began to rise. Either I was in the middle of a dream, or I was locked in here forever. *Let it be a dream, let it be a dream.* If it was a dream, it would mean I was actually getting some sleep. I'd wake refreshed, and ready to tackle another day. I didn't yet feel the relief I thought I would feel from pressing the buzzer. Instead, a horrible feeling of disappointment ran through me. Still, I no longer wanted to be here. I looked around, but it didn't *feel* like a dream. Or *look* like a dream. I glanced down and saw the sticky coffee on the floor, some of it on my hands and legs. I was awake. I was awake.

"Hello?" I called out. My voice was croaky. I hadn't used it in a while, other than the small mutterings to myself. "Hello?" I tried again. "I'm ready to come out."

The door opened, and I almost fainted with relief. It was Larry.

"Larry?" I whispered, not daring to believe. There was still a big possibility that he was not really there, no matter how real he seemed to me at the moment.

He smiled. "It's okay, Ryan. You're fine. You can come out now. You did well."

He reached for my hand and helped me up. *I did well. I did well. I did well.* I knew it. I knew it. I trailed after him, relieved when I stepped out of the pod for the first time. He sat me down, and I ran my hands over the soft sofa, happy to be feeling a different material again. I knew I was being dramatic. It wasn't like I had been inside for years, or even months, but I couldn't help the emotions. I felt close to tears. Larry had rushed off to get me some water, and I took a moment to compose myself. I was in the same waiting area I had been in when I'd first arrived, and I was surprised once again to find that the place was not swarming with the TV crew. Why was Larry—the show's *creator*—doing everything? He was back before I had a chance to fully question it all, and I sipped the water as if I hadn't had anything for days. Again, this was crazy, and over-dramatic, as drinking water was perhaps all I had been doing in there. How could I feel so different after two weeks? It was strange to know that this place had been outside my pod the whole time. I wished I could've held onto that thought in there, but I had felt vacuumed inside. I smiled gratefully at him.

"You did well," he said, and the words filled me with joy. "Would you like a cup of coffee or tea? We can sit and chat for a while before I call your cab."

I chuckled. I assumed he'd witnessed the coffee granules on the floor. Things didn't seem as serious now that I was out. Whatever I had felt inside had been multiplied by a thousand, while back in the real world the common sense part of my brain was starting to kick in again. It had been difficult inside, but it would've been the same for anyone. We weren't meant to live in a vacuum. I was fine.

I wasn't going insane. "Coffee would be wonderful."

He left again, and I gazed around. The room wasn't much to behold, just a small area with sofas and a potted plant which looked like it could do with some attention. I resisted the urge to get up and give the place a proper once over, mostly because I knew it would mean having to pass by the big mirror on the side. I hadn't noticed it when I first came in, and now that I was sitting, I was just outside of its viewpoint. I was happy to be out, but I wasn't quite ready for that yet.

Larry seemed to take forever to come back, but I wasn't sure whether my sense of time was still messed up. When he returned, the first thing I noticed was the strong smell of coffee, which was so different to the smell from inside the pod. This was proper coffee, percolated to perfection. As I reached to take it from his hand, I noticed my palm was still sticky from the wet granules, and I hoped nobody would notice. I couldn't see any cameras around, but I was pretty sure this part was still being filmed. The understanding that this was all for some big reality show dawned on me, and I felt instantly ashamed of the way I'd acted inside. Part of me wished I could go back and do it over, just to redo the image the world would now have of me, but another part was still too grateful to be out. I kept reminding myself that everyone would've done the same in my position.

"How ya holdin' up?" Larry asked.

"Uh, a little disoriented to be honest, but the coffee is good," I said and with each sip I found a bit of the old me return.

"I'm sure. It's tough in there. I tried doing it myself once, and I didn't do well at all. So, don't be hard on yourself, mate. I know you hoped to stay the whole hog, but being completely alone is a lot harder than anyone can imagine, hey?"

I nodded. Took another sip. Nodded. The more normal I felt, the more aware I was of my failure. It wasn't my proudest moment.

"Ryan, ol' boy, you did well. You should be proud. All right?"

I nodded. "Sure." I'd floated out as excited as a balloon ready to take flight, but I was deflated now, a broken mess I was afraid would never be fixed again.

"So, mind if I ask you a few questions? Or would you like a moment to yourself?"

I wanted to get out. "Now is fine."

"Ah, wonderful. We'll chat again in a few weeks, once you're all settled again, but I'd like to get a few questions while you're still in this mindset. Let me get my camera set up."

That made me feel better. If he was fetching his camera it meant none of this had been recorded yet. Which meant I still had time to look somewhat decent. I asked for the bathroom, and splashed water on my face without looking into the mirror. I still couldn't bring myself to. I ran some water through my hair and gave it a good rustle. Not quite my usual beauty regime but it would have to do. At least I no longer had coffee granules stuck to me. I wiped my face, then headed back to the room.

"Righto, let's get straight to it." Larry had mounted a tripod in both corners of the room, but told me I could look at him. I wasn't sure if the one camera was there in case the other one failed, or if having different perspectives of my face was important, but I tried to ignore them. "Naturally, the first question on my mind, which I'm sure is on yours too, is how long you think you've been in there. I'm surprised you haven't asked me that already."

I was surprised too, but I could guess my reasons why. I was afraid of the answer. I licked my lips, then stopped and stuck my tongue back in my mouth. It was a nervous twitch I sometimes had, something that was pointed out to me during one of my live video streams, and I'd been conscious of it ever since. Had I done it while in the pod? I hoped not. "Uh, it's so hard to tell. Clearly I didn't make the full two weeks, but I have a feeling I was close. So, I'm gonna estimate eleven days." I was pretty sure it was twelve, but I didn't want to seem over confident.

Larry seemed surprised. "Really?" He jotted something in his pad while I waited impatiently for him to confirm my timeframe. He looked up, and pushed his glasses back up his nose. I involuntarily did the same, but I wasn't wearing any. I must have left them in the pod, although I barely remembered wearing them inside. It didn't matter. They were only for show. The idea of wearing them seemed so ridiculous to me now.

"So, uh, you might be surprised to hear that you were inside for six days. Well, five and three quarters, but let's not get bogged down by technicalities, aye?"

I didn't dare look into the camera at this point. I stared instead at Larry trying to figure out if he was joking. I hadn't had much human interaction lately, but even if I had, I wasn't sure I'd be able to read him. He was an odd character, a tall jittery man who seemed ill at ease in his body. He looked like he had been locked up for a while too, his pale skin—paler than I remembered—and white hair made his red-rimmed eyes stand out. He was clearly happy though; he seemed to be about to jump out of his skin. It was like Skeletor had come alive. Was he joking, though? Was that why he seemed so excited? I kept waiting for him to yell, "I fooled ya," but it never came.

"Ryan, you okay?"

"Six days?" I asked. I'd forget about the five and three quarter bit. That was a little uncalled for, to be honest.

Larry offered me a sympathetic smile that immediately told me all I needed to know. "Don't feel bad. That's a long time to be alone."

I nodded. "It felt longer." And I now felt humiliated. I'd told him eleven days. Eleven! I'd lasted half of that time. I had another burning question I was too afraid to ask but blurted out anyway. "The others? How'd they do?"

"They're still in there," Larry said, and instead of feeling happy with this news I felt worse. So, I was the only idiot who couldn't survive? Was that it? Was I that pathetic?

"What part did you find the hardest in there? Was it the constant light, the cameras, the boredom?" Larry seemed completely unaware of how mortified I was, so hopefully it wasn't coming across on camera. I wasn't sure. Larry didn't seem to be very socially adept. He might not see my humiliation, but the rest of the world wouldn't be fooled.

The hardest? The fact I thought someone was in the room with me. The inability to look into my own eyes. The assurance of what a failure my life had become. The knowledge that I was a nobody. The fear that I was slowly losing my mind. I blinked a few times and tried to focus on Larry. I couldn't change what had happened inside, but I could control how I came across in this interview. I tried to rearrange my face into what I hoped included an ordinary smile. "You know, it was the lack of sleep, I think. It was tough to sleep in there, but at the same time it was the only thing I wanted to do. I guess that frustration got to me in the end." The answer surprised me. It wasn't a lie, but it barely touched the surface on what it was really like. I was impressed. Which only proved that it was easier to lie when there were other people around. The truth only reared its ugly head when I was alone.

"Yes, let's talk about the end quickly. I have not seen all the footage myself yet, but I did notice a bit of decline in the last few days. The constant need to wash your hair. What happened there?"

Smile, Ryan. Smile. I forced my lips up even though I was certain it hadn't reached my eyes. I shrugged. "Just never felt clean in there."

"Funny the things that will get to you, eh?"

I nodded.

The conversation moved slower than I'd have liked, but I finally got through the interview. I felt more and more uneasy with every question he threw my way, but I hoped a bit of charm came through somehow. I'd been called charming many times before. Although, that was when I did my own videos, with perfect hair, and carefully edited segments. I was only really charming when it was curated. How would the real me come across? Larry didn't seem upset that I was out early. Then again, why would he? It would be boring TV if everyone remained until the end, and more money for them to dish out.

"Where's everyone else, by the way?" I asked just before the car arrived for me.

"Everyone el…oh, the crew. Ah, they're on a break. Sleeping. We've been taking turns so someone is always awake in case a buzzer is pressed."

"Right. Well, uh, so you'll be in touch?"

"I'll be in touch. And, don't worry, Ryan. You did good in there." He sounded sincere, but I couldn't get rid of the suspicion he was judging me. If he were an emoji, he'd be a thumbs down. No, he'd be a laughing face.

Good for nothing. No good. The good, the bad, and the effing ugly. That was me. "Thanks."

16

Elton

I sat in front of the camera. It was time for yet another episode of the PodBook, which had, as of late (I think), turned into some sort of weird reality social media thing I kept forgetting wasn't real. The moment I talked into the little screen, it felt as if a light had gone up on stage for me, a cue for me to begin my performance. Then, whenever I was done, it would feel as if I was walking off stage, and back to the confines of my own space. Just yesterday (two days ago?) I'd 'signed out' of PodBook, then said, "Thank God that's over" and let out a giant fart. I'd snapped out of it the moment the sound, and smell, permeated the room, and made a joke of it as if I had planned it all along. Thankfully, I'd snapped out of it in time. I had honestly forgotten about the other cameras. I thought I'd love the constant attention, but having to stay on form at all times was proving to be difficult. The only downtime I had was in the bathroom, but even then I'd end up worrying that I was in there for too long. I kept imaging the words 'One hour later' popping up onto the screen as I finally made my way out. The last thing I wanted was to be seen as the guy who went to the toilet a little too many times. I was meant to be doing another camera session now, but I sat there too long, looking forlornly into the camera as if in a trance. It was as if I kept losing touch of reality. It wasn't the first time I'd found myself open-mouthed and vegetative. A joke came to mind but I wasn't sure how the audience would take it. That was a first for me. I didn't usually care how low my jokes got. Why did I care now? Nobody was watching? Or was everyone watching? Or…I blinked. Coughed. The stage was lit.

"So here's what I've been thinkin' because, let's face it, what else would I do in here. What is humour? Do you know the Americans spell it without the u? What does that mean? If the letter u is you then who makes the jokes?" I paused. I had practiced that one in the shower at least three times and it had sounded so much funnier then. Or had I said it all wrong? I suddenly couldn't remember what was funny about it anymore. It no longer made sense. There was meant to be a punch line that was going allow me the segue I needed for a long joke about Australians living in America and vice versa. Now I couldn't remember it, and the more I tried to figure it out the more confused I became.

This wasn't the first time I'd gotten stage fright. This year marked five years since the worst day of my life. I turned every bad thing that happened to me into a joke I could one day tell up on stage, but I still hadn't shared this one yet. No matter how many times I looked at it, this one still wasn't funny to me, and I found *most* things funny in life. The gig had been meant to be life changing. I guess it had been, just not in the way I'd wanted it. The presenter was an old friend of mine. One of the very few 'before I became well-known' friends I still had. He was the one who had gotten me the gig in the first place. I thought I'd owe him forever. Now I hated him forever. To this day I could remember those few minutes as if they had only just happened.

"I'd like to welcome on the stage a very good friend of mine, and one of the best comedians I've ever met, Bob Store." He'd said the name with so much ease, that he hadn't even realized what he'd said, and when I didn't go out, he still hadn't realized. Someone had to push me on, and the moment he saw my face as I basically tumbled up to the front of the stage, he understood. He laughed and reintroduced me. But the damage was done. All my jokes had disappeared along with my dignity. I'd tanked that day, all my jokes as unfunny as the next, and I had never quite managed to forgive him for what he had done to me. He'd said a million sorry's to me once it was over, and promised to get me back on again, but I hadn't found it in myself to forgive him. The anger was probably not deserved, but all I could think about was that he still thought of me as that boring kid with the boring name.

It was all I could think of now as I stared into the camera. Bob Store. Bob Store. Who the fuck was Bob Store?

"Joke book time," I said nervously as I blinked myself back to reality. Reality? This pod was not real life. PodBook was not real life. I really needed to focus. I couldn't tank again. I was *not* Bob Store. I flipped randomly to a page. "Ever tried to eat a clock? It's *time*-consuming." I laughed. Funny. Funny. Funny. Elton Rigby is hilarious. "Speaking of clocks," I said. I almost said 'cock' which would've probably sent me into a fit of laughter that I wasn't ready for yet. Pity, because I had a lot of cock jokes. Was this the audience for it, though? Who *was* the audience? *Focus, Elton. Focus.* "My time is almost done in here, I mean with you. Not with here. I probably still have a good week to go. Time is money and all that." What on earth was I talking about? I was no longer in control of my own mouth. "Let's see if I can fit in one more joke." Another random flip through the book. My hands shook, and I could only hope the camera hadn't picked up on it. What the hell was going on with me? I knew it wasn't going to be easy, but I figured I'd just get bored. I didn't expect my mind to take a holiday to la-la land. I was not prepared for it, and with no distractions I had no idea what to do to make it better. My headline was changing. "Want to hear a joke about pizza? Never mind, it's pretty cheesy." Then I stared into the camera a little too long again and mumbled something about being a comedian god, which was not quite the way I wanted to get that headline into people's minds. I just hoped like hell that my mumbling had been incoherent.

I got up and walked away without 'signing out'. I should've gone with a cock joke. I had seriously *cocked* that up. I laughed a little. *You see*, I told myself, *you are funny.*

<u>17</u>

Ryan

I spent two nights at a nearby bed and breakfast, and time flew by. I could've gotten a flight back the very day I got out, but I didn't want to go home yet. It felt too much like defeat. I lay in bed the whole first day, just watching the telly. It was ridiculous. I'd gone from one pod to another. I once read about a guy who had spent thirty years in prison, and the first thing he did when he got out was to go to a Macca's for a burger. He then robbed the place the following day and ended up being back behind bars, but that was beside the point. I couldn't believe that anyone would do something so mundane after getting a taste of freedom again. I had been gone six days (or five and three quarters to use Larry's crude words), so the comparison felt a little wrong, but here I was doing very much what I had done in there. Only instead of the wall, I was watching reality shows. Same thing, really. It was the shame I couldn't shake off. I only looked at my phone on the second day, and even then I couldn't bring myself to get back onto social media. I wasn't sure what was worse, not knowing what to say to everyone, or seeing all the posts I had saved to send off when I returned. I had two different posts planned, based on me either seeing the challenge through to the end—which I'd assumed I'd do—or seeing it through *almost* to the end. I didn't have anything planned for not even lasting a week. I didn't have the heart to do a video, or to smile into the camera, or to spend a few hours choosing the right photo. Fake.

Fake. Fake. Fake. I was a fake. I guess I had always known that. My biggest fear had come true. My façade had come crumbling down, and it had happened in front of the whole world. No, even worse, it was still going to happen. I had no idea when the show would broadcast. How did these things even work? This wasn't going to be like ripping a Band-Aid. This was going to be as long and painful as a trip to the dentist. And, just like a tooth extraction, I'd be left with a gaping hole where my dignity had once been.

It was now day three, and my flight was booked for that evening. I had a long day ahead of me with nothing to do but sit and think. I didn't want to think. I wanted to do everything except think, but the thoughts wouldn't stop coming. The way the sweet old owner of the B&B had looked at me when I walked in, as if I was a tiny bird who had fallen from her nest. The way I had looked at myself in the mirror for the first time and seen what she had just seen. I had never seen myself look so vulnerable before. I seemed to have shrunk, except for my eyes which had grown larger. It was this image that kept coming back to me. Knowing that this was what all my friends, families, and followers were going to see when the show came out was a tough pill to swallow. I wasn't sure what was worse, that I had failed or that some foul-mouthed annoying comedian had beaten me. Was he still there? Was this all a part of his comedy skit? Hell, at least he would finally have someone to laugh at his jokes.

I was being mean, but I didn't care. The guy had bothered me. He was too loud. Too crude. Too fake. Fake. *Shit*. I was fake. The thought brought me crashing back to reality. Did other people look at me the way I had looked at him? I reached for my phone again and typed in his name. I couldn't remember his surname, or if he'd even told us, but it didn't take long for me to find him. He hadn't done anything for a while, but I managed to find one of his old videos. I couldn't watch too long. It was…embarrassing. I sighed. If he made a fool of himself in the pod it wouldn't really matter. The man clearly had no sense of self. Unlike me. I was far *too* aware of what others thought of me. I skimmed through a few articles on the guy, some good, some bad, some I was pretty sure he'd written himself. Then I turned off my phone. That was enough. I needed to get out. From the glance I'd had out the window, I was wasting a perfectly good day. Also, this was my last chance to check out the area. Soon I'd been back in good ol' Newton, sipping coffee from the downstairs café. But not before I took the perfect photo of it. I balked. Maybe I should just throw away my phone. What I didn't know couldn't hurt me.

Bessie sat in the living room by herself playing a game of solitaire, and for a brief moment I thought I had been transported back to my little pod. Was I Bessie? I snapped out of it when she looked up and smiled.

"Good to see you up and about," she said.

"Uh, yeah. It's good." I'd lost my ability to talk to people.

"You're not checking out now are you?"

"No, only later. I thought I'd go out and get some lunch. Any good places around here?"

Bessie described a café nearby. She said it was close enough to walk to, and I supposed it was, only I took forever to get there. She'd told me that 'with my long legs' I should be there in ten minutes. It took me twenty-five. Time kept speeding up and slowing down. I spotted it before I saw the sign. It was the sort of place someone like Bessie would frequent. Apparently, they had the best coffee in the area. "None of those flat whites and moccachinos, and whatever other nonsense they keep coming up with," she'd said. "It's why I never go to the city anymore. I always end up arguing with the staff about the unnecessary new variations that keep popping up everywhere. Do you know that I saw them advertise *charcoal coffee? Charcoal!* Whatever for? No thank you, a regular coffee works just fine for me. Strong and simple." I'd backed away then. Her eyes had sort of glazed over as she spoke, and the interaction had become too much for me. Seemed I didn't want to be in the pod, but I didn't want to be out it either.

There wasn't anything special about the place, but the coffee *did* smell good, and I drifted toward it like a cartoon character. Nose up, following the smell. The moment I sat down I was greeted with a familiar face. It was the girl from the park, the one who had known Larry. She didn't seem to remember me, but I didn't hold that against her. I wasn't the most memorable guy in the world, no matter what my Instagram feed might tell you. 10,000 likes on a post does not equate to the same in real life. She bounced over to me, all smiles, a little like Tigger from Winnie the Pooh. The red hair only served to boost this image. Man alive she was pretty.

"Oh, hey there," she said as she handed me a menu. "Enjoyin' the sunshine?" Her voice was just as cute as her image, so chipper I found myself smiling back.

"I am. I've been stuck indoors, so it's good to be out."

"Too right," she said. "Well, let me know if you need any help deciding."

"Actually, I heard the coffee is really good here."

"It sure is," she beamed. "We only have one kind, served one way, but we've had no complaints."

I grinned back. She reminded me a little of Bessie there, despite the age gap. "I'll take one of those."

"Can I interest you in a brownie? The place is known for them."

"Sure, why not."

"Wonderful. You'll be helpin' a girl out. I've already had one of these today, and I shouldn't have another one. I'm trying to sell them off so I'm not tempted."

"I'll take two then. One now and one to go." I figured I'd give one to Bessie and regain a bit of my depleted reputation.

"You *are* a life saviour." She gave me a strange look, then shook her head and strolled off.

My hands immediately flew to my hair, as if I'd forgotten to wash it, and I had to resist the urge not to get out my phone to check. You know that thing you do, when you pretend you're taking a photo of something but you've actually reversed the camera so you can make sure you look okay? I glanced around at the café. I had a strong suspicion nobody here had ever done something like that.

"Here yer go," she said as she put a heavenly smelling coffee and brownie down for me.

"Wow, that looks and smells incredible."

"Oh, it is. I'll bring your other brownie in a takeout box. Uh, I know this is weird, but you really look familiar to me. Do I know you? Or, are you famous or something? We don't get many famous people around here. Not that I know of, of course. I'm not the most clued up with popular culture, to be honest. We once had that *Friends* guy, David Swimmer here and I had no idea who he was until he left and everyone told me. Oh, sorry, I'm babblin'."

God, this girl was cute. I didn't have the heart to tell her it was Schwimmer. "Actually, we've met. Sort of," I said. "Sorry I didn't say anything earlier, I wasn't quite sure myself," I lied.

"You met David Swimmer?"

I laughed. "No. I've met you."

"You have? Here?"

"At the park actually. You knew Larry. It was a few weeks ago," I said then shook my head. "No, it was a week ago. Sorry, getting my timeframes mixed up."

"Of course! Hey, weren't you wearing glasses?"

I prayed I hadn't turned the same colour as her hair. I *had* been wearing glasses that day, but they weren't even real. I just got them because I thought they suited me. I had left them behind in the pod and had pretty much stopped wearing them on the second day—or what I had probably thought was like day five or something.

"Contacts," I lied.

"I'm so glad you're here actually."

"You are?"

"I've been wondering where Larry has been all week. I was worried he was ill or somethin'."

"Oh, does he come here often?"

"Every single day. He's always here at 8.30 without fail. Two boiled eggs, white toast, and a cup of coffee. Like clockwork. Have you seen him?"

"I have. Uh," I was about to tell her about the show, but we'd signed forms about not telling anyone until the show aired. Not that it had stopped Jon from telling me. The urge to tell someone about the show, and what I had been through, was suddenly strong, especially someone as kind looking as the waitress, or Tigger as I was calling her in my mind, but I resisted. "I saw him the other day. He's fine. Just busy. He's working on a project."

"He is? Ah, I knew it. He's smart that guy. The last time I saw him he was talking to me about neuro…uh, wait, what was it… neurotransmitters I think. Something about coffee releasing them. I don't know now, but I always pegged him as the mad professor type you know."

"Yeah, I suppose you're right." I didn't know much about the guy, but mad professor seemed appropriate.

"So, how do you know him?"

"Oh, uh…"

"You're one of his students, aren't ya? Is it for his new project?"

"It's top secret," I said. This really was the easiest route to take right now. "Honestly, I'm not allowed to say."

Her eyes widened. "No way! This is exciting. Okay, well I'll let you get back to your coffee. Do me a favour and tell Larry to pop in when he's free again. I miss seeing him."

"I'll do that."

I sat for a while, sipping my coffee—just as delicious as promised—and enjoying my brownie (not sure I wanted to give the other one to Bessie anymore), and reading through the newspaper that had been on the table. I felt a million years older, or that I'd perhaps transported back in time when cell phones didn't exist, and it felt good not to spend time taking the perfect photo. I'd lost count of the amount of cold coffees I'd had because of that. When I finished, Tigger was nowhere to be found, so I paid up at the counter. As I was about to leave, I spotted her sitting in the corner reading her book, and eating a brownie. She saw me and waved me over.

She put down her book, Jane Austen's *Emma* I saw on the cover and smiled. She seemed like a classics sort of girl. "Guilty as charged," she said as she pointed to the brownie. "I couldn't help myself."

"I'll be honest, I'm probably going to eat this one on the way home," I said as I held up the box.

"It was lovely to meet you. I just wanted to say good luck with that secret project. Oh, and I'm Sarah by the way."

"Thank you. I'm Ryan," I shook her hand. "It was a pleasure to meet you too."

I walked back to the B&B a lot quicker than I had gone to the café. Sarah's bounciness must've been contagious. I was still mortified about the past week, but chatting to Sarah had made me feel better. Maybe things wouldn't be so bad after all.

<u>18</u>

Jon

Something was wrong. I was sure of it. I just didn't know what it was, and I didn't want to speak to Keri about it again. She had been acting strange lately, and it was hard to talk to her without the conversation moving to introspection. She was asking me probing questions, like what I really thought of her hair (*I love your hair, Ke. Ha! Hair. Ke. It even rhymes*), and if I ever thought about the future (*Back to the future? Nah, I'm more of a present sort of guy. Live for the moment and all that*), and whether I had known it was love when I saw her that first day (*Well, you were bleeding profusely, so love might not be the right word. Still, I thought you were hot as all hell*). Odd questions but none of my answers seemed to satisfy her, and I didn't know what to do about it. Right now, I figured the best thing to do was to leave her alone. I knew from past experiences that Keri was stubborn, and that nothing I said or did would help. The whole thing was ridiculous anyway. Of course I loved her. Why would I be with her if I didn't? Telling her she was good eye candy and that I'd known it even with blood gushing down her leg was not the right thing to say. I thought for sure it would make her laugh. Instead, she went off at me, telling me there was more to her than just looks. *That* particular argument had happened not so long ago, and she still sat fuming in the corner of the room. I glanced at her now, and wondered if I should console her, but there wasn't any point. If she wanted to sulk then let her sulk. Maybe for once in my life people would see that I wasn't the cause of all arguments.

I desperately needed to visit the bathroom. I couldn't remember the last time I had gone, and I'd been drinking more water than necessary. I felt hungry all the time, but Keri was so sure I was eating too much that I tried to appease her by filling up on water. It didn't help. Man alive, why were they taking so long in the bathroom? I was going to pee myself. Keri made a funny little noise, another one of her puffs to remind me she was upset, and the sound somehow snapped me back to the reality that I was going to wait forever for that person to finish up, because there was nobody in the bathroom. *There. Was. Nobody. Else. Here.* A bead of sweat dripped down my face, and I wiped it off with my sleeve. Who was this imaginary person I kept waiting for? I better not tell Keri about this again. Soon she'd think I was waiting for another woman or something. Lately she twisted all my words.

It still took me a while to make my way to the bathroom, mostly because I wasn't sure how well my legs were going to work. I felt unstable and unsure of myself, and this lack of control was unlike anything I had ever experienced before. Still, a lack of control in my mind might be a little better than a lack of control with my bladder. That thought finally got me up, and I made it to the bathroom in record time. After relieving myself for what felt like forever (which in here could mean two minutes or two hours), I splashed cold water on my face and gave myself a little talking to. I'd always laughed at those people who said mantras to themselves every day. One of my previous roommates, during the pre-Keri days, used to sit on the bed each day and repeat: *you've got this, you're stronger than you think, you're smarter than you think, you've got this.* Over and over again. I had thought it was a joke at first, something he took offense to, of course. He hadn't stayed with me long, but I hadn't minded at the time. I thought he was a whack job. I'd told him, too. The day he moved out I asked him if he needed help with the boxes. He said he was fine. I replied, "Of course you do. You've got this. You can carry those boxes yourself. You're stronger than you think. You've got this!" I never saw the guy again. Now here I was chanting something similar to myself in the mirror. The only difference was that I wasn't sure how much I believed my own mantra.

When I got back out, Keri was still on the floor, her gaze to her lap, almost as if she was meditating. She'd been trying to get me to start meditation classes with her for a long time, but I had always refused to go. Why the hell would I want to waste my time doing nothing? Our time on earth wasn't long, and I had every intention of making the most of that time. If I wanted quiet time, I could just go to bed. I turned away from her and made myself a cup of coffee. The sound of the kettle soothed me, and as I poured the contents into the mug I wondered if we would really run out of coffee before the end of our time in here like Keri said we might. Larry had assured us we had extra provisions, and it looked to me like we still had enough to keep us going for a while. I thought of making a small cup just in case, but instead found myself doubling up the coffee dosage just to prove a point.

I didn't want to sit on the bed, but Keri was already on the floor, so I went back to my usual spot. I grimaced when I noticed a mark against the cream wall from where I always sat. Keri would have a fit if she saw it, so I propped up a pillow to hide it from her view. I took a sip of coffee, recoiling slightly from the intensity, and then grinned as it danced down my throat. Wow. Two spoons of this stuff was totally the way forward. Maybe after this I'd finally tackle a round of exercises. If I didn't use those kettlebells soon Keri was never going to forgive me for convincing her to bring them in.

"Did you just make yourself coffee without even offering one to me?"

I glanced over at Keri, who was now leaning forward with her elbows on her knees. "I didn't think you'd want any."

"Is that so? You know that's the first cup you're making for yourself, don't you? I've made heaps for you. In fact, I've made every single other cup for you but that one. But you don't even think of making me one. Nice."

"No, I made us one that first day, remember?"

She rolled her eyes, and as she did her elbow slipped off her knee and she almost whacked her chin. I wished she had. Comedy. Now that's what this place was missing. I let out a little chuckle.

"Are you laughing at me?"

"Come on, Ke. You almost hit yourself in the face with your own knee. It was funny from where I'm sitting. Trust me. If the roles were reversed you would've laughed at me. Do you want some coffee? I'll make you one." *Say no. Say no.*

"No. I'm fine. Thank you very much for thinking of me."

"Wow, sarcasm does *not* suit you."

She didn't reply at first, and the two of us went back to what we were doing. The coffee tasted a little too bitter now. It needed some extra water, or some more of that powered milk they'd given us, but if I got up she might expect me to make her one. I wasn't really trying to be nice. I just wanted her to think I was. Reverse psychology and all that. I drank it as it was and tried to enjoy it.

"You really didn't think of offering me one?" she said again. Clearly this was not a topic that was just going to go away on its own. I wasn't surprised by this. Keri didn't let things go as easily as I did. She would tell me she was fine, and then she'd bring it up out of the blue again, sometimes even after days had passed. Then she'd get angry when I was not as upset as she was.

"I just did."

"Not *now*. When you made a cup for yourself, did it not even cross your mind?"

"You looked like you were meditating. I didn't want to disturb you. I thought I was doing the right thing. Wow, Ke, you don't have to turn everything into an argument."

"Meditating? Since when do I meditate?"

"You've been badgering me to do it with you for months. I

figured you were giving it a go."

"Oh, so I *badger* you now? Nice, Jon. Nice."

"Come on, let me make you a cup." I was safe because there was no way she'd say yes to this now. Her stubborn streak would take over, just as it always did.

"No thank you."

"Okay then. Suit yourself."

She sighed. "Jon, I'm tired of this. Why is this so hard? I thought it would be easy. Well, not easy, but not nearly as hard as this. I'm going out of my mind from boredom."

Guilt washed over me. I probably *should've* made her a cup. Keri was a tall and confident woman on the outside, but right now she looked so small. "Come on, bunny, cheer up. Join me here." I patted the space next to me. Sometimes I was bunny and she was funny, sometimes it was the other way around.

She laughed and surprised me by getting up and joining me.

"Hi, funny," she said.

"When did those nicknames start?" I asked.

She shrugged. "I have no idea. I guess I always thought you were funny, and as cute as a bunny."

I wiggled my nose at her. "Is this our first romantic moment in here?"

She smiled. "You know, I think it might be." She sidled in close to me. "How ya holdin' up, Jon? Honestly."

"Why do you say it like that?" Had she noticed that I was starting to lose it? And was it because she knew me so well or because it was obvious? I didn't want to unravel in front of the whole nation, or, at least, however many people end up watching this show.

"I guess I don't want to feel like I'm the only one that's losing my marbles in here," she said.

"Aye? You too? You're the strong one. I figured you were fine. Other than constantly annoyed with me, of course."

"You think *I'm* the strong one? I wish." She sighed, then sniffed.

I hoped she wasn't getting sick. That was the last thing we needed. "Nah, I'm not strong at all. I'm having a hard time in here. It's not easy, and," she gestured around her, "these cameras don't help."

"I'm struggling, too. I mean, when's the last time I went without exercising for so long?"

"We should've brought something else other than those damn kettlebells," she said.

"You say that, but if we're not using those, then what makes you think we would've used anything else that we brought in here? It's like this place sucks the energy out of you. I've never felt so lethargic in my life."

"Lethargic? Nice word. You been doing crossword puzzles when I'm not around or something?" she teased.

"You serious?" What the hell? Was she really just calling me stupid right now? Is that what she thought of me?

"Oh come on, I'm kidding. You're just not a big word sort of guy, that's all. You're a big muscle kind of guy," she said as she reached over to touch my bicep.

I flinched. What a way to make me look in front of the cameras. "Nice, Ke. Nice."

"It was a *joke*. Wow, there goes the honeymoon period."

I stood up, suddenly desperate to get away, and as I did my pillow fell down. I'd forgotten about the dirty mark on the wall until I heard Keri gasp.

"What the hell is that? Is this your sweat? Gross. Wait, were you hiding this with the pillow? That's disgusting, Jon. You know you have to put your face on that thing each night? Don't you think?"

Wonderful. Now I was dirty *and* an idiot. "I wasn't hiding anything. I didn't even see it. It's just a bit of dirt. It's not the end of the world. I'm going to shower."

"You do that. You *need* to."

Fuming, I stormed into the bathroom, and the moment I opened the sanity line into the small room I felt as if I'd been vacuumed inside. The bathroom had always felt like our safe place, but for the first time it felt just like an extension of the rest of the pod, only more extreme. I usually used this space as a place to clear my head of unwanted thoughts, but those very thoughts seemed to sudden multiply. Keri was having a hard time in here too, but did she also feel as if she was losing her mind? No, that was all on me. I stood there for a long time trying to figure out whether I should shower, or just pretend to, but Keri's nose had taken on some sort of superpowers lately, sniffing out anything dirty. Unfortunately, while we had ventilation in the room, it wasn't enough, and I was pretty sure the two of us were emitting some rather rancid odours in here. Maybe being in a pod alone was a better idea after all. I stepped under the shower, and thought once again about Larry. It disturbed me a little that he was my first thought right now, especially considering I was completely naked, but something about the guy irked me. Left with nothing else but my own thoughts, I naturally gravitated toward him. Something was up with him, I was sure of it. But what? I was a tall guy, tall enough to be annoyed that the shower didn't come with its own separate ceiling. The bathroom had clearly been built as an afterthought. Either that or they'd wanted to make sure we still felt mildly exposed. I'd already searched for hidden cameras, but hadn't found any. So, unless they'd been hidden *that* well, I was safe to be in here without clothes on. But why then did I feel so exposed? Why could I still see Larry's beady eyes on me? The camera on the wall! The thought hurtled its way to me, and I got down to the floor. Was that it? Was the camera just high enough to still get a good view of the bathroom? Was Larry watching me right now? Fuck him! I wouldn't let that weirdo creep get any more footage of me. I spent the rest of the time on the cold tiles, while the warm water cascaded over me. The contrasting temperatures made me feel strange, yet good. I reached up to switch the water off, then both dried and changed while still sitting down. I felt restored, like a reset button had been pushed. New thoughts were running through my head. *Stay ahead of Larry. Stay ahead of Larry.*

19

Elton

Elton Rigby, picks up his towel
In the shower where he got clean.
He's not what he seems.
Waits in the bedroom, wearing a shirt,
That he picked for the pod.
He's a comedian god.

The song played over and over in my head, until I wasn't sure which words I had made up and which were real. Was anything real? Eleanor. Elton. Who even cared? It wasn't my real name anyway. I kept trying to figure out how the Beatles song ended. I thought it would be a nice touch to change the whole song to my own words by the time I reached the last day in here, but whether I had two or five days left I was no longer sure. Also, it wasn't easy trying to figure out how to change the song when I could barely remember how the actual one went anymore. I tried to sing the real song again, but each time I did I'd start mixing in the words I had come up with in here.

"Eleanor Rigby, picks up her towel…" I started, then stopped. No, she didn't pick up her towel. What did she pick up? "La-la-la, lonely people," I improvised. There was something to do with loneliness, I was sure of it. God damn this was annoying. I'd formed my name around this song and I couldn't for the life of me think of the lyrics anymore. And how the hell did it end?

I tried to busy myself by cleaning the pod, which wasn't easy without any products. Could they not have at least given us a broom? Or were they hoping for some sort of solo version of *Lord of the Flies*? Did they want to watch us turn into animals? I wasn't even much of a neat freak back home, but I didn't know what else to do with myself in here, and no amount of cleaning seemed to be enough. I would clean for an hour and feel like all I had done was transfer the dirt from the pod onto myself. Yet I continued to do it, even if only to make myself feel better. My joke book lay face down on the floor. I picked it up and examined it. For an old book it was in great condition, which was surprising considering the amount of times I had flipped through the thing as a teenager. Except for one double page where tiny specks were dotted all over from a Cola explosion. I remember being so pissed off that day, especially when I found out that my 'friend' Lenny had given the can a good ol' shake before going home. He'd phoned me later that day asking me how my drink had been. It had splattered over my new white shirt too, and my mum had been so angry at me. She'd only gotten me that shirt after I'd promised to do the dishes for a week. I barely remembered the shirt now, but back then it had felt so important to me. God, that felt like a long time ago. It *was* a long time ago. Why did I remember something like this but forget my lines when I went out on stage? Why did I still feel like that angry little kid when I was already forty-two? Almost forty-three actually. Which was close to forty-five. Which, really, was close to fifty. I put down the book, and continued with my cleaning. I made the bed, stopping every now and again to do something silly even though my heart wasn't in it. I was supposed to be here to entertain. To bring Elton Rigby back onto center stage. But I felt more like Bob Store here than Elton Rigby, and it was getting harder and harder to pretend. The worst part was that I barely knew who Bob Store was anymore, so every reminder of him only made me confused. He hadn't been a bad guy.

Just…well, just boring. I tucked the duvet around the mattress like a hotel, then told my 'audience' what the correct way of doing things should be. That immediately gave me an idea of pretending as if I was in some sort of hotel show, and I spent some time showcasing the place as if it were worthy of five stars.

"This room even comes with a Michelin-star restaurant," I said as I opened the fridge with extravagance. "Think of it as part Blumenthal, part Ramsay, and maybe even a little bit of Oliver thrown in. You know, minus the taste." I picked up a box and held it out to one of the cameras. "Or, actually, the presentation. Who am I kiddin'? This place is more hostel than hotel."

I wasn't sure when I had switched from cleaning, to giving a tour, but I was exhausted, and neither one of those options appealed to me anymore. Hadn't I given a tour of the place before? The Blumenthal part seemed familiar, and I was now pretty sure I'd said those exact words before. Was I rehashing my jokes? Was that the sort of comedian I had become? They weren't even good jokes. My gaze fell on some peeled paint in the corner, where the floor met the wall, and I bent down to examine it. I scratched at it and some of it came off, so I scratched at it some more, watching as tiny bits of paint fell to the floor. The more I took off, the more it annoyed me and the more I scrubbed. I stopped when a small pile of cream paint had formed in front of me, like a little mountain for ants. I scrubbed so much that a bit of blood formed at the tips of my fingers, just under my far too long fingernails. Gross. I should've cut them before coming into this place, but I'd forgotten, and now they were all I was going to think of. Thankfully the camera probably wouldn't pick up on them. Just in case I needed not to draw any attention to my fingers. A drop of blood fell onto the ant's mountain, snapping me back to the weird reality of what I was doing. I laughed a little then, the sound odd and forced. Then I made a few jokes about the place being *apeel*ing, and how being in here was like watching paint dry. Ha ha ha.

The ending of the song came to me. Not the exact words, but the idea. Eleanor Rigby died in the end. *Buried with her name* were the words I could remember. An image of a tombstone came to mind, and for the first time I wondered what name would be put on mine. Elton or Bob? What name would I want on there? I stared at the buzzer. Should I hit it? I wanted to. The thought of seeing another face again other than my own was overwhelming. I thought having a mirror in the pod was a good idea, but I was now so sick of seeing my own face. Maybe I didn't look at myself all that much, but the long moments in front of the mirror had made me see myself in a different life. When I thought of myself, I imagined a twenty-something-year old up on stage. Not surprising considering the amount of times I re-watched old videos of me doing standup. Sometimes that mental image was so strong that for a few seconds I'd still see that guy in the mirror. The longer I stared at myself, the more I began to morph into the forty-two-year-old man everyone else saw.

There was more to the end of the song. I didn't want to think of them, but they came regardless as I stared at the buzzer. One line played over and over again in my head. I needed to get up and do another PodBook skit, but this place seemed to have sucked out all of my energy. I hadn't even done one yesterday. I was supposed to be in here to entertain, but I'd become the world's most boring comedian. Unless, of course, everyone found it funny that I was spending most of my time staring at the wall, or counting wrinkles on my hands. I should just press the damn buzzer but the line kept playing in my head. *Nobody came.*

<u>20</u>

Melanie

It just took that one dream of Andy for him to haunt the rest of my nights. I tried to resist it at first. I prolonged my meditation as much as I could, I drew more, and I tried to stack happy thought upon happy thought on top of the memories. Still, they seeped out, oozing like dirty liquid from a sewerage pipe. Even if I stopped them from escaping, they were still inside me, festering more each day. If I didn't deal with them, I'd one day explode. I didn't need a therapist to tell me that. This was Basic Humanness 101. The pod wasn't the place I wanted to get down to the heart of my issues though, but it had some up sides to it. For one, Andy couldn't get to me. I was safe. Even when I was out of the pod, I would remember what it felt like to be in here, walls protecting me like arms. I'd forgotten what that felt like. For years I'd lived with the sort of deep fear that nobody should ever experience. As I lay in bed now, my hands moved over my stomach, just like it had when *she* was inside me. I'd never given her a name, I'd never even truly known if she was a girl, but she'd felt like a girl. With every kick of her little foot, and wriggle of her body, I'd feel the sort of love that made me understand what love was for the first time. It was different to any other love I'd ever experienced, and even though I had no idea what the future held I wasn't sure if I would ever feel that again. I sometimes felt bad that I had never given her a name, but I supposed a part of me always knew she would never see the world the way I had. When she'd died a part of me had been relieved.

"Oh." A little sound puffed out of me. It sounded like the air that escaped a balloon that you were trying to tie.

It took me by surprise. I turned to face the wall now, where the camera couldn't see my face. I didn't mind being vulnerable in here, but these tears were not meant for anyone but her. I felt around for my sock and tied it around my eyes again, pretending to be fast asleep. Sometime in the night I must've pushed off the eye mask. I pursed my lips tightly, scared that if I made enough sound it would turn to sobbing. This was the first time I was admitting to that relief. She'd been my little secret for so long. I didn't even care she was half of Andy. She was mine, and that was all that mattered. That was, of course, until the day he found out. Then I did care. I cared a lot.

"A little Melanie. A tiny little Melanie," he said as he put his hand on my stomach.

For a brief moment I thought this would make him change. Babies did that to people, didn't they? Not to monsters, though. Monsters never changed. By then I knew that I was living with one. Unfortunately, I made the mistake of flinching at his touch. He sneered.

"I hope she's just as feisty as you are," he said. "When were you planning on telling me?"

"I didn't know," I had whimpered. I was upset with myself then. Just before he found out, I had told myself that I had to start sticking up for myself more. Something about Andy reduced me to a person I was ashamed to be. I'd stood up for myself many times before. I'd tried to leave before. You never knew how hard it was until you were in the situation yourself. I had judged many women who were stuck in relationships they said they couldn't get out of. I would never judge anyone ever again.

"You didn't know? You think I'm a fool, do ya? Bloody stuck-up bitch." He hit me then, so hard I thought my nose was broken. I didn't care. He could knock me around like Tyson, as long as he stuck to my face, and not my belly. *Just leave her alone.*

I lay there for a while, my eyes shut tight by the sock around my head.

The darkness was pleasing at first, but soon became unbearable. I pulled it off, then sat up, and strolled as casually as I could to the bathroom. Once there, I allowed the emotions to come. *Just leave her alone.* He didn't leave her alone. He didn't only hit my face. I always knew it was coming. I switched the shower on, then slid to the floor. The water mingled with my tears, and I cried properly for the first time since I lost her. I'd been angry, but I'd never allowed myself to be sad. In a way, we had both escaped him. Still, even though I never got to meet her, I missed her. For the short time that she'd been inside me, I had never felt more whole.

I wasn't sure how long I sat on the shower floor. For the first time since being in the pod, I wasn't in tune to the time passing on the outside. The other contestants came to mind. Were they lost in this strange place, suspended in time and uncertainty? I didn't like the loss of control I felt, but knowing how quick my mind could slip in here, made me snap out of it. I scrubbed my face, then got out, ready to start over. I felt lighter from the release of emotions, and more prepared for their inevitably return. As I changed, I thought again about the others. Was Jon without the h still as cocky as he was when he first went in? He reminded me a little of Andy. Not that I thought he was a monster—I didn't—but he was one of those guys who took up a lot of space in this world. He moved with a surety and sense of entitlement that made it obvious he was not sure of himself at all. He was so typically blokey too. All about his muscles. All about him. Maybe this was why I hadn't liked him from the start. I didn't like people who had to hide. Then again, wasn't that what I was doing all the time? Wasn't that what we all did? We all just did it in our own ways. Who was I to judge his method? Keri must've seen something she liked in him, so he couldn't be all that bad. Unless Keri wasn't the nice girl she seemed to be. I doubted it. They all seemed like decent people. Just all a little messed up in their own ways. But maybe you had to be a little messed up to agree to a show like this. Or would money make people do anything? What about Ryan? How was he doing? I had liked him from the moment I met him, despite him being in cahoots with Jon. Unlike Jon and Keri, I felt I could relate to him. He was younger than me, and I had a feeling he hadn't been through all that much in his life. At least, not as much as I had. Yet, despite this, he seemed so unsure of himself. I hoped he had some coping mechanisms for this place, because a guy like him might not be able to handle the silence. Although, maybe I was wrong. Maybe Jon would be the one to fall first. Cocky people usually didn't have much inner strength to rely on. I hoped Ryan did well. I knew he had the strength in him, but I just wasn't sure how easy it would be for him to find it. And that buzzer was so tempting. Even to me, and I enjoyed being in the pod. I was certain Elton had long gone. What would he do inside once the jokes ran dry? Or was I too quick to judge? Hopefully he'd prove me wrong. From the short meeting I'd had with all of them, it was hard not to judge from first impressions. What had they thought of me? Probably not much. I didn't mind. I liked not being noticed. There was a party I'd attended soon after I'd finally left Andy, some work function I couldn't weasel out of. The following day three people came up to me and asked me why I hadn't been at the party, even though I had been there almost to the end. My light grey shirt had matched the shade of the wall that evening. Maybe I'd simply become one with it. I didn't feel sorry for myself then, and I definitely didn't feel sorry for myself now.

I'd had three weeks to prepare for life in here. It wasn't much time, but I made the most of it. I researched, and watched a lot of videos, and I knew how easy it would be for your mind to slowly unravel in a place like this. Most of the videos I had watched were based on solitary confinement in prison, which was a whole different story to what we were going to go through in here. We had a shower, a bathroom, a bed, a supply of food and drinks. We even had our one allowed item to keep us entertained. In that sense, we were luckier. There was, however, one thing that made our life harder than prison. We had cameras on us. Every minute was being recorded, and everything we did was going to go out for the rest of the world to see, and that no amount of prison or solitary videos could prepare me for it. Would the constant feeling of being watched help us, or would this be the thing that made us fall apart? Still, the research had helped. I'd stuck to my schedule every day, and had done my exercises and meditation even when I didn't feel like it. Today's dream and cry in the shower was something I hadn't expected, but I would not let it deter me from continuing what I had started.

The days had gone by relatively quickly for me, and even though I always thought I would do well, I was surprised at the ease at which I'd gotten through them. The meditations had been easier than they were back home, the silence a fantastic backdrop to the Zen-like state. Maybe one day I'd even go on a meditation retreat, or visit a Buddhist temple. It would be interesting to see how I did with others around me. I chuckled every time I finished with a meditation routine. I imagined the editors of the show cutting to another contestant each time. There was probably a lot of eye rolling and plenty of "why did we choose *this* girl?" every time they saw me sitting still for an hour. I couldn't imagine my yoga routine or even my exercise session was anymore riveting. There were only so many times you could watch someone doing the same thing over and over again. Because of this, I got the feeling I was going to get little air time. This suited me greatly. The odd nightmare, and the cat drawings, were probably the only things that made me interesting. Even the alphabet game was dull, and because I did it in my head instead of saying it out loud, I probably just looked like I was meditating again. "God, there she goes again," they'd say. "Quickly, switch to Jon without the h."

I made myself a cup of tea, then sat on the floor with my back against the bed. I looked at the date at the top of the book and smiled. If my calculations were correct, I only had two more days in here. Three at the most. I was going to walk out of this place a better person, and richer too. I had come in here for the money, but I'd gained a whole lot more. I flipped through the book and smiled at all my drawings. I had improved since I started. With so little time left in here, I might even skip one or two of my exercises and spend some more time with my drawings. The first thing I drew was Todd in the Pod. He wasn't doing much. Just lazing about on the floor. Without thinking I found myself drawing a little kitten, a little fluff of a thing so small and so furry you could barely make out its features. I drew it again, and this time I drew Todd in the Pod lying next to it. Paw to paw. And just like that, Todd was a father.

21

Elton

Nobody came. Nobody came. Nobody came.

I did something stupid the night before. It might have been in the middle of the damn day, but in the real world all my bad decisions were done at night, only now I couldn't blame the booze. Or the drugs. Maybe that's why I was going crazy in here. Without stimulants the world was flat. I'd tried to go up on stage without a hit of coke, or a swig or ten of vodka, but it always made everything more difficult, as if my words had to move through a heavy smog before reaching the audience. My mind, and my delivery was always a lot more concise with a little helping hand. What I could've done for something in here. It would've made this whole experience so much better. Why was it so bad? If it made me more confident, and funnier, then what was so wrong about it? Who was I hurting? I'd done quite well without it at the start of this experience, but maybe I'd used up all my energy reserves too quickly. With no drugs, and no more jokes, I was falling apart. The whole thing didn't feel worth it to me anymore, and last night had only amplified it. That's when I knew I had to get out of here, because out of all the hilarious moments I'd had in here, I knew without a shadow of a doubt that the one moment they would play over and over again was my stupid meltdown.

It had all started quite innocently. I sat on the floor, flipping through the joke book for inspiration. I had my back against the wall to avoid looking at the scratched-off paint. After scraping it until my finger bled, I had an odd desire to keep at it. Without wanting to be obvious, I'd taken a 'stroll' around the pod every so often, making as if I was walking through a park. I'd stop to 'rest' at my imaginary water station, and I'd use this time to casually scratch off a bit more with my back to the camera. I'd do it quickly, so that even if I was caught it would be too fast for the viewers to see it. I'd splash the imaginary water on my face, and then stroll off again, only to come back later and do it all again. I must've done it more times than I thought because there was now a massive section of the wall without paint. This was why I found myself with my back against it the night before, sitting with my knees up and my joke book in front of me. The more aware I was of the wall the more I wanted to continue peeling the paint. I had been looking through the joke book, wondering why I had ever found it so funny, when I noticed how raw my nails were, especially my forefinger, which I'd used almost exclusively in the peeling. I kept glancing at my finger and then back at the book, over and over again until I could no longer remember why I was looking at the book in the first place. And then, just like that, I imploded. One minute the book was in my hand, the next it was shredded to pieces on the floor.

I couldn't remember when I had fallen asleep or how I had moved from the floor, but when I woke, I was in bed. The first thing I saw was pieces of the joke book scattered over the floor, and the end of the joke book seemed to signal the end of my time in here. I no longer wanted to be funny. I no longer saw the joke. Only my ego had kept me in so long, but I needed to get out before I made an even bigger fool of myself. Maybe I could even turn this around for me. I could finally tell the world who I was, and say that Bob Store had emerged in the pod. Boring ol' Bob Store. Elton Rigby was too big a personality to be in such small confines. Maybe they'd appreciate my honesty. I stared at the buzzer now, which seemed to have grown overnight. *Nobody came. Nobody came.* Then I stood up, and walked dramatically over to it, using my last shred of comedy to end it for me, and pressed it.

At first, nothing happened. Even though the room was already silent, it seemed to get even more silent, if such a thing was possible. I stared at the door, and waited. This was the time to make a joke. To look into the camera and say something amusing, something that would make everyone watching laugh, and my whole stay worthwhile. Like the devastating joke book melt down, this was definitely going to be shown on the telly. This was the part all the producers wanted to happen. Yet, despite this, I couldn't bring myself to even crack a smile. The silence had been replaced by the loud beating of my own heart, a forceful reminder of being alive and having failed. I no longer cared. I just wanted to get out of this hell hole. As I reached over to press it again, the door opened, and I jumped to my feet.

"Sorry, sorry," said a harried sounding Larry as he pushed open the door like a man battling a boulder on an uphill. He looked exhausted and pale, as if he'd been doing the same pod challenge as I had. He turned to me. "You okay?" he asked.

I frowned. "Uh, I'm fine. Are *you* okay?"

"Yes, sorry, I'm a little unwell, that's all." Then a big smile formed on his face that was obviously fake. I knew it because it was the same smile I had used a million times before. "Come on out. You did well, Elton. Very well. I was sorry to see you press the buzzer. Come on, take a seat."

I followed him out, and a million emotions cascaded through me, from happiness, weariness, and disappointment. Most of all though, I felt tired. I was sure I looked the same as Larry did. Man the guy looked bad. Whatever he had, I didn't want to catch it. Maybe I had gone into the pod with his germs on me. That would make a lot of sense. That could explain why I hadn't been myself. Larry had gone, fetching me water, which really was the last thing I wanted at the moment. I wanted vodka. A lot of it.

"So," he said as we sat down to chat. "Let's talk about how you're feeling."

His voice was flat, and the whole thing seemed staged. This wasn't the exit scene I had been anticipating, and while I didn't want to go back inside, I felt a desperate urge to get away from all of this. *Me?* I wanted to say, *how about we talk about how* you're *feeling?*

"We'll conduct a proper interview at a later stage, but I do have a few questions for you if you don't mind. I'm sure you're desperate to get home."

"Sure, go for it," I said.

"Let's start with the obvious one. Why did you quit?"

I sighed. "Dude, it was hard," I said as I ran a hand through my greasy hair. "It was…"I struggled to find the right word. "Boring," I decided. I laughed bitterly. "And I'm not a man who likes to be bored. I guess the place was a little too small for me."

"Did you feel a loss of control?" He was sipping water in between his questions and a bit of colour had returned to his face.

"I guess you could say so. I just didn't feel like myself in there." I felt like Bob Store, that's who I felt like, but I didn't say it out loud.

"You did very well," Larry said.

"I did? I was trying to go for the comedy angle, but it was hard. It…" I gulped. Emotion gripped hold of me, and for a brief and terrifying moment I thought I was going to burst into tears. Was I on camera right now? I looked around.

"You okay?" Larry asked.

"I…I'm just drained," I said.

"Don't worry, I'll set you up in a hotel tonight and…"

"No, I think I'll just go home," I said.

"I understand, but flights…"

"It's fine," I interrupted. "I'll go straight to the airport. I'll figure something out."

"Are you sure? You might feel better if…"

"I'm sure," I said a little too harshly. I didn't want to be here right now.

"So, now comes the fun part," Larry said with forced enthusiasm.

"Fun?"

"How long do you think you were inside for?" The question perked Larry up. That saying 'death warmed up' seemed appropriate for this moment. Maybe he'd just been bored to death before, and having me out had given him something to do.

"Where are the other guys?" I said, ignoring the question. "Not the contestants, the…" What was the word… "crew."

"They're working on the footage as we speak. So, time…this is the part I find the most fascinating. How long do you think you were inside?"

"You never opened up for me, so I clearly failed," I started.

"Failure is not a word I like to use. You did well, Elton. Go on, give me your best guess."

While in the pod I had been certain I only had a few days left, but now that I was out, I wasn't sure. My sense of time had shifted, and as I struggled to come up with an answer I wondered if I was about to make a fool of myself all over again.

"You know, I have no idea," I said. "I'm going to say I was in there for ten days, maybe eleven."

Larry beamed at me. "Impressive. Eleven and…" he looked at his watch then. "Almost twelve actually."

"Shit! So damn close."

"Can I ask though, if you thought you only had a few days left, why did you leave?"

This one I knew the answer to immediately. "I no longer wanted to be in there."

"So the money was no longer a driving force?" he asked.

"Maybe it never was," I said.

"Interesting," he said as he wrote something down.

We spoke a bit more, but I soon asked to leave. This might be interesting to him, but every second with him was another reminder of my failure. Not that he seemed to mind. I'd managed to book a flight online, now that I was back with my blessed phone. Just having the phone in my hand again made me feel more connected to the world again. We stood to leave.

"What about…" I was surprised he hadn't told me about the others. Was it because I was the only one out? I'd been so stuck in my own little bubble I'd forgotten about them. Did I even want to know? "What about the other contestants? How's Jon?" I asked.

"He's…they're…they're doing okay," he said. "Jon is fine. Ryan came out a while ago."

"He did?" I said with too much excitement.

"It's tough in there," Larry said in Ryan's defence.

"It sure is."

I perked up a little then, and as I made my way to the cab waiting for me outside, I couldn't help but feel happy I wasn't the first one out. The others would surely make it now, but none of that seemed so bad knowing that Ryan had come out first.

***

The first step inside my house was strange, as if I was coming home after being away for years rather than days. The air inside was damp and musty, and I rushed through the house to open everything up. Cool air mingled through the pungent smell, and it didn't take long for everything to feel like home again. As I sat in the living room, I gazed around at a place I thought I loved but which no longer felt right for me. The house was big, and showy, and everything I had once thought to be impressive now seemed boastful. My big white wall was covered with huge block letters, the type you'd see up on stage: ELTON RIGBY. I groaned. I had never felt less like that guy.

I got up onto the sofa, my body heavy from years of excess, and took down each letter. I lost my grip on the B which came crashing down to the floor and smashed into pieces, but I didn't care. My cleaner would sort that on her return. I left the Y up. It seemed fitting. I sat back down and stared at my mostly bare wall. The white was so different to the cream I'd stared at for so long. I needed something else white now. A little pick me up to remind me who I was again. I pulled out my phone and called my dealer, the only number I knew by heart.

<u>22</u>

Ryan

The familiarity of home was comforting. I lay on my beanbag, watching some ridiculous show about home improvement. A man with a face made for radio was weeping at the sight of his new kitchen, which had been revamped in two days. The presenter, who had a face for TV, had a hand to his heart as he watched the weeping man while knowing the camera was on him. It must've taken a team of at least twenty to get the place done in two days, but the only man to take the credit was the presenter. His name appeared on the screen, and under it were the words 'Dream Maker'. I cringed but didn't switch it off. I still hadn't gone onto social media, which was an all-new record for me, but I spent an alarming amount of time watching the telly. I was like an addict who had cured one problem by replacing it with another. The other thing I kept doing was looking at my phone, which I kept as close to me as possible. The two weeks were up today, and seeing as though I still hadn't heard from Jon or Keri, I knew they were going to make it. Part of me was desperate to hear from them, just to speak to someone who had been through the same thing as me, and another part of me wondered if I'd even pick up the phone if they called. Keri would be sympathetic; Jon would laugh. I imagined them telling me how easy it was, then putting the phone down and gazing pitifully at each other as they spoke at length about my failure. Keri would probably insist on still giving me some of the money, while Jon would insist it wasn't part of the deal. Then I'd insist I was fine, when really I wasn't. I almost wished they had failed, although I wouldn't admit that to anyone, especially not to them. The man on the telly gazed into the camera, and launched into a monologue about how good it had been to help someone less fortunate. As if he had done it all by himself. I still didn't switch it off. My phone rang and I almost tumbled off the beanbag, which would've been quite the feat considering how snug I was inside. It wasn't Jon or Keri, but my mother, who assumed I was back from my 'retreat'. Answer it. Don't answer it. Answer it. Don't answer it.

"Hi, Mum."

"Darling! You're back. I was just telling your father you might be back, but I couldn't remember if it was today or tomorrow. You should've called us. How are you? How was it? How long have you been home?"

"Oh. Fine. Yes, very nice. Uh, I've not been back long. Just…"

"What's wrong, Ryan?"

"What? Nothing's wrong? Just a little tired, that's all."

"Darling, I know when you're upset. Did something happen? Was it not as good as you were hoping?"

"No, it was fine. I'm just tired. I promise." Damn her motherly instincts. My father would never have picked up on this.

"Why don't you come over? I'll make us tea and biccies, and you can tell us all about it. You can even sleep over if you don't feel like the drive back."

"It's okay, Mum. I think I need a bit of rest."

"We'll come over then."

"No. It's fine. You don't need to do that. It's far, and I know Dad hates driving all this way." I couldn't think of anything worse than having my parents interrogate me in my own home. Especially since I hadn't even done the dishes from the night before, and I still couldn't locate the source of the odd smell coming from the kitchen.

"Nonsense, you're not *that* far. I'll speak to your father now, and we'll come over as soon as we can. Just need to put the washing up and then I'm good to go." Her tone was firm and I knew her well enough to know she would not let up on this.

"You know, maybe a drive *will* do me good."

"That would be great, Ryan. While you drive here I can get the biccies ready," she said. "They'll be fresh out the oven as soon as you arrive." I hated it when she used the word 'biccies' just as much as she hated it when I said 'cookies'. She said I watched too much American TV, while I told her that biccies sounded like something a five-year-old would say. I decided now wasn't the time for this argument, especially since the show I was currently watching was American.

I noticed she hadn't insisted on coming here. Perhaps me going to see her was her plan all along. She was good.

"Okay. I'll see you soon, Mum."

***

The whole drive I thought about what I was going to say to my parents. I'd told them I was going on this two-week retreat without signal, and had always planned on wowing them with the truth when I got back. I figured they wouldn't mind the lie when they knew that not only was their son going to be on a proper TV show, but that I'd made a whack of money in the process. Now I had to figure out whether I wanted to tell them the truth, or continue with the retreat story. What was the point? They'd find out soon enough. Knowing Jon he'd call them the moment he was out to make things worse for me. Why was I even friends with Jon? If it wasn't for him I never would've done this stupid thing in the first place. I pulled up to their driveway still unsure about what I was going to say, and trudged up to their door as slowly as a man walking to his demise would. Thanks to my exhaust, my car announced my arrival before

I did, and my mother opened the door before I had even had the chance to knock (or compose myself).

"Ryan, you're so skinny. Didn't they feed you in this place?" She pulled me in for a hug, and I wanted to say the same thing to her. Since when had she lost so much weight? Or had I just never noticed? Despite her tiny frame, her skinny arms wrapped around me with so much force I felt as if I'd been transported back to being a kid again. The smell of freshly baked goods coming from inside only added to the illusion.

"Smells so good in here, Mum."

She released me and smiled. "They're about ready to come out of the oven. Come on. Your father's finishing up in his shed. He'll join us soon."

"What's he making now?" I followed her inside. My father was always working on some new project or another. I was sure he took proper offense to the fact that I hadn't turned out to be much of a handyman.

"Oh you know your father. He has a million things on the go. I'm sure he'll tell you himself when he comes in."

"I heard my name." My father's voice boomed behind me, and I jumped. He frowned when he saw me. "Don't tell me you're on another one of those silly diets are you? This wasn't some hippie retreat, was it? Where you eat lettuce leaves all day?"

"Darling, let Ryan do what he wants to do. Anyway, I'm about to fatten him up," she said as she opened the oven door.

The smell that hit me was so homely it almost made me cry. I steadied myself against the kitchen counter and tried not to look my father in the eye. It was bad enough that I wasn't good with my hands, or that I had lost weight, but he'd lose it if he saw me crying over the smell of my mum's baking.

"Hi, Dad," I said casually.

"What's wrong? Did something happen?"

God, how bad did I look? "Nothing is wrong. I'm just tired.

Good to see you, though. Uh, Mum tells me you've been in the shed. Whatcha working on?" Change the subject, change the subject.

Thankfully my question saved me, at least for a while, and my father spoke at length about some bookshelf he was building for my mum. We all made our way to the living room to eat (I ate lots to prove I was fine) and drink our tea, and I threw question after question at my father to keep the conversation away from me. It was inevitable that this couldn't go on forever, especially since my mum had been eying me all through the exchange. She wasn't a fool.

"Tell us all about this retreat," she said and offered me a big smile to show she was not concerned, but curious.

"Yes, tell us," my father added. "You've certainly come back looking very different."

"Skinny. I know," I said.

"No, not just skinny. You're more…what's the word?" He eyed me. "Disheveled."

"Ah, way to feel welcome," I mumbled.

"It's a good thing. You know, other than the raccoon eyes and skinniness, it's actually good to see you not looking so polished. I haven't seen you without products in your hair in years."

"Darling, leave him alone," my mother said firmly.

"Why? I'm complimenting him. You look… well, you look good and bad at the same time," he said then laughed. "This place must've been quite something to be your undoing in such a short space of time."

I just stared at the two of them, wondering why I had bothered to come. They were meant to make me feel better, not worse. Wasn't that their job? I must've stared at them a little too long, because the lines on my father's forehead deepened as a look of concern formed on his face to match my mother's.

"Uh, Ryan, are you okay, boy? I was only kiddin', ya know. You look fine. You mustn't take anything I say seriously. You know what

I'm like. Your mother is always telling me to stop joking around, but I can't help myself. If you want to talk, you can talk. You know that."

I nodded, but I couldn't speak or smile because any sudden movement would make me cry. I didn't want to cry. My father was looking more and more uncomfortable. I turned to look at my mother but the small movement forced a tear. Once one came, the rest followed. I wiped them away while muttering my apologies, and my father jumped up and ran out of he room. I thought he was trying to get as far away from me as possible, but he was only getting me something I could use to wipe my face.

"Thanks." I took the toilet roll from him.

"Toilet roll? We have face cloths," my mother said.

"No, this is perfect," I said as I tore off a piece and blew my nose. "Thanks, Dad. Sorry. Sorry about this."

"Come on, darling. It's time to tell us what's going on. Is it drugs?" My mother's voice was rife with concern. It reminded me of the time I'd told her I wasn't going to college, and she'd been convinced I'd joined a gang.

I laughed. "I wish."

"Worse than drugs? Oh no. You've made some girl pregnant, haven't you?" my father contributed. He seemed unsure whether to sit or stand and hovered between both until he finally sat down.

I sighed. "No, I haven't made any girl pregnant. There's no girl."

"Oh, come on, there's surely a girl."

"No, there's not. Thanks for reminding me." My voice was sharp. This was a such a stupid thing to fight about right now but the deflection was a relief.

"Darling, now is not the time," my mother said and gave my father a look so hard it could break rocks.

"I didn't mean anything by it. I'm just trying to figure out why he's crying," he said to my mother, as if I wasn't in the room.

I sighed. My poor father was not equipped for anything

emotional. "Sorry. I…I messed up."

"Do you want some more tea? Then you can tell us everything."

I nodded. "Okay."

My parents both jumped up at the same time because apparently it took two people to make tea. I could hear them whispering to each other in the kitchen, and I was pretty sure I heard them talking about drugs again. They came back to the living room carrying a tray of tea and wearing big smiles, and after a bit of coaxing, they asked me to tell them what was going on. They listened with surprise as I told my story, which had nothing to do with drugs or girls, and clearly not what they had expected me to say. I couldn't figure out what they were thinking while I spoke. My father kept nodding and my mother's mouth had formed the shape of a tiny letter o.

"So, here I am," I finished.

"And *that's* why you're upset?" my father asked, clearly relieved that I hadn't become a heroin addict.

"I didn't make the full two weeks. Hell Dad, I made six days. Or, as it was so kindly put to me, five and three quarter days. And, well, I wasn't exactly doing well in there. So now, not only do I not get the money, but I'll also have the whole world watching me fall apart within days. Days!"

"Do you need money? Is that the problem? Because we can help you—

"No," I interrupted harshly. "Thanks, Mum," I said more gently this time when I saw the look of surprise on her face. We may have our differences, but I had never raised my voice to them. "It's not about the money. The money would've been nice, of course, but…I guess I'm ashamed."

"But why? I suppose the point was to break you down. That's the whole premise of the show, surely? What happened was normal."

"Jon did fine," I pointed out.

"Jon had Keri with him. You can't compare yourself to him.

Anyway, Jon was probably trying to prove à point. You know what he's like. At least you were willing to show that you're human." My father had never been a big fan of Jon, and never bothered to hide that with me. My mother, being best friends with Jon's mother, was always sticking up for him, even though I gained the impression she wasn't his greatest fan either.

"I suppose." I thought of the other two contestants but didn't say anything. I didn't mind Melanie beating me. But Elton? That frustrated me even more than Jon.

"Don't worry about it. First, the whole world is not going to watch you. There are a million shows on the telly these days. Second, you'll be famous for a little while before everyone moves onto someone else. You know how it goes."

"He's right, darling. I barely remember the contestants who left from *Strictly* and I watch that religiously. Some guy made the news the other day because he deliberately tripped someone up on stage, but already people have moved on. You'll be fine. Why didn't you tell us you were doing this?"

I shrugged. "We were told it was a secret. I guess they don't want the media talking about it until the show is officially released."

"When does it come out?"

"I'm not sure."

"Which company is it running through?"

"Uh, I'm not sure."

"Do you know which channel it will be on?"

"Uh, no."

"You weren't told much, were you? What about the place? What was it like? Did you meet the producer? Ellie Thompson, you know, Hettie's friend, well her cousin is a TV producer, or something like that. Maybe it's him. You said you went to Queensland?"

"Yeah, Victoria Point," I said.

"Viccie Point," my father replied. "That's an odd place for it. I would've thought it would've been in the city or something.

So, who did you meet while you were there? Must've been quite overwhelming with all the cameras. I become a different man when a camera is pointed at me."

My mother laughed. "It's true. Your father had a few seconds of fame once, when some interviewer asked him a question in the mall. He went completely blank."

"Really? I didn't know that," I said. A few seconds was nothing compared to what I had done, but I felt a sort of kinship with him anyway.

"I lost the ability to speak. Ever since then I've had a new respect for people on camera. Although I'm assuming it's different with what you did. Those reality type shows don't usually have the cameras shoved in your face. They're hidden, aren't they?"

"Well, there were cameras in the pod, and I was pretty aware of them unfortunately. They were hard to avoid in such a tiny place."

"The pod. That's what it's called? The show?"

"No, that's just what Larry called our small rooms. The show is going to be called *The Void*."

"*The Void*," my mother said. "Good name. How on earth did Jon come across this whole thing? I haven't heard anything about a show like this."

"I don't know. He said he came across some advert for it online. I…well…I guess I never asked him much about it. He just gave me the email to apply."

"And you got in just like that? Wow, that's lucky. Who is this Larry guy?" My father asked.

"He was the creator of the show. Bit of an interesting character. Uh, he met us all at the park. There were five of us. Keri and Jon were the only couple. I guess they were in there to see if having a partner makes a difference in solitary."

"Of course it will," my mother said.

"Sure, but imagine spending two weeks in a tiny room with Jon," my father scoffed. "That's torture in itself. Those two will probably be interesting to watch. What on earth did you do with yourself in there? It must've been so boring."

"Oh, it was. I don't know to be honest. I sat a lot. Thought a lot. Showered a lot."

Mum gasped. "Did you get privacy there?"

"Of course. That's why I was always in there. Honestly, I didn't do much. I…It was hard." It was too difficult to explain it. Now that I was out in felt almost as if I was talking about someone else. I wouldn't watch the show when it came out. I'd rather pretend it wasn't me in there.

"I'm sure. This Larry guy, you said he met you at the park? That's a bit of a strange place to meet."

"I thought so too. Something to do with them not wanting us to all know the location beforehand. I guess they wanted the whole thing to remain as secretive as possible."

"And the actual *creator* met you at the park?"

"Yeah, I guess he was excited about the whole thing."

"But you must've seen where the place was when you arrived?" my father asked. I'd never seen him so interested in anything I had done in my whole life before. Pity I had been such a colossal failure at it.

"Not really. The van had black-out windows, and—

"Black-out windows? Dramatic!" my mother exclaimed eagerly. I resisted the urge to tell her not to get too excited that her son was about to be on the telly. She seemed to have forgotten what a fool I'd made of myself.

"I guess so. When we got out, we were in some garage, and then we were taken straight to a waiting room and then to our pods. I didn't see much at all."

"What about when you left?" my father asked. "You surely didn't go through the same procedure?"

"Well, no. He had a cab take me to my hotel. But…" I shook my head. "I wasn't really concentrating on where I was, you know. The whole thing was so surreal."

"I can imagine, but…" My father seemed to be deep in concentration, the way he did whenever he was working on a project in the shed. "What about the other people? Who else did you meet?"

"Nobody. Just Larry."

"Just Larry? You're telling me the guy ran the entire thing himself? That seems a bit odd."

"No, he said the rest of the crew were sleeping when I got out. You know, they took turns watching the monitors when we were inside. I guess they didn't need too many people. They just need footage from the cameras. But…" It was my turn to pause. The more I spoke the stranger the whole thing seemed to me. My father and I were staring at each other in a way that made me feel oddly connected to him. It wasn't often that we had the same thoughts.

"Ryan, who exactly is this Larry guy?"

"I…I have no idea."

<u>23</u>

Keri

I had officially lost track of time. Jon was convinced we should've been out yesterday, and for once I agreed with him. Not that I told him this. I'd never felt less connected to him as I had been in here. We'd been so disjointed. Whenever he was feeling one way, I seemed to be feeling the opposite. It was as if were sitting on one of those seesaws at the park. He went up when I went down. Although his ups seemed to be more manic than happy, which was where he seemed to be for most of the morning (Afternoon? Evening? Middle of the freaking night?).

He was in the shower now, singing some weird, made-up tune about staying ahead of the game. I'd peeked in to ask him a question the other day and found him sitting on the floor while he showered. He didn't tell me why but advised me to do the same. I'd never seen him so crazed before, and I wondered if I would ever be able to forget this side of him. Lately, he'd been even worse, but that was because he was certain the two weeks were up. Somewhere along the way our timeline had fused because I also thought we'd be done by now. I thought we'd be out yesterday, so I figured it was going to be today. I kept staring at the door, wishing it would open. Jon was probably showering to get himself camera ready, which was ridiculous considering we'd been on camera the whole time we were in here. I never thought it was possible, but we did actually forget most of the time. At least, *I* certainly did. Jon seemed to be acting all of the time. I'd mentioned it to him once, told him that he should just be himself, and he'd turned it around and accused me of trying to portray him in a bad light. I left it now. For the most part, it was like we were in here alone. If only that were true. I was sure I would've had a far easier time without him.

Jon let out a huge cough, the sort that smokers have, and I cringed. I was glad he was showering. The last thing I needed was for one of us to get sick in here, and lately I'd been convinced that something was infecting us. It wasn't normal to be stuck indoors for this long, breathing in each other's sweat and bodily odours. I swept and cleaned as much as I could, but it wasn't easy without anything to clean with. I used one of my shirts as a rag, and spent a lot of time 'mopping' the floor and then cleaning out the rag in the shower. We barely had any soap or shampoo left, so I mostly just rinsed out the rag under warm water. The shirt was one I had bought specifically for the show, and ironically had the word *Fresh* emblazoned on the front. I didn't care. I wasn't sure I'd keep any of the clothes I had worn in here once I was out, and I'd rather be one shirt down and have a clean pod. I was going to leave that shirt behind when we got out, and I was also going to get myself fully checked by a doctor. I did not feel healthy in here, and neither did Jon. Not that he told me that, but I could see it in the new yellow undertone of his skin, and the slightly rancid smell that now permeated his side of the bed. I was glad he hadn't exercised as planned. He was already sweating too much. Those stupid kettlebells lay under the bed, and neither one of us mentioned them. When that door eventually opened, I was going to leave them behind.

When Jon got out of the shower, I pointed to the part of the floor I had mopped so he didn't walk there. He glanced at the floor, then at me, and groaned.

"Cleaning again?"

"Of course I am. Do you want to get sick in here?"

"We're not going to get sick in here. The two weeks are up. Today. We're getting out. Who cares about cleaning? Although, you should probably have a shower if you want to come out looking good."

"What are you trying to say?"

"Nothing. I'm not saying anything."

"You think I don't look good? Wow, nice." I was on my hands and knees, scrubbing a part of the floor I had already cleaned. For some reason this part of the floor was slightly darker than the rest, and even though this was just some design flaw, I kept cleaning it in case I was wrong. I couldn't remember if it had looked that way when we had first come in. What if some sort of fungus was coming up from the bottom?

"Ke, stop cleaning, for fuck's sake."

I glared at him. "Don't swear, Jon. I'm only cleaning to make the place look nice."

"Whatever," he said and then deliberately walked over the spot I had told him not to. He sat on the bed and stared at the door as if it was going to open at any moment.

As much as I wanted to clean up after him, I knew he would only do it again. I hated to admit he was right, but I did really need to shower. I hastily got up and snatched some clothes. I had brought enough clothes for the duration, but I had already worn shirts more than once, so my timing was definitely a little out. Nevertheless, I grabbed the shirt I had worn yesterday to wear again, only because it was the outfit I had decided would be my exit outfit from the beginning. We might not have been released yesterday, but today *had* to be the day.

"I'm going to shower."

"You don't have to announce it."

"You don't have to…"

There wasn't a point in arguing. I stormed off as best I could in a space that allowed only a few steps to get from one end to another and turned on the shower. Crossing the sanity line wasn't as much of a relief as it used to be, but I was still glad to be away from Jon. I turned on the water and scrubbed my entire body as if I were the floor of the pod. Even with the water running, I could hear Jon coughing, and if he'd somehow managed to infect me, I needed to do my best to stay germ-free. My body was raw from the scrub, but it felt good. I cleaned my rag while I was there, then hung it up to dry. Hopefully I would never have to use it again. I brightened at the thought. In fact, the very thought of never having to shower in here again myself me feel better. I spent some time getting dressed and felt a little more normal for the first time in a while. I avoided the mirror, not wanting to burst the illusion. I might suddenly feel good, but I wasn't sure if I looked it. I hadn't been allowed to bring any makeup in here, and even though Jon had said it made me look younger on the first day, I wasn't sure the same could be said now. I'd seen him glance curiously at me a few times.

When I got out the bathroom, I found Jon still on the bed, staring at the door.

"Jon, that might have been the last shower I will ever take in here," I said as cheerfully as possible.

It would be nice to make amends right before we were going to leave. Perhaps we could even turn this whole thing around and end with a dramatic twist in our forgotten love story. Two people torn apart then brought together. I'd been feeling sad about how we had conducted ourselves these past two weeks, sad that my whole family—because who really cared what the rest of the world thought—would see the way we had treated one another. But there was still time. That door could open at any second, but if we played things well, we could end in the same positive and loving way we began. I wanted to sit next to him, but I was so clean, and the bed had become the place I enjoyed the least. How could they not have provided us with spare bedding? I could swear Jon sweated more during the night than at any other time. Even though he'd showered before me, I chose to sit on the little chair by the diary camera. "How about some coffee?" We barely had any left but there wasn't any point in rationing anymore. Jon didn't answer. He continued to look at the door as if it wouldn't open without his laser focus stare.

"Hello. Earth to Jon."

"Yeah?" he asked without looking away.

I inhaled deeply. My immediate response was going to be to snap back at him, but I needed this all to end well. "Would you like a cup of coffee? I thought it would be nice to spend some time together before the door opened."

He laughed. "Spend some time together?"

Deep breath. Deep breath. "You know what I mean."

"Coffee sounds good. Make it a double."

"You sure? A double means you might not get another cup." I held up the jar. "Actually, I'm pretty sure you won't get another cup. How much coffee have we had in here? Didn't Larry say he'd given us extra?"

Jon shrugged. "Larry is a liar."

I didn't know what Jon meant by that, but I wasn't going to ask. Jon said a lot of strange things these days, and his fixation on Larry seemed to grow with every passing minute. I wouldn't be surprised if Jon had been drinking double the amount of coffee when he made it, because that was the only way we had run out. I had meant to avoid this very thing. Either that, or Larry hadn't given us extra, but right now I was leaning more toward Jon as the culprit.

I made him a double anyway, but only because our time was almost over, and chuckled as he took a sip and smiled. Had I been too harsh on him? I sat back down on the chair to drink my own and wondered briefly if I should do a diary entry. We'd both done a few in the beginning, but they had felt so awkward. I pushed my chair forward so that the camera wasn't on my face and saw that Jon was watching me.

"Why don't you come sit on the bed?"

"Oh, I don't know. I like this chair."

"You do? I thought you said it was uncomfortable. Didn't you say it reminded you of a waiting room chair?"

I gestured toward the door. "Well, that's what we're doing, isn't it?" I smiled a little to show I still had a sense of humour.

"Thought you wanted to spend some time with me."

I smiled even though my humour was fast disappearing. "I do. I am. Jon, I don't want to fight with you just before we leave. This whole thing has been tough, but we made it. The two weeks must surely be almost up. We did it. We should be impressed with ourselves. And hey, we didn't kill each other. I'm proud of you, Jon." It wasn't entirely true. Proud wasn't really the right word I'd use for all the things he'd said and done while here. But we'd almost made it, and *that* at least was something to be proud of.

"You don't want to sit here because you think the bed is dirty. I'm right, eh?"

"What? No. Of course not. Jon, come on, let's look at the bright side in all of this. We did well. I'm glad I did this with you. One day we'll look back on this and laugh. What do you think? Aren't you proud of us?" *Come on, Jon. We're on camera. Remember we're on camera. Say something nice about me. About us. Say something that will make me understand why I'm in here with you.*

"We'll get even more money than you think."

"What are you on about?" I asked as I looked curiously at the man who was looking less and less like the man I thought I knew.

He laughed then shook his head. "Don't worry, Ke. I won't let them get away with this."

"Jon, what are you talking about?"

He looked up then, as if seeing me for the first time. His gaze changed, and as he stared at me he seemed to slowly morph back into the old Jon. He glanced back at the door, then sighed. "Sorry.

Nothing. Nothing. I'm just so ready to get out of here."

"You and me both, Jon. You and me both."

And just like that I knew what was going to happen. We weren't going to recover from this. I had no idea what was going through Jon's mind anymore, but the more time I spent with him the more I saw our future. A future that did not involve us together. I guess I had always known this. Everyone had known it. They'd told me over and over again until they decided to stop and let me figure it out on my own. I watched him now as he was studying the door. My gaze traced the outline of his face as it had done so many times before, but even though it was so familiar to me, it felt as if I was looking at a stranger. When had he changed from that confident but cute boy who rescued me from my fall, to this man who barely noticed me at all?

"Any minute now," I heard him mumble, still staring intently at the door with frightening intensity. "Any minute and we're free."

Free. I sighed. Jon had been my first love, no matter what other people might have thought of him. I thought coming in here would be one of the biggest love stories of my life, something to share with our kids for years to come. Instead of a wedding video, we'd play this reality show to them. I had the whole thing mapped out in my head. I even knew what our kids were going to look like. I tried to picture them now, but their faces had turned fuzzy; their bodies had blurred. This was it. That door would open, and everything would change. I thought about trying one more time, but as I was about to say something, he turned his head ever so slightly and burped. Then he laughed and continued to stare back at the door, his gaze even more manic than before. I wanted to tell him to stop being such an idiot. I wanted to tell him that it could very well be four in the morning and that the door might only open later that day. I wanted to tell him to take a step back to remember that the whole world (or, Australia at least) would see this moment of madness. I wanted to tell him to look at me and tell me that he loved me. To prove to me that all of this was worthwhile. I didn't say any of that. Instead, I got up, and scrubbed my mug, over and over again until not a speck of dust, dirt, or coffee was left inside it. Then I did the same with my hands, washing until my skin was raw. The door could open now. I was ready to leave this place.

24

Jon

Today was the day. I could feel it in my bones. Even Keri knew it. She was wearing her exit outfit and seemed to have made more of an effort. She'd worn the same outfit the day before, which meant she thought we'd be released yesterday, but time was one big blur now that I actually wasn't sure anymore. There was something in the air today, a sensation that had not been there yesterday or the previous days. Something was happening. Perhaps I could sense movement from behind the door even though I couldn't hear anything, or maybe being in this pod for so long had heightened my other senses. I laughed at the thought, and the sound bounced from wall to wall, almost as if it were a tangible thing. I tried it again and tried to slow the sound down with my mind.

Keri's head popped out of the bathroom, and she looked curiously at me. From where I sat, it looked like she only had a head, and no body, and that only made me laugh even more. She frowned, and the floating head disappeared. Keri was acting so strange. She kept looking at me in the same way a mother would look at their child who had done something wrong. She disapproved of something I was doing but she didn't want to tell me. Not that I asked, of course. I had enough things to worry about without having to worry about Keri. I'd already told her a few times about the camera watching the shower, but she refused to listen. That was her problem. If she wanted some strange man watching her in the shower, that was on her. When I got out of this place, I was going to demand to get the entire footage. If I found even one video of myself, Keri or any of the other contestants in the shower I was going to sue them. I would also let the whole world know Larry was a pervert. I was sure of it more than anything I'd ever been sure of before. Outsmarting him had been the one thing keeping me sane in here. I had two theories about the creep. Either he had cameras in the bathroom to watch us doing our thing, or he was pumping something through the air vent to mess with our minds. Or both. Probably both. Why else was Keri going so completely crazy with cleaning? She wasn't like this back home. I was always finding bits of her hair all over the place, and keeping the apartment clean had never been her top priority. She wasn't dirty, but she wasn't a neat freak. Not like she was in here. Something was happening to her brain to make her this way. It was why she'd gotten so emotional on me, too. That's why I had to be the strong one. I would protect the two of us from this crazy place. We would get let out today, and the first thing I would do was make them show me the tapes. I wouldn't leave until they showed it all to me. We were going to be rich from all of this, and this stupid reality show would never see the light of day. I glanced up at the air vent now. *Don't you dare mess with my mind, Larry, you sicko.*

A deep rumble caused me to jump, and for a moment I thought the door was about to open. I could only laugh when it happened again, and I realised it was coming from my stomach. That always happened to me when I drank coffee without food. I made my way to the fridge and looked inside. Keri had been strict with the food, so we had a bit left. I picked up each box and looked at them. We'd gone through everything now, and all that was left was just duplicates of previous meals. I guess there were only so many freezer foods out there and, even though they promised to offer all the nutrition the body needed, I wasn't sure. The food was delicious and disgusting at the same time. It was hard to put it into words, but it reminded me of a plane crash you couldn't stop looking at. I would chew, swallow and almost always gag at the first few bites and then I'd immediately dig in for more. It was as if my mouth and my brain were telling me two different stories. I couldn't wait to go home and have a proper meal again. Nevertheless, despite the despair I felt while trying to choose between boxes, I was still ravenous enough to pick out two. I chose a BBQ chicken, mash and slaw dish, and a butter chicken. I called out to Keri to let her know I was having two of the meals today. Her floating head popped out around the corner and I wondered what she was doing in there. Probably cleaning. Always cleaning.

"Yeah?"

"I said I'm having two today. I'm starving, and we have plenty."

She shrugged. "Sure."

Her response surprised me, but she'd given up caring about what I ate in here. The door would probably open mid-meal anyway. I warmed up the meals, watching them turn around and around in the microwave, and then made my way to the bed. That was another thing Keri hated me doing, as eating in bed would only cause more germs, and I resisted the urge to smear sauce all over the sheets. She came out of the shower, her hands pink as if she'd scrubbed the skin off, and didn't say a word about the little bed picnic I had created.

"Ah hell, I'm going to have more too," she said and sat down to choose between the meals that were left.

"Nice, Ke. You see, it's good to live on the edge a bit sometimes."

She snorted, and for once the sound seemed genuine. "Is this what our life has boiled down to? Doubling our meals and calling it living on the edge? Wasn't this what we called being a porker before?"

"Hey, speak for yourself. I've lost weight since being in here." It was true. Although, technically I'd lost muscle, but that little detail didn't seem important.

"Don't remind me." She sighed. "I wish I could say the same for myself. Which should I have?" she said as she laid out a few boxes on the floor.

"Go for the veg ones. Less calories."

She snapped her head up. "Are you being serious right now?"

"Ke, you just said you've put on weight."

"Oh, so I'm fat now?"

I groaned. "Come on, I'm only kidding with ya. Holy shit Ke, it's not a big deal. You always choose those veg ones anyway. I thought you liked them. What's with them dagger eyes?"

"What's with *the* dagger in your eyes! Speak properly, for God's sake."

"Oh yeah? Since when is the way I speak a problem?"

"Since now."

"You know, I'm starting to think you've had enough of me." I was about to take another bite of my food when I saw the container was empty. When the hell had that happened?

"Maybe I am, Jon without the h. Maybe I am."

"What's your problem, Ke? Do you want to break up with me? Right here? On camera? Really?"

"You know what, I do! I do."

"Fine by me."

She got up and stormed back to the bathroom.

"Where are you going?"

"To shower," she said, and moments later I heard the water running. Oh well, if she wanted to spend all day showering, I would spend all day eating. I made my way to the floor, picked up another box of food, and warmed it up. I'd gained three meals, and lost one girlfriend in a very short space of time. I no longer cared about anything. I was certain this show would never air anyway, so what did I care? I took a bite of her food and laughed. Her so-called healthy veg meals were covered in a layer of cheesy oil, and my stomach turned, but I sat on the bed and continued to eat. With a flick of my fork I watched as bits of vegetable and oil flung to the bedspread.

I laughed. "Oops."

25

Melanie

Up until now I'd had a firm grasp on time, but something had shifted lately. According to my calculations, I should've been out by now. This pleased me. I liked that I'd managed to lose a bit of control again. I'd felt it happening too. The first week everything had been so rigid, to the point where my time guesstimate wouldn't have been out by more than an hour. It was the second week where things started to change. I still made sure I ticked everything off my list, but I did things in whatever order I felt like doing them, and if that meant drawing for an extra fifty minutes, or exercising for only ten, I was fine with that. I'd stopped counting, too, which felt almost like being free again. I wasn't sure when I had first started with the counting. I could remember the moment when I was first made aware of it. I'd been at work, and I was waiting to be called in for an important meeting. My boss had mentioned something about needing to talk to me, and I'd been so sure that I was about to get fired. I didn't know when the meeting would be, only that he'd let me know as soon as he was ready and that it would be before lunch time. The closer it got to twelve, the more I counted. Maybe when I got to 100 he would call me in. Could I make it to 150? I was on three hundred and twenty when someone walked past and asked me what I was counting. "Oh, just trying to work something out," I'd said and had thanked my lucky stars that working in an accounting firm would help my case. After that, I noticed I counted often, and for no particular reason but to pass the time. I looked it up once, and I wasn't alone in this weird obsession. Not that it made it any more normal. Counting as much as I did was definitely a part of a neurological issue, and was thought to be a way to calm other thoughts. If I was counting, then I was giving my brain something else to do instead of focusing on the problem at hand. How long had I been trapped in my own mind?

I knew I'd enjoy my time away, but I didn't expect to like it for these reasons. I had learnt so much about myself. The person I was before, the person I had become, and I now knew the person I wanted to be. I was ready to leave now, and ready to face reality again. I needed to make some big changes in my life, and the first one would be a new career. No more watching the clock for me anymore. My new life was going to be about enjoying my minutes, instead of wishing them away. How much time had I already wasted? What would I do with my newfound freedom? I'd always wanted to go to Paris. I could go anywhere really, but Paris was my dream. It was the sort of place I imagined only people who had their lives together would go. A romantic notion, but in a way it would mark the change in my life in the best way possible. When last had I done something for myself? I had once planned on moving to Paris, in pre-Andy days. I had been young, and foolish. Or so I thought. Doing spontaneous things was not foolish. It was... Well, it was living. Something I had one day stopped doing. The idea of Paris wasn't just mine. It was a culmination of endless drunken conversations with my then best friend. Back then I had been a little more impulsive, and despite having only enough money for a ticket and a month of accommodation, I agreed to it. I met *him* two months before my departure date. He convinced me to stay a little longer. Promised me he'd buy me a new ticket and that if things worked out with us, he'd come with me. Taz, my friend of over ten years, was angry when I'd told her my decision.

"You're staying behind for a *guy*?" she'd asked. I could still remember the look on her face. Incredulous, disgusted, disappointed. It was the first time I'd ever seen her look at me that way, but not the last. "He could be the one, though."

"He's not the one," she'd insisted.

"How do you know?"

"I *know*, Mel. I know. Call it best friend's intuition or something. I just know. Don't do this. Come with me. If he really wants to be with you, he can come and visit you. Let him come after you. Paris, Mel. You've always wanted to go. You're going to regret not going with me. You've only just met this guy. You've known me forever."

"I'm still coming. I'll just be a little late, that's all."

"You're really going to stay behind?"

"I'm not staying behind. I'm coming to Paris. I'll be there in a few months, that's all." It had felt like I was trying to convince myself as well as her.

"No, you won't. Come now, or you won't come at all."

"I'm going to come," I had insisted.

"I don't understand why you're doing this. Tell me honestly, Mel. Are you in love with this guy?"

"Love? I only just met him."

"But you're choosing him over me."

"I'm not."

"Look at me. Do you promise you'll still come to Paris? With or without him?"

"I promise."

I hadn't gone to Paris, not even with Andy. Not once throughout our relationship did we leave our city. Even from the start, he'd had a hold on me. It was the one thing that angered and embarrassed me the most about that time of my life. Had I been so weak a person that the smallest bit of affection from a man would make me abandon my friend, as well as my hopes and dreams? How foolish had I been? Being here, in this pod, with no distractions but my own mind, was the reawakening of a person I had almost forgotten about. I was ready to take responsibility for what I had done. I couldn't just blame Andy for this. He wasn't the only one in the wrong. I had let him do this to me. When I left this place, I was going to leave behind all the problems I had entered with. For the first time, I made my way over to the diary camera. I took a seat, and looked into the blinking light, then smiled.

"Hi, I'm sorry I've been so quiet. I guess I'm finally ready to talk." My voice felt a little odd to me, mostly because I hadn't spoken out loud for a long time, and also because I wasn't sure who I was speaking to. To Andy? To the general public? Or to my future self who would one day watch this show. Maybe a little to each. "I'll be honest, I thought I had this time thing down. I'm pretty sure I did at first, but life in here is very different to life outside, and I'm now not so sure anymore. I thought that door would've opened yesterday, but it remains closed, and I'm not sure if today is my last day, or whether I still have a few to go. I'm going to give it a good ol' college try and say that I'm still in here for another day. Wow, talking is weird," I said with a nervous laugh. I lifted my feet and propped my head on my knees. I should probably care about the way I was presenting myself, but after two weeks of not worrying about the cameras I definitely wasn't about to start now. "Oh, and I'm getting myself a cat."

<u>26</u>

Ryan

Surprisingly, speaking to my parents had made me feel better. My father had opened up to me more during that short afternoon than he'd ever done in my entire life, and I'd seen a side to him I didn't know existed. We spoke at lengths about what I referred to as my 'meltdown' but which they said was just a normal part of being human.

"This isn't a bad thing," my father said. "Look, I don't pretend to understand your life and what you do. I know it's very different to the way I used to do things, and I'm not saying that's a bad thing. Things have changed, I know that. I've actually seen some of your videos and photos, and I've read your…uh…log…"

"Blog? You've read my blog?" I wasn't sure whether to smile or cringe at this. I probably would've written things very differently if I knew he'd been reading them.

"Of course I have. It's great. I could never have done what you have at your age, but it's very…how do I put this?"

"Curated?" I offered.

"Good word. Yes, it doesn't feel real. I know you went through a bad time, and I know you're ashamed it happened on camera, but at least it's real."

I drove home with a lump in my throat, especially after Mum gave me a bag of groceries to take home, which she'd gotten by nipping out to the shop while my father and I had a heart-to-heart. She'd claimed only to be going out for milk, but returned with enough food to last me a week, and my father gave me some sort of weird half hug followed by a pat on the back. With a clearing of his throat, he told me everything would be fine. Of course, my parents were kind people, and not everyone in the world was going to be so nice about me. I knew that. I'd be mocked, teased, and laughed at, but hopefully there'd be some people that match the reaction of my parents.

As I got home, I decided to pop in to the downstairs café to get a cup of coffee. Marty, the owner, was short and slow, and moved around the café with heavy footsteps. If Sarah had been Tigger, then he was definitely Eeyore.

"Mr. Ryan," he drawled. "We haven't seen you here in a while." He took off his glasses and examined me, which was so counterproductive it made me want to laugh. "You look different."

"Good to see you, Marty. I've been away."

"Ah, what it must be like to be so young and free," he mused. He wasn't that old, but seemed to think he was. "Messy hair," he pointed out with a bit more enthusiasm. "That's it!"

I ran my hands through my hair. Since coming back I hadn't applied any products. I had no idea why. Doing so would almost be like getting back into character, and I wasn't sure how much I wanted that role anymore. "Messy hair, don't care," I said and surprised myself by smiling.

"I like it. The usual?"

I nodded. "Yes please. Uh, but I'm going to pay for it this time. I don't have my phone," I lied. "So no photos today."

"Nonsense, it's still on the house. Just don't tell the others," he said with a wink.

The coffee took forever to come, but that was because Marty stopped along the way to talk to other customers, and moved so slowly I thought he might never get there. I couldn't complain. Getting free things meant having to accept the imperfections that come along with it. Coffee in front of me, I took a sip before it cooled.

"Thanks Marty. Hey, you by any chance seen Jon around?"

"Jon?"

"You know, the tall guy I'm sometimes with. Dark blond."

"Ah the one with the pretty girlfriend."

"That's the one." This made me happy. Jon wouldn't be pleased to know that he was simply thought of as the guy with the pretty girlfriend. He spent a lot of time in the gym making sure he was the one that stood out.

"No, not in a while. You've all been quiet. Was he away with you on this holiday?"

"Uh, yeah, but we're back now. I thought that maybe he'd come in."

"No, not as far as I know."

"Okay, thanks Marty."

As I drank my coffee, I thought about Jon. Why hadn't he contacted me yet? If he had made it to the end his first thought would've been to phone me and rub it in my face. Then again, the first thing I would usually have done was to do a video for social media, and I still hadn't done that. Maybe he'd changed too. No, that didn't sit well with me. If Jon had made the full two weeks, he would be telling the world the moment he got out. So where was he? I wanted to look at my phone, but I'd told Marty I didn't have it with. I snuck a glance under the table anyway, but neither Jon nor Keri had tried to contact me. Maybe I'd gotten my time frame wrong. I redid the same calculations I had been doing all day. No, they should be back already. I'd hear from them tomorrow. Maybe they were just too exhausted to call anyone yet. Maybe Keri had convinced Jon not to call me and make me feel worse for not making it. Tomorrow I would finally hear from them. I already knew how the conversation was going to go, but after speaking to my parents I felt more ready to deal with it. Anyway, I had a very strong feeling that Jon and I weren't going to stay friends for much longer. If that was all the pod did for me, that was probably not such a bad thing.

***

I thought about them the moment I opened my eyes that morning. Like a dull throb before a headache sets in, they knocked away in my thoughts until I could no longer take it anymore. It was late when I got up, the most I had slept in a while, and when I reached for my phone I was almost certain this time there would be a message from them. I stared at my phone with trepidation but the only message waiting for me was from my father. That was a surprise. My father was a one-finger typist and left everything phone related up to my mother. It was a nice message but overshadowed by the messages I hadn't received. For the first time since coming out I decided to check Instagram, not because I wanted to look at my own account, but because I wanted to see if Keri had put up anything. It was the one account I knew she used often. For a moment I was lost in the sea of my own account, notifications from people who had liked previous posts, a few people asking if I was okay. I was transported back to the Ryan of before, the one who thought this translated to real love and real meaning. I stopped when I noticed I didn't have a clue who these people were, and that not one of the people I knew in real life had bothered to ask where I was. These were probably just people who wondered when I was going to do another giveaway. I did them often. It kept people coming back. I almost clicked on one of my old videos to remind myself of who I could be if I wanted to, but I didn't. I wasn't ready. I clicked, instead, on Keri's name. Her last photograph had been posted the day before *The Void*. It was a beautiful black-and-white image of a tortoise, his head just about to duck into his own shell. Only Keri could've come up with such a clever way of telling people she was going to be in solitary for a while without really telling them at all. After that, there'd been no more photos. I checked her phone, but her last seen date was from the day of going in. What was going on?

I tried to ignore it for the rest of the day, which wasn't easy. I busied myself at home by cleaning. Now that my parents knew what was going on, I had a sneaky suspicion that they might unexpectedly stop by. Mum would say they were just in the area, but they were *never* just in the area. Thankfully, I located the awful smell, some old cheese that had fallen in between my fridge and oven. I hadn't had any cheese since coming back, which meant it was from before the pod. Just finding it and throwing it away made the place smell better. I felt as if I could breathe for the first time since coming home. With my apartment more 'parent ready' I thought about what to do next. One of these days I was going to have to face the reality of my dwindling bank account. I did quite well with all the product endorsements I got, even though I was mostly paid in things rather than money. Still, I rarely had to pay for food, coffee, or beauty products, so the small bit of money that came my way was stretched quite far. However, without a large sum of cash in my account each month, I was unable to save. I had enough freebies coming my way to lead a good life, but I had nothing to fall back on. I'd always known this, but I hadn't really understood my lack of a safety net until now. No wonder my poor father was always worried about me. What was I doing with my life? I would deal with this another day. I was desperate for coffee, but I didn't want to go down to the café again. Marty would give me free coffee, and I would be forced to post my first photo. I couldn't keep getting free drinks from him without doing something in return. That had been the agreement from the start. Instead I took a long walk, past the café and down several roads until I reached a small internet café. I was surprised to see the computers were all occupied. Who didn't have their own computer these days? Didn't people own phones? Weren't phones small computers in their own right? The café was the sort of place where I would usually never set foot. There was no flow to the aesthetic, no interesting quirks to look at, or unusual menu items. A black board stood on the counter with the words 'soup of the day' on it, and then no mention of what that soup might be. I took a seat in the corner, a good place to observe, and ordered a cup of coffee. It was strong, bitter, and a little better than Marty's. I spent most mornings telling my 'friends' about the BEST COFFEE IN THE WORLD, when really it was the best *free* coffee in the world. I thought about ordering food, but remembered my lack of incoming funds, so ordered a second coffee instead. Two cups of coffee were the same price of one of Marty's so I didn't feel so bad. I powered back on a caffeine high, and wolfed down some cereal the moment I got home. Food and coffee done, I felt a little more ready to face the day. Still, no matter how much I tried to get on with it, the nagging sensation something was wrong continued to plague me. Mum rang, so my parents must've been feeling the same.

"Darling, I called Alison this morning," Mum said. Alison was Jon's mother, a woman so sweet it was hard to imagine Jon had come from her.

My heart pounded. "Is…uh…how's Jon?" I managed to ask after a pause.

"She hasn't heard from Jon in a while. The last she heard he was going away for some television show, but he was very secretive about it. Said he wasn't allowed to tell anyone about it. She thought he'd be back by now but he hasn't been in touch."

"Did you tell her about the show?" I asked.

"No. I wanted to, but I didn't want her to worry. I said I'd call you and see if you've heard from him. She seemed a little worried. She said it's not like him to not call."

"Jon calls his mum?"

"I don't think Jon is nearly as strong as you think he is," she said. "Have you heard from him yet?"

"Nothing. Not even Keri."

"Have you called?"

"I figured they'd call me when they got out, but nothing. Maybe they feel bad that they made it and I didn't."

"Keri would've phoned you. She's got a heart of gold that one," my mother said. My mother had taken such a shining to Keri that I had often wondered if she wished she'd had a daughter instead of me. I didn't blame her, though. Keri *was* lovely. Mum was right. She would've called me.

"Maybe I got my days mixed up, or maybe they decided…" Decided to do what? Stay in there longer? Not a chance. "I don't know. I…"

"Darling, why don't you give them a call? Alison is going to worry if she doesn't hear from them, and I'm sure Keri's parents are thinking the same." Keri's parents didn't like Jon, and none of us knew whether they were still on speaking terms. She didn't talk about them much so it was hard to know for sure.

"You don't think I should wait a bit longer?"

"What for?"

What for? To mentally prepare myself for the embarrassment. To relive the very thing I was trying so desperately to forget. "Okay. I'll call now."

I stared at my phone after that, unsure of who to call first. Either way they would probably be together, and the phone would more than likely get passed from one to another. I clicked on Keri's name.

"Hi," came her cheery voice and I breathed a sigh of relief until she carried on. "I'm not available to take your call right now, but please leave a message after the beep."

Shit!

I tried Jon's but, as expected, didn't get through either. His message made me groan.

"Hi, you've reached Jon, but I'm too busy doing something *I really* enjoy to take your call right now. Some like it back and forth, but I like it up and down….(a pause)…so when I'm finished brushing my teeth I'll call you back."

"Jon, it's Ryan. You back? Call me."

Okay, so the challenge was over and neither one of them had their phones. Had something happened to them on the way back? Maybe they'd gotten into an accident. What if they were lying in some hospital somewhere without any form of identification on them? That wouldn't make sense. Surely they would've had their phones on them when they left. Had they been mugged? Hurt? Something had been nagging at me since yesterday, but I hadn't allowed myself to worry about it yet. Now that I'd actively tried to call them, the mild unease that I had been feeling was turning into full blown panic. When my phone rang I dropped it from fright, and struggled off the beanbag to retrieve it. I was so sure it was going to be Keri or Jon, but I probably should've known it wouldn't be.

"Mum," I said. "Sorry. I dropped my phone."

"Did you call them?"

"Both their phones went to voicemail."

"What on earth is going on?"

"I have no idea," I said. "It doesn't make sense. They should be back. Look, maybe we're worrying for nothing. I'm going to Jon's now. Maybe they lost their phones or something. They're probably at home, completely unaware that we're worried about them. You know what Jon's like, he wouldn't even stop to consider that I might be wondering where he was." Keri *would* though, I thought but didn't say so.

"Okay, that's a good idea. What about the others? Do you know who they are? Can't you contact them?"

"Let me try Jon and Keri. Don't say anything to Alison yet."

Jon stayed close by, a little too close I used to think, and wondered once again why I was friends with the guy. I pushed away the thought. If anything *had* happened to him, the guilt from these thoughts would get to me. I was sure nothing had happened to them. Surely we would've heard something by now if there'd been some trouble. I wished I'd gone by foot rather than car, even though it was a little far to walk. My hands trembled as I drove, and I clutched the steering wheel like I was learning to drive for the first time. Everyone seemed to be out on the roads today too, but that was normal for the area, I hadn't noticed it before. Jon and Keri stayed in a small apartment, with only one parking space, which meant one of them always had to park outside. This, most of the time, ended up being Keri because Jon claimed his car couldn't handle the sun damage. Finding parking as a visitor was always a problem, and most of the time I ended up around the block. This time was no different, and once I eventually found parking I had already wasted a considerable amount of time. I'd have been better off walking. Keri's car was parked outside as usual, but I couldn't tell whether it had been used lately. Still, the sight of it gave me hope, as if nothing bad could've happened if the car was still there. It was amazing what small things you held onto when you wanted some reassurance. When I got there, the first thing I noticed was the closed windows, and all my reassurance faded. I knocked, then knocked again. Nothing. I waited several minutes in case they were sleeping before knocking once more. Then I tried calling out their names. Nothing. As I turned to leave, a door opened, and I jumped around in surprise.

"Can I help you?"

In all close-knit apartment living there is always that one person who knows everyone's business. Where I stayed it was Anne, or Ol' Miss Wobbly as I preferred to call her. She was always 'just walking by'. Great when you were curious about someone else's business, but not so good when you wanted to be left alone. Here it was Wrinkles, not the most original name, and not even the most accurate. Her clothes were more wrinkly than her face, but she was one of those people who presented themselves in a way that made them seem older upon first glance. She was far worse than Ol' Miss Wobbly when it came to her curiosity, and I had no doubt she'd watched me knock the whole time. She was most interested in Jon and Keri, partly because she lived right next door to them, and partly because she was fascinated that Jon wasn't with a white girl. Also, unlike Wobbly, she wasn't all that nice. Then again, if anyone would know if Jon and Keri were back, it would be she.

"Hi Wri…uh…hi. I'm Ryan, I—"

"Yes, I know who you are. You're friends with the tall boy with the muscles." Despite knowing so much about everything that was going on, she still hadn't managed to learn their names. Jon was always the tall boy with the muscles, and Keri was usually the girl with the hair. I had no idea what she called me, but I didn't really want to know. She didn't seem to like me much. She only had eyes for Jon, but that was because he flirted with her non-stop. If only she knew the sort of things he said about her behind her back.

"Yes, have you seen him?"

"I have not. I was hoping you were him when I heard all the racket going on out here. He told me he was going away on holiday, lucky boy, but he's not back yet. He must be loving his time away. Probably won't even want to come back, not that I blame him. This place is too small for a boy like him, although I dread to think who will move in if he moves out," she rattled on. Unfortunately, as with most busybodies, she had a willingness to divulge every thought that popped into her mind.

"So, he hasn't come back yet? What about Keri?"

"Who?"

"His girlfriend."

"Oh," she said without bothering to hide her disgust. "The girl with the hair? Maybe they broke up."

"Her car is still outside."

"I haven't seen her either. Are they okay? Is there trouble?" She perked up at this idea.

"No trouble, I was just wondering if they were back from their…uh…holiday. If you see them, tell them Ryan was looking for them."

"Ryan, yes," she said as she assessed me up and down. I wondered how many seconds my name stayed in her mind before she reverted to the name she had for me. Or maybe she didn't have a name for me at all. Perhaps I wasn't memorable enough. I said my goodbyes to her, backing off one step at a time while she tried to tell me about two cats in the building who'd recently had a late-night fight and kept her up.

"I have to go," I said as I went.

"They shouldn't allow animals in this place." She seemed unaware that I was walking away from her.

"Sure, see ya," I said as I rounded the corner, and dashed down the road to get to my car. I half expected to turn around and see her coming after me.

When I reached my car I was out of breath. I flopped into the driver's seat and considered my options. Jon and Keri had not returned, and I had no idea how to find them. It wasn't as if I could simply return to Victoria Point and start knocking on doors. I got out my phone and typed in 'The Void' and 'Larry, TV Producer,' but nothing took me to the right place or the right person. Had I really gone into this whole thing without any information? It hadn't even occurred to me at the time to question it, but now I felt so stupid. I knew nothing about Melanie, so I couldn't look her up either. Elton Rigby! Now there was someone I could find. I typed in his name and scrolled through every bit of information I could find, then I frowned. This article said his real name was Bob Store. Bob Store? That name didn't match the man I had met at all, but I wasn't surprised. He seemed the sort who would change his name.

A part of me found it sad. It would've been far better for him to rely on his comedy rather than his name to make it big. Perhaps I would've liked Bob Store. It didn't take me long to find a number for him.

<u>27</u>

Elton

I rushed out with more energy than I thought possible when I heard the faint whisper of my doorbell making its way through my loud music. Any softer, and I would've been too aware of my thoughts. I eagerly opened the door and grinned like a kid at Christmas.

"Good to see you again, Tripps, come in."

"Thought you'd found another dealer," he said.

Tony 'Tripps' Turner, or TTT, was not what you would expect from a dealer. Not only was he in his late fifties, and balding, but he looked like the sort of man who would be most comfortable sitting in an office cubicle. Everything about him was drab, from the brown of his suit, to the tan of his shoes.

"Never," I said honestly as we made our way to the kitchen counter. He'd been here enough times to know exactly where to go.

"What the hell happened here?" he asked as his gaze moved from the big Y on my wall to the smashed letter on the floor. I hadn't had the energy to clean it up yet.

"Redecorating," I said as if it was the simplest answer in the world.

He shrugged, because, really, as long as he got paid he didn't care what I did. "Okay, well, I have your order. Double, you said?"

"Yes please." I eagerly watched him deposit two bank bags down for me. It always amazed me how something so small could bring me such large amounts of joy.

"Want anything else while I'm here? Pure MDMA, I've got two extra pills," he said, even though I knew he'd brought them along with him to sell. I wasn't much of an ecstasy fan; the highs were too high. I liked happy but even-tempered drugs that wouldn't make me too obvious to the outside world. "Trust me," he continued. "This stuff will guarantee you hours of happiness."

"I'll take them." I didn't need much persuasion. Hours of happiness was exactly what I needed right now.

I shoved money into his hand and waved him out in eager anticipation for the afternoon ahead. Thankfully, Tripps had no intention of hanging around. I gained the distinct impression he didn't do drugs himself and that he didn't like the people he sold them to. What he liked, and what he probably had in abundance, was money. This sort of relationship suited me just fine. I waited until I heard his car drive off, and then I locked the door, put the music back on and took my stash to the living room. First things first, the coke. I made a line far fatter than usual, rolled up a note with the dexterity of someone who had done this many times before, and sniffed the white powder without a moment's hesitation. Then, with a hop to the kitchen, I got myself a glass of water and popped a pill. Back in the living room, I lay down on the floor, the rug softer and more expensive than even the sofa, and stared up at the whiteness of the ceiling. It didn't take long for the familiar feeling to kick in. The pill had yet to work, but the powder was already working its magic. Not an extreme high, or overwhelming waves of emotions. Just the steady normality I had missed so much. I glanced down toward the big Y on the wall. *Now* I felt like Elton Rigby. Hey, there was an idea for a new show, a group of people in solitary doing drugs. Now *that* would make for good viewing. I sat up, and smiled into my imaginary camera.

"G'day, Podsters, and welcome to another episode of PodBook. Status update: Elton Rigby is back."

I lay back down, closed my eyes, and smiled. I ran my hands over the softness of the rug, and reminded myself I could be whoever I wanted to be. I'd been through worse things before, and every experience both good and bad could be turned into comedy. The worse things were, the funnier I could make them. It was a *good* thing I had come out early. What was funny about a guy sitting in solitary for two weeks and coming out with money? Nothing really. People wanted someone to relate to, and what better than a man who pretty much fell to pieces inside. It was so incredibly unfunny that it was now funny. Between the music, my beating heart, and the millions of happy thoughts now running through my mind, I almost didn't hear my phone. I thought it was just part of the music. The number on the screen was unfamiliar, so I decided not to answer. Then I sat up, missing my coffee table by an inch. What if this was someone phoning me for work? What if it was Jon, calling to tell me that not only had he made the full two weeks but that he now wanted everyone to know how hilarious I was. What if…damn, the phone had stopped ringing. I was about to lie back down when it rang again.

"G'day, Podster," I said.

"Uh…hello. Uh, Elton? Elton Rigby?"

"The one and only." I liked the way my voice sounded. It had a sing-song quality to it when I took drugs. A happy, pleasant voice. I made a mental note to record myself later. "Who's this?"

"Oh good! You're out."

"Out?"

"This is Ryan Milton. I was one of the other contestants—

"Ryan! My man," I said loudly. First the drugs, now *this*. I knew things were going to look up for me. "I hear you didn't make the two weeks either. Shit mate, it was hard, wasn't it? Way harder than I thought it would be. Damn it was boring as f—

"You didn't make it either?"

He seemed surprised, which pleased me. It bode well with me

that I came across as the sort of person who would've coped. Yet another proof that people still saw me the way I wanted them to. "I was close, but I got to a point when it didn't seem worth it to me. How about you? How long were you in there for?"

Ryan mumbled something I couldn't understand. It sounded like he was talking with his hand over the receiver.

"I didn't catch that. The line's gone fuzzy."

"Six days. Pretty poor."

"Six days!" I exclaimed with excitement and then instantly felt bad for the guy, but happy for me. At least I'd almost made it. I wouldn't be seen as the guy who couldn't even make a full week. "Ah, don't worry, mate. Like I said, it wasn't easy in there. Hey, how'd you get my number? That weirdo, Larry, give it to you?"

"No, I…I looked it up."

I grinned. I hadn't pegged Ryan as the sort of guy who appreciated good comedy.

"You did? Cool. So cool," I said as a new wave of joy hit me. For a moment I'd forgotten I'd even taken that pill. I closed my eyes to allow the rush to run through me. I zoned back in at the sound of Ryan's voice which had blurred for a little while.

"Hello? You still there?"

"I sure am. Sorry. Just…well…what can I do for you Ryan Milton?"

"Actually, I was looking for my friends, Jon and Keri. I haven't…"

"Your friends? You knew them before going in?"

"Uh, I did. It—

"Cool! I liked Jon. That guy was hilarious. And his girlfriend was hot as fuck."

"She's very pretty," Ryan said stiffly, and I knew straight away this was not the sort of guy you could joke around with. In other words, boring. Not the sort of guy who would take kindly to the fact that I was lying in a happy, drug-induced haze while I spoke to him. The thought made me chuckle.

"So," I interrupted whatever it was he was telling me. "Why are you calling?"

"Like I just said, I haven't heard anything from Jon and Keri yet. Were they still in when you left?"

"They sure were. Happy as two peas in a pod, I'm assuming. Oh hey, that's a good one," I jumped up to look for a paper and pen. "Hang on…" I said as I located a scrap of paper and quickly scribbled the idea down. This would make for a fantastic comedy skit.

"Right, I'm back. You were saying?" I was slowly losing grip on what this conversation was all about. 'Jon and Keri!" I said happily as it came back to me. "Yes, they were still inside. But hey, the thing is over now. They should be back."

"That's the thing. I can't get hold of either of them."

"Maybe they took the money and eloped."

"No, they wouldn't do that. Look, it's probably nothing, but it's just weird that I haven't heard from them. They live nearby, but they're not home and nobody has seen them."

"Ooh, do you think that creepy Larry guy murdered them and buried them in their pod?"

"I'm actually a little worried, so I don't think—

"Sorry, sorry. That was insensitive. I'm just messing with ya, mate. So, no sign of the two of them, huh? That *is* odd. It might've been easy for them, but I'm pretty sure they would've been dying to get back to normality. Proper food, proper shower, privacy and all that. Unless they were bonking like monkeys in there, of course. Not that I'd blame them. Would make for great telly."

"Okay, never mind. I just thought I'd see if you'd heard anything," Ryan said. It was pretty obvious from the tone of his voice that he no longer wanted to converse with me. Pity really, the guy was boring as all hell, but it was nice having someone to talk to.

"Hey, sorry, I was just messing around with ya. Listen, I've heard nothing, but why don't you call Larry and find out what's going on?" I suggested.

"I don't have his number. Hey, do you?"

"No, just his email address. You should try that."

"I have. No reply. Do you know his surname? Or the name of the production company?"

"No. Actually, come to think of it, I know very little about it all. Well, I guess that's the way they wanted it to be, huh."

"I guess." Ryan's voice did not match my own. This was a boy who very much needed a bit of my magic white powder.

"Ryan Milton," I said as a new wave of joy hit me. "Why don't you come over and join me for a drink or two or three?"

"A drink? Don't you stay in Melbourne?"

"Sure. How about you?"

"Sydney."

"Oh. Well. Pity."

"Uh, I'll call you if I hear anything," he said wearily.

"You do that. I'm sure they're just off on their next adventure."

And with that, I worked on my next line, rolled up my bank note, and got ready to go on an adventure of my own.

<u>28</u>

Jon

"Hello! Hello! Can anybody hear me?" I called out.

"Anything?" Keri asked.

What felt like a full day had passed since we'd broken up on camera, and I could no longer take the torture. In that time I'd paced the length of the room at least every half an hour, counting my steps each time, as if somehow the space would miraculously get bigger. Eight regular size steps. That was how long it took me to get from one side to the other. Shouldn't we get a sixteen-stepper if we were in here as a couple? Between every pace of the room I would sit for a while, wondering what to do with myself. I had thought fighting with Keri had been torture, but this weird silence was even worse. It almost didn't feel like silence, but that was mostly because I could hear her huffing and puffing like a bloody dragon every few minutes. This was Keri's way of saying she wanted me to apologise to her, without coming right out and asking me to do it. Well, I wasn't going to say sorry for something I hadn't done. She was the one who said she wanted to break up with me in the first place. The only thing I wanted to do was to get out of this place, and I no longer thought we had our times wrong. The two weeks were up now, I was sure of it. If anything, we had been in here longer than we were supposed to. So either we were going completely insane, or we'd been forgotten about. Or…or…a million more ideas came to mind, each one worse than the one before. I pounded on the door again, ignoring my ex-girlfriend. If she wanted to know if there was someone calling back on the other side, then she could come over here and knock herself.

"Hello? Hello? Our time is over. Can anyone hear me? Hello!"

"Jon, I'm going to press the buzzer," Keri said.

I turned around and stared at Keri, who was now making her way over to the buzzer. Ten steps. That was probably how long it took her. She was tall, but not as tall as me, and her steps were shorter. What a stupid thing to be thinking of right now. "Don't!" I called out before she got to the buzzer.

"Why not? Maybe they're not outside the door. What if they're in some office somewhere?" she said.

"They should be watching us on the monitors. They must see that we're calling for help. What's the point of pressing the buzzer?"

"What's the point of *not* pressing it?" she asked. "Jon, you think we've been in here longer than we're supposed to, don't you?"

"Well, yes, but…"

"Then why can't I press this buzzer? Give me one good reason."

"Because…" Why not? She was right. I did not have a valid reason for it. And yet… "Because it would feel like we've failed." Even I realised how stupid that sounded out loud.

"Failed? But the time is up. You said so yourself."

"But…" I hated the thoughts that were coming to me now. "What if it isn't?"

"Are you kidding me right now, Jon? You've been going on and on about time being up for days now. And if you really don't think our time is up, then why the hell are you hitting the door like that and calling for help?"

I slid to the floor. "I don't know," I mumbled.

"You don't know? I'm pressing it."

"Don't!" I yelled. The sound was so loud it startled me. It clearly startled her too because she was staring at me in shock. We might have our differences, but I'd never once raised my voice at her.

"Sorry."

"What has gotten into you, Jon? You've gone crazy, you know that? You've gone absolutely bonkers on me. You. Have. Lost. Your. Mind," she said as she made her way back to the bed and flopped down on it. She sat down with so much force the edges of the mattress rose. My first thought was saying something about her putting on weight, but I caught myself in time. I held onto the fact that I could still make jokes. If I could do that, then surely I was okay.

"I haven't lost my mind," I said slowly. "I haven't."

"You sure act like you have."

"Yeah, well, what do you know?" This was the sort of conversation teenage siblings would have. I had never felt less in control of my mind before, and I had always thought myself to be an extremely controlled person.

"Okay, I have an idea," she said.

"You do? Don't tell me you want to exercise."

She laughed. The first genuine laugh I'd heard for a while. "Of course not. Why don't we wait another day? Then, if we still haven't been released, *then* we hit the buzzer. What do you think?"

"Another day? Well, okay, that's not a bad idea. Just in case we *are* wrong about the time frame. I mean, it doesn't really make sense. If the time was up, they would've opened up for us by now. And surely they can hear us. If they had forgotten about the time then we would've reminded them. Maybe we're in some time warp here where two weeks feels longer than it really is. But…if it's not over now, then it should be soon. I'm sure of it. One day. I can do that," I said. "I can do that," I said again to reassure myself.

"You can. You've done worse things in your life. Imagine what Ray the x-ray would've been like in here? He would've been far too weak to do something like this."

I looked at her in surprise. I had names for all my clients, and Keri was always telling me to stop being so mean about them. This was the first time I'd ever heard her say something even remotely not nice about one of them. "Ray the x-ray," I mused. It was good to think about our life outside of this place. The thought of going back to the gym and getting back into a routine seemed almost impossible, but it was a good thought regardless. "You know," I said. "He's actually a pretty sweet kid. Skinny as a motherfucker, but sweet. And hey, at least he's trying." I waited for Keri to reprimand me for swearing, but she didn't.

"He's better than us right now," she said instead. "We haven't done any exercise in here. Not even once."

"I told you I could last two weeks without exercising."

She laughed. "You call this lasting?"

I chuckled, then sighed. "Hey, bunny…"

"Yes funny," she asked sadly.

"Have we really broken up?"

She looked like a cartoon as she sighed, the heaviness of it dragging down her shoulders. "I don't know, Jon. I really don't know."

"I'm so sick of being here," I said.

"Me too."

"Can I ask you something?"

"I guess," she said wearily.

"Why do you keep showering?"

"Do I?"

"You know you do," I said.

Another world-weary sigh. "I just never feel clean in here."

"Me neither. Do you think they're pumping drugs into the vent?" I had this sudden desire to talk about everything that had been bothering me lately, which wasn't like me at all.

"No, I honestly don't think so. Do you really believe that?"

"I don't know what to believe anymore. I just know I don't like it here. Hey, remember that time we thought our apartment was tiny?"

That got another laugh out of her. "God, I'm never going to

complain about that again."

We fell silent then, and I wondered if she was thinking the same thing as me – were we even going to be living together when we got out of this place? We sat there for a while, both of us lost in thought, neither one of us wanting to discuss the situation further. I wanted to get up, my legs were starting to cramp from the position, but I didn't know where to go. The only place I really wanted to go was out of this pod. I hoped the door would open while I was leaned against it, and every now and again I could swear it moved. I'd look back and be surprised to see it still shut. Keri was in the same position, and every now and again our gaze would meet and we'd both look away. The two weeks hadn't done much for our relationship, but in a way I was glad to have her there with me. We'd spent the entire time not really getting along, but feeling angry and annoyed was probably a lot better than feeling lonely.

"Wonder how the others have gotten along?" she said all of a sudden, and I was grateful for the sound. The silence was horrible. Sometimes I thought I heard the sound of a ticking clock when the two of us weren't talking. Then I'd realise that there was no clock, and I'd instantly think it was a bomb.

"I've been wondering the same thing too. Think we're the only ones left?"

"I honestly have no idea. I sometimes forget there are people right here next to us, which sort of makes me think banging that door is no help. I mean, I haven't heard a peep from either side of us. This place is completely sound proof."

"Sure, but they're all in there by themselves. Who would they talk to?"

Keri shrugged. "Themselves? The diary camera? I don't know. I haven't heard anything. Not even the sound of their shower. Sometimes I feel like you and I are the only ones going through this."

"Sometimes I feel like I'm in here alone," I said.

"Without me?"

"Let's be honest, Ke, we're not going to win couple of the year after this."

She sighed. "No, we're definitely not. Let me ask you something then, was this worth it? This whole experience. Was it worth it?"

"When we walk out with the money I'll probably say yes. Right now, I'm going with no. How about you?"

"Hell no," she said firmly. "I'm not even sure I'll feel differently when we get the money."

"Why not?"

"You really think this was worth the money?" she asked.

"It's a lot of money, Ke."

"And that, right there, is the difference between you and me. Money isn't everything to me."

"Seriously?" I stood up, but the room closed in on me and I immediately sat back down again. My legs were aching from sitting on the floor, but I no longer knew what to do with myself. They should've made these rooms according to our height. The taller you were, the more space you were given. "You really think money is important to me?"

"Yes, I do. Why did you do this then?"

"For the experience. Of course for the money too, but that's not the only reason. And you said yourself, winning that money would be great for you. We spoke for hours about what we were going to do with it when we got out. Don't act like I'm the only one in here who thought about winning. It's not fair to put that on me."

"You're right. The money would be wonderful, and yes that's why I came in here. I figured two weeks was nothing for such a large sum. Want to know why it's not worth it anymore to me, though?"

"Because you've put on weight?" I said like a petulant teenager talking back to his mother.

She sighed and let out one of her little laughs. The one she reserved for every time she was disappointed in me. The one I'd heard so many times before. "No, not because I've put on weight. None of this was worth it to me because I'm walking out of here without a boyfriend. I gained money, but lost you. And *that*," she said as she stood up, "is why you and I are so different. I've always cared more about you than you have about me. Unfortunately, these two weeks have taught me that you and I are not destined to be. Everyone was right about you. You *are* an asshole." She stormed, as much as she could in the little space she had, into the bathroom.

I didn't say anything. Neither did I get up to console her. I didn't hear the water running so I had no idea what she was doing in there, but I couldn't bring myself to go and find out. I wanted to get out of this place. I glared up at the camera, which seemed to be looking right at me, and narrowed my eyes at it.

"What day is it?" I asked. "What day is it?"

I heard a sound and thought someone was answering me back. I almost jumped up with elation until I realized that it was Keri crying in the bathroom.

<u>29</u>

Keri

I was sure I had now been wearing my exit outfit for two or maybe three days. Even though I'd showered a few times in between, I kept putting it back on. It might be silly to have a planned outfit for the day we were getting out, but it was the way I had wanted it to be. Sure, the whole world had seen me wearing my most comfortable clothes, and no makeup at all, but I wanted to go out in style. I wanted, for the first time since being in here, to feel like I still had control over the way I looked. I had stormed out of the room after Jon had called me fat. I expected him to come after me, to tell me he was only joking, but he never came. Instead, I heard him talking to himself again. Was that the sort of guy I had chosen to be with? One who didn't care at all about me when I cried? We had two mirrors in this pod, one in the room and one in the bathroom. As I gazed at myself I knew it was two mirrors too many. I may have a nice outfit on, but I looked awful. Also, the clothes felt tight on me, and a definite odour was emanating from them. I sniffed under my arms and grimaced. I took the shirt off and scrubbed it under the sink with what was left of our soap. Then I took off my skirt and did the same. Washing clothes in here wasn't the wisest thing to do, because there was nowhere to hang them. We had a wash basket in the corner, where all of our clothes were going to be seen to on the day we got out of here, but whoever had come up with that idea clearly hadn't thought it through. No wonder the place smelled so bad. Two weeks of clothing now lay one on top of each other, the fumes moving through the air with nowhere to escape. I couldn't take it anymore. I grabbed the basket and dumped the entire contents into the shower. Then I pulled off the shower head, and hosed them down. I noticed that there was still a bit of shampoo left, so I threw that in too, and continued to clean. The shampoo had been a bad idea, because no matter how many times I tried to get rid of it, the clothes remained heavy with the stuff. This was unlike any shampoo I had ever used before, and I now wasn't even sure if it was the real deal. What the hell had we been putting in our hair every day?

"Shit," I murmured as I poured water over the clothes. Nothing seemed to help. The clothes were laden in the soapy mixture, and the water cascaded over them. I was also making more of a mess than I intended, and water and soap oozed over the edge of the shower. I noticed water trailing under the shower curtain and out the room. I threw a towel down on at the edge of the sanity line to stop any more from escaping. As I did this, Jon stuck his head in and gasped in surprise. It was only then that I realized how crazy this must look to an outsider. I was completely naked, my clothes from earlier now wet and hanging to dry, and at the base of the shower lay a heap of all our clothes covered in shampoo. I kept saying Jon was the one going insane in here, but now I wasn't so sure.

"What the hell is going on in here? Are those all our clothes?"

I looked at them again, the soapy mixture still oozing down the sides. It looked like a school volcanic project gone wrong. "I…I…" What could I say? I sat down, but even the edge of the shower was covered, and I almost slid right off. I held onto the pile of clothes, and grimaced as the slime touched my skin. "I just want everything to be clean."

Jon came in, making sure to close the curtain securely so that the cameras couldn't see inside. Out of all the things he'd done so far, that was probably the nicest. He knelt down, then took my hands in his. "Ke, this is crazy. You know that, right?"

I nodded. "I know. I just want to get out of this place."

"We will," he said and for the first time he spoke with so much conviction I believed him. "In fact, those doors could open any minute now. You don't want to leave without any clothes on do you?" he smiled at me then and I glimpsed the man I had once fallen in love with.

I smiled back. "Definitely not." A few droplets fell then, and I looked up to see my exit outfit hanging on the towel rack. "Oh no, my clothes. They're all wet. Why did I do that?"

"Come on, let me get you something to wear. These aren't all our clothes, are they?"

"I still have my pyjamas," I said. "Oh, Jon, I can't go out in my pyjamas." I felt the weight of what I had just done sit heavy on me now. Cleaning those clothes had felt like someone possessing me.

He squeezed my hand. "Your pyjamas happen to be very cute. Wait here, I'll get them for you."

Jon returned with a towel and my pyjamas for me. The towel was slightly damp, but that wasn't unusual. We'd been given quite a few in here, and I assumed it was so that while one was wet, another would be dry. But I had showered so many times since being in here that I seldom had a towel that was completely dry anymore. Jon helped me dry myself, and even helped me change. We didn't say anything to each other the whole time, but I could tell we had reached a breaking point. We were either going to come out of this stronger, or we really had broken up for good. He put down the towel, and we both sat down with our backs against the wall. The room was so small that even with our legs bent they still touched the edge of the shower. I leaned into him, feeling his support for the first time.

"I'm so glad that none of this was on camera," I said to him as I eyed the mounds of clothes sitting on the floor of the shower.

"Yeah, I hope not," he said.

I glanced at him, and frowned. "You hope not? There's no camera in here."

"Hmm."

I stiffened at his response. Did Jon know something I didn't know? "What do you mean, Jon? There's no camera here, right?"

He sighed. "I don't know, Ke. It's been bugging me for ages."

"Really? You think there's a camera here? But where?" I gazed around the room, but I couldn't see any evidence of a camera. If he'd found one and not told me I would never forgive him.

"Not in here. I don't think so at least. I've looked. Oh, trust me, I've looked."

"I don't understand."

"Up there," he whispered.

"Jon, you're freaking me out. Up where?"

"That camera in the room. It's pointed this way. What if it can see over this wall? Maybe that's why they didn't build the shower walls all the way up. What if Larry now has tapes and tapes of us showering?" He was whispering, but it was almost as loud as if he were speaking. He'd clearly given this a lot of thought.

"What the hell? Oh my god, is that why you've been sitting when you shower?"

He nodded. "Yes."

"Why didn't you tell me?"

"I tried to. A few times. You kept telling me I wasn't making any sense."

"Well, you weren't making sense. Shit. Do you really think they would do that?" I glanced up at the camera, but I couldn't see it from where we were sitting.

"I don't know, Ke. It's been driving me insane. But don't worry, 'kay?" He squeezed my hand. "I'm going to demand we see the tapes as soon as we get out of here. If I find even a few seconds of footage of us, or the other contestants, in the shower, I'm going to sue the hell out of them. I'll also make sure that none of this gets shown on the telly. There's not going to be a reality show. *The Void*, or whatever the hell Larry called it, is *not* going to ever see the light of day."

My usual reaction to this would've been to either laugh, or to tell Jon that he was completely insane. Maybe I was going crazy too, but something about what he was saying made sense. I wasn't sure if the shower thing was true, but there was something about this place that didn't sit well with me. I couldn't quite figure out what it was, but over the past few days I'd gained the suspicion that something wasn't right. We sat there in silence, finally together.

"Jon?"

"Hmm?"

"I'm not sure they're ever going to come for us."

30

Melanie

Something was wrong. After what I thought was an hour-long meditation I tried to draw Todd. The previous illustration was of him sitting by a window, looking out. Today I couldn't find any way to position him, and I knew it was because he shouldn't be in the pod anymore. And neither should I. I thought I'd lost a day or two, and to be honest, I'd been quite proud of that. It had been good to let go of the control. I flipped through the book and saw Todd in various stages, and without realising it, almost all the drawings reflected my own mood at the time. This book was like a diary only I would understand. Maybe that's why I didn't want to draw Todd today. I didn't want to see how panicked I really was. I no longer felt safe in here. I felt bored and lonely, and I missed being in the outside world. For a long time I had forgotten how to live, but I was ready now. I was ready to do all the things I had always wanted to do. Go to Paris, take a drawing course, take long leisurely breaks at various cafés with a book in hand, take more photographs, maybe even meet someone. And get a cat. Definitely get a cat.

I drew Todd now, just to give myself something to do. He was perched up against a door, his claws deep into the wood as he tried to claw himself out. I put down the pen, stood up, and went to the door. I needed to get out too. I pressed my ear against the door, which was a little ridiculous considering I hadn't heard a thing from outside since being in the pod. I wasn't sure what I was hoping to hear, but I knew that even the slightest sound would reassure me. I suddenly became aware of my beating heart, which seemed even louder in the still of the room. I put my hand on my chest and reminded myself everything was going to be fine. Maybe I had gotten the story all wrong. Maybe they didn't come to get us when the two weeks were up. Perhaps they wanted to see how long we would last, even if it was over the allotted time frame. Could I have pressed the buzzer days ago already? Was I staying in here longer than was necessary? I tried to recall the conversation I'd had with Larry when he'd first taken me into the pod. I was pretty sure that he said he would open the door after two weeks, but the more I tried to think about his exact words, the more they disappeared. With all the excitement of starting, I might not have heard him right. I stared at the buzzer.

The buzzer had been positioned in such a way that made it obvious in the room. Like a bright beacon on a misty day, it was meant to beckon us toward it. I'd noticed it the first few days, but it had soon blended in with the rest of the room.

"Screw it," I thought and marched right over to press it. Even if I had gotten it all wrong, and walked out without the money, I didn't care. The money would've been great, especially since I could no longer get the thought of Paris out of my head, but it wasn't the most important thing to me. I was ready to leave. I *needed* to leave. If I left now, I would still be leaving in the right frame of mind. Any longer and I was sure I'd start to unravel. Losing control was one thing, but going crazy was another. I had done enough exercises, meditations, games and drawings. Even my pad of paper was almost full, and Todd had grown from happy to desperate near the end.

With the buzzer pressed, a lightness came over me. It was over. It was all over. I calmly walked over to my bag, threw a few things in, including Todd, and zipped it up. Then I sat on the bed, and waited for the door to open.

And waited.

And waited.

I wasn't expecting the door to fling open the moment I pressed the buzzer, as if the two were connected to each other. However, I did expect someone to open the door relatively soon after. I stared at the door, willing it to open, but nothing happened. There was an eerie silence in the room now. The silence had turned from peaceful to unnerving, and the longer I sat there, the louder my breathing became. I could feel the panic rising inside me. *Come on, just open up.* How long should I give it? Was this all part of the plan? To see how we would cope when the door didn't open right away? It was a cruel game to play with people who had already gone through a lot of emotional distress. There was no chance of meditating or drawing my time away. If Todd were real, he'd be clawing at more than the door now. Had they forgotten about me? Were the others out? I hadn't thought much of the others since being in here, except for Ryan who had been on my mind every so often. I wished we'd all met beforehand and exchanged numbers, with promises to all message each other once we were out. But why would we have done that? It wasn't like anything was supposed to go wrong. This was a TV production. There were probably rooms filled with staff all around the clock. Wouldn't there be producers, and editors, and whoever else they needed for the show?

I thought of Larry then, his white hair, and the excited way he had about him. He'd seemed eccentric to me when I'd first met him, a bit of a social outcast whom I'd felt a bit of a connection with. It was Jon who'd whispered that the guy was a weirdo, and Elton had agreed. I'd thought nothing of it at time, because, well, they were Elton and Jon…the two people I wouldn't usually consider as reliable sources for anything. Were they right to be suspicious? Was something more sinister going on?

"Calm down," I whispered to myself. I was no longer looking at the door, but staring intently at my hands. As much as I tried to relax, I couldn't get rid of the building anxiety, and my thumbs made circles in the air. My foot was tapping now, the sound matching the beating of my heart. My foot tapped faster as I grew more and more nervous. They should've answered by now. I got up and hit the buzzer again, then did it again. Three times now. That was enough for someone to have heard it. I waited a few minutes, then stared into the camera.

"I think my buzzer is broken. Can you hear me? I have pressed the buzzer. I'm ready to come out now. You can open for me. Thank you." My voice sounded strange in the room. I sounded like the few times that I had been forced to do some sort of public speaking, the shakiness of my voice betraying my otherwise calm exterior. Although, judging by the way my body could no longer be still, I was sure my exterior now matched what was going on inside. Pure panic. I waited again, but still nobody came.

I walked over to the door and tried to open it, which was ridiculous, but I no longer knew what to do. Why was nobody coming for me? What if the cameras and the buzzer were broken? I waved into one of the other cameras just in case. Then I rushed over to open my bag, pulled out my notebook and scribbled 'LET ME OUT' in big block letters. I stood on the bed, and held it front of the camera. Then I jumped off, and did the same into the other cameras, hoping at least one of them would be working.

"Hello? HELLO! Can anyone hear me? HELLO? It's Melanie. I'm ready to come out." I banged on the door, over and over again. Then I fell to the ground. "Help me," I whispered. "Help me."

31

Ryan

I paced my small living room, trying to figure out what to do. I'd told my mother not to worry and asked her to stall Alison while I made a few more calls. I seemed to be going around in circles. Jon and Keri were still not answering their phones, I wasn't getting replies from Larry through the email I had for him, and Elton Rigby had been no help at all. In fact, Elton had sounded strange on the phone, a hyped-up version of his already hyped-up stand-up persona. Bizarre. It was one thing them not phoning me, but it was another thing altogether that they weren't answering their calls. Without knowing what to do, I called Jon's place of work, to see what he had told them.

"Jon? Yeah, I haven't heard from him. Been trying to call him all day. He had a client scheduled for this afternoon, and I have no idea if he's coming in or not," Thomas, the gym manager, said. "Do you know if he's coming in?"

"Uh, I have no idea," I said. "I'm struggling to get through to him, too. Maybe he got his days mixed up."

"Maybe. Hey, any idea where he was these past few weeks? He was all secretive about it when he left, but said he'd tell me when he got back. Something about being famous or something."

I rolled my eyes. Only Jon would think that a show like this would make him famous. "I'm not sure," I lied. "He said the same thing to me."

"Well, if you hear from him, tell him that his client will be in at three."

"Okay, I'll tell him."

The phone calls were not getting me any closer to the truth. I sat down because the pacing was doing nothing to clear my head, and tried to figure out another way to get hold of them. Keri worked for herself, so there was no work colleague or boss I could call, and Jon's work hadn't been helpful at all. The only thing that I could think of was to fly back to Brisbane, make my way back to Victoria Point, and see what was going on for myself. But what was I going to do? Knock on every door in the hopes of finding the right place? I was nervous about the whole thing, as if I had been a part of some weird plan I hadn't been aware about. The only logical explanation I had was that something had happened to Keri and Jon. I grabbed my laptop, retrieved the names of all the hospitals in and around Victoria Point, and then called each one to ask if a Jon Mann or a Keri Linden had been admitted. When that didn't get me anywhere, I called more places further out, thinking that maybe they had decided to go sightseeing upon their exit. This seemed like something they would do, especially with Keri spending two weeks away from her camera. Maybe something had happened the day they had gotten out, and they were lying in some hospital bed somewhere. I got the same result each time. No, nobody with those names had been admitted. I was a nervous person, not that you'd think so by my social media presence. There I was all positive vibes and witty comments, but in my real life I constantly felt as if I were drowning. This was not helping my anxiety levels, especially since I hated nothing more than being in a situation I had no control over.

"Mum, what should I do? Do you think I should call the police? If they stayed the full two weeks, then they've only been missing for a few days. Is that long enough?"

"It's never too early. Call them. It's worth a try."

"Okay, I'll call you back."

Talking to the police wasn't nearly as easy as I thought it was going to be. Weren't these the guys who were meant to serve and protect us? I got put through to three different departments until I finally had someone to talk to. The woman sounded bored, and I wouldn't be surprised if I had caught her at a bad time – like in the middle of a nap at her desk or something. She perked a little when I explained the reality show to her.

"So, let me get this straight. The premise of the show was to stay in solitary for two weeks? That's it?"

"Well, yeah, but…"

"And you lasted four days?"

"Almost six really, but—

"What I would give for two weeks of peace and quiet like that," she mused. "And to get paid for it, too. Bliss. Maybe your friends decided they really liked the solitude, you know? I wouldn't worry about it. A few days, you say? Hell, I have friends who don't use their phones for weeks at a time."

I inhaled deeply. "Is there anything I can do to find them? Can't you—

"Don't you have the number of the production agency, or, what did you say that guy's name was? Lenny—

"Larry," I tersely corrected even though the name was clearly not going to make a difference.

"Can't you call Larry? He's the one that set this whole thing up, isn't he?"

Did this woman only talk in questions? "I told you already. He's not replying to his emails. Isn't there someone who can track this?"

She sighed. "Look, I'm going to be honest with you, this doesn't sound like anything to worry about just yet. Give it another day or two. If you still haven't heard from your friends, then we'll see if there's—

I cut the call. That was the biggest problems with mobile phones, the inability to slam the phone. Cutting a call didn't have enough aggression to it. I phoned my mother, knowing she was waiting for me.

"They won't help me. Apparently, it's not urgent enough."

"Are you kidding me?"

"Nope."

"Ryan, I don't know…Hang on, your father wants a word."

"I don't have a good feeling about this." My father's voice was so much louder than my mother's, and I pulled the phone away from my ear. "Something is up. Are you sure this whole thing was legit?"

"I mean, yeah, I think so. I was in there, so it wasn't made up or anything. Also, I pressed the buzzer, and I was let out. Larry even interviewed me after."

"Just Larry?"

The same strange feeling came over me every time I thought about *The Void*. I had never been on a reality TV show before. I'd never been on the telly at all. With nothing to compare it to, I liked to think everything was normal. The odd feeling I got was nothing more than my own anxiety flaring up again. Wasn't it?

"Just Larry. Is that odd?"

"Ryan, something about this doesn't sit well with me. You must've at least seen one other crew member while you were there."

"I was locked up most of the time. I did meet the other contestants, though."

"Have you heard from them?"

"I phoned Elton, but he wasn't much help. The other woman, Melanie, well, I don't even know who she is. We didn't have time to exchange numbers," I said.

"So, how did you phone this Elton guy then?"

"Have you heard of Elton Rigby?"

"No? Should I?"

"I guess not. I mean, I hadn't either before this. He's a standup comedian. His real name is Bob Store, but he goes by Elton Rigby. Anyway, he was one of the other contestants. He was easy to look up. He also left before the time was up."

"And you called him?"

"I did. He didn't seem to know much. He invited me over for a drink," I said as I recalled the strange conversation I'd had with him.

"Did you go?"

"No, he's in Melbourne. Although, even if he lived next door I wouldn't have gone. He's not my cup of tea."

"Call him again. Ask him if he met anyone else but Larry."

"Okay. Uh, Dad…" I paused. "Do you really think something is going on here? I mean, Elton and I both got out. So if anything, uh, you know, bad was supposed to happen, then surely it would've happened to us too."

"I guess. Still, I'm not going to feel comfortable until we hear from Jon and Keri."

"I'll call Elton now."

I wasn't looking forward to speaking to Elton again, and braced myself for the boisterous voice that would boom loud into my ear. I'd never done well with loud people. The more noise someone made, the more I retreated into myself. It took a certain type of person to make me come out of my shell, and Elton was definitely not it. I retrieved his number from my phone history, and waited for him to answer. The phone rang and rang but he didn't pick up. Ten minutes later, I tried again. This time he picked up as I was about to cut the call.

"Eh?"

"Uh, hello? Is that Elton?"

"Hmm."

"Sorry, did I wake you? It's Ryan. Uh, from uh…*The Void.*"

"Oh. Yes. Hi. What's up?" he asked with as much enthusiasm as a popped balloon. Compared to the conversation we'd had the time before, it was as if I was speaking to another person.

"Is this an okay time to talk?"

"Sure."

"Well, okay, uh, I was just wondering if you saw anyone else when you got out of the pod that day? You know, when you hit the buzzer. Did you see anyone else but Larry?"

"Nah."

I squeezed my eyes in frustration. What the hell was wrong with this guy? I regretted wishing he wasn't so flamboyant. A little bit of enthusiasm would've been nice right about now. Or, at least, more answers than one word each time. Either I'd just woken him, or something else was going on with him.

"So just Larry?" I clarified.

"Just Larry."

"Don't you find that a bit strange?"

"Eh? Don't know."

"Elton, uh, is everything okay? You seem a bit distant."

"I'm in Melbourne," he said and chuckled ever so slightly. This was the most animated he'd been so far, so maybe we were getting somewhere.

"Good one," I said with a forced laughter. Stroking his ego was not what I wanted to do right now, but if it got some answers out of the guy it was worth a try. "I was just thinking, don't you find it a little strange that we didn't see anyone else there? I mean, this was for some reality TV show, a show where each of us could've walked away with money if we'd stayed in the whole time. Which means whoever was hosting this thing needed to make sure they could pay us all." I sighed. "What I'm trying to get at, is that surely a proper TV show would've had more people around? Isn't it weird that we only met Larry? And he said he came up with the show's concept, which is cool and all, but why would the creator of the show fetch us from the park, take us into the pods, and interview us when we get out. Why only him?"

"God, you're giving me a headache."

I frowned. "Wow, sorry," I said sarcastically. "Don't worry about it then. I was only—

"No, I'm not saying *you're* giving me a headache. Ah, listen, Ryan mate, you just caught me at a bad time. I…let's just say I've been partying a little too hard lately."

"Partying? Oh, well, that's not a bad—

"Alone," he interrupted. "I've been partying alone. How's that for comedy?"

"Oh. Sorry." What was I supposed to say to that now? I'd called about one problem and he was giving me another.

"So, let's go back to the issue at hand. Larry. Yeah, you know, it *is* a little bizarre that he was the only one we met. I didn't think about it at the time. I was far too concerned about the fact that we were about to enter two weeks of isolation. Also, I'd never done anything like that before, so I had no comparison. Then, coming out, I was a little…well…a little bummed out I guess you could say. I'm not sure I made a great impression in there."

I felt an immediate kinship with the guy, and I wondered if I'd perhaps been a bit too harsh on him.

"Hey, at least you lasted longer than I did. Not only did I last a few days in there, but I had a bit of a meltdown just before coming out. So, yeah, I know what you're going through. I'm so angry at myself all the time now. I want to go back and redo it all, and I hate that everyone is going to see me like that. I was a mess in there. I honestly never thought it would be so hard. Now that I'm out I feel like I could've done better, but inside that place…it was…I don't even know how to put it into words."

"It was like the room sucked the life out of you," he said.

"Exactly." I felt better than I had in a long time. My parents had been encouraging, but speaking to someone who had actually been there was so much better. "Hey, are you okay?" I asked a bit more gently this time.

A heavy sigh resonated through the phone, and if he wasn't all the way in Melbourne, I'd swear I felt it. "I'm okay. I'll be okay. How 'bout you?" he asked. Not that I wanted Elton to be depressed or anything, but I really preferred this side to him. Was this Bob Store?

"I'll be okay, too. I'm just worried about Jon and Keri. Like really worried. It's not like them."

"So you really knew Jon beforehand?" he asked.

"Yeah, he's the one who told me about the show. He swore me to secrecy. We thought it would be clever to both go in and share the money if only one of us made it."

"Ah, so you're still getting money!"

"No, we had conditions. I didn't make it long enough. Anyway, I don't even care about that money now. I just don't know why they haven't been in touch. Neither Jon nor Keri."

"Are you guys close?"

"I've known Jon since I was a kid, and Keri and I have been friends since they've been together. My mother and Jon's mother are best friends, and Alison—that's his mum—is worried because he hasn't been in touch. It's just weird, you know. For *both* of them not to answer their phone like that. For *both* of them not to be in touch. I called the police and they say it's nothing to worry about. But I know them. This isn't like them. For one, Jon would've called me the moment he walked out just to boast that he'd made it. Keri would've called to see if I was okay. What the hell is going on?"

"Shit. Do you think they've been in an accident? Maybe they're in some hospital somewhere."

"I've tried that. I called every hospital in that area. I've gone to their house too, and nobody has seen them. It's like they've just vanished."

"You don't think…nah…"

"What?" I asked.

"This probably sounds stupid, but you don't think they're, well, still there?" he asked.

Elton's observations mimicked my own fears. Each time one of the hospitals told me that they weren't there, I wasn't surprised, because I had a strange suspicion that they were still sitting in the same pod. But why? "Why?" I asked him. "Why would they still be there? I mean, we got out."

"I don't know. Shit. This is weird."

"What about Melanie?" I asked. "Do you know anything about her?"

"Melanie?"

"The other contestant."

"Oh, yes. I forgot about her. Quiet one. Bit bland. I wonder why they chose her."

And just like that I was back to talking to Elton. There had been something about Melanie that I had liked, even with such a short meeting. I thought she was the opposite of bland. "You obviously didn't know her then. Damn. It's not like I can go around calling every Melanie in the phone book. So, how do we find Keri and Jon?"

"I don't know, but damn this is exciting."

I cut the call. I didn't even bother saying goodbye. If he thought it was exciting that my friends were missing, then I didn't want to talk to him at all. My phone rang, and I saw his number flashing on my screen, but I didn't pick up. I was happy to talk to Bob Store, but not a guy who thrived on disaster. Instead, I spent the next hour searching on the internet for anything that might catch my interest. I tried everything. I put in Keri and Jon's names. I checked out all the social media pages. I looked up people in the TV industry called Larry. I did a street view search of Victoria Point hoping to find something familiar. I'd watched the movie *Lion* not so long ago. If that guy could find his home town from Google Maps, then maybe I could find this, too. I was about to give up hope when something came to me. I typed the name into the search bar, then dragged the little yellow man onto my marker. I zoomed in, moved the cursor around, and there it was.

32

Elton

That Ryan kid was an asshole. Selfish little prick. I'd been having a good conversation with the guy, and just like that he put the phone down on me. Why? Because I said that Melanie girl was bland? How should I know that Ryan had a crush on her? Oversensitive idiot. I'd always been good at English, back in the day before my comedic days. Bob Store had wanted to be an English teacher once upon a time. He always thought he could rid the world of illiteracy, one young kid at a time. When I become Elton Rigby, I thought I could use my English in my skits, but I soon noticed the low-blow comments were the ones which got me the most laughs. Despite coming out of a long drug induced comedown, I was ready for another line. I had some left in a small container, which was impressive. It wasn't often I was left with anything after a binge night. I must've known I would need some more. I took a line, then lay back down, thinking of Ryan. My English skills couldn't be gone, could they? He probably thought he was better than me, but he wasn't. I needed a unique way to describe the asshole that he was. Butt nugget? No, that was too juvenile.

"You're an abominable excuse for a human being, a vile, opprobrious, obnoxious, arrogant, boorish, uncouth…uh… millennial!" The last word made me smile. I hated most millennials. Someone once told me I didn't like them because I wished I was one myself, but that wasn't true. I didn't mind not being young, especially if it meant not being someone who cuts a call in the middle of a conversation. My parents may have been boring, but they'd at least taught me how to behave. Maybe that was my problem. Perhaps I needed to stop marketing to the youngsters. Fart jokes could only get someone so far, no matter how funny I still found them. I'd wow them all with my great command of the English language. Maybe I'd rebrand myself. I'll call myself…what would a good name be for someone who doesn't bend to social constructs? I grinned, sat up and took another line. Bob Store. That's what I'll call myself.

I stared at the big Y on my wall and decided it would stay. It would remain as my constant reminder to always question myself and the world around me. I had lived too long as a man I didn't like, a man most people didn't like. Maybe that's why Ryan had cut the call, too much Elton going on. I couldn't avoid the show coming out for the world to see, but I could use my breakdown as Elton Rigby as the end of one era and the start of another. I'd gone on the show in the hopes that I would show the world what I was really made of, and reignite the dwindling flame of my career, and that was exactly what I intended to do. I felt a slight moment of panic as it dawned on me that I had no more drugs left, but then I stopped. Maybe this new me didn't even do drugs. I grinned as the title of my first stand up show as Bob Store came to mind: *Avoiding The Void.*

33

Jon

I woke in a panic, and for a moment I didn't know where I was. For some reason I thought I was at the gym, and I couldn't figure out why on earth I would've fallen asleep there of all places. Had I passed out?

"Hey, what's going on?" I asked as I sat up, expecting to see another gym instructor, or a client peering down at me. Instead I saw Keri lying on the bed, and I suddenly knew exactly where I was. "Shit."

"What? Are they here?" Keri shot out of bed as quick as a fox, then stood there searching the room in confusion. She must've fallen asleep too, and by the way her gaze darted around the room, I could tell she was in that half-sleep, half-awake phase she often got when she woke abruptly. I usually found it funny, but right now I didn't want to look at her for fear of seeing my own crazed look in her eyes. It was better to pretend I didn't look quite so harried.

"We fell asleep," I said to her.

She sat down so hard on the bed I thought she was going to break it. "Ah no. I thought—

I nodded. "I know. I know. Me too. I woke up thinking I was at the gym. I wonder how long we've been asleep for."

"It feels like a long time, but who knows." She curled her feet up into her, and wrapped the blanket around her. It wasn't ever cold in this place, but it wasn't hot either. It was that perfect temperature that you always thought you wanted. "What are you thinking about?"

I looked at Keri, surprised by the sound. I kept fading in and out. "Huh?"

"You looked so far away."

"I was thinking about the temperature."

"What do you mean?"

I waved my hand around. "Here. The way it's not too hot or too cold. I remember hearing once how you can never appreciate the good without the bad, and I never believed that. I sort of get it now. I want to feel cold enough to crawl into bed with layers upon layers with you, drinking hot coffee and watching old movies like we used to. Or so hot that we walk around without clothes on and hope like hell that Wrinkles doesn't spot us."

A small smile danced on Keri's face, not as wide as it usually was, but a smile nonetheless. "I've never heard you talk like this before."

I shook my head. "Sorry, I'm losing it a bit."

"No, don't be sorry. It's nice."

"Nice?"

She nodded. She was so curled up in bed now that you'd swear it was the middle of winter. "Jon, have we really broken up?"

I stared at her then, trying to figure out what the right answer would be. My first response was to be sarcastic, or maybe even nasty to her, but how could I when she looked like a lost child? More than that, for the first time in years, I truly felt she needed me.

"I don't know," I said. "Do you want us to be broken up?"

"Life would be pretty boring without you."

I smiled. "I'm sorry for always being such a dick," I said. Then I shook my head. "I mean, an idiot."

"You can say dick."

"You hate it when I talk like that. Or do you think the name suits me?" I teased.

"It has a certain ring to it. Although, I prefer funny."

I sat up, and joined her on the bed, crawling under the cover with her. I could tell why she didn't want to get out of this blanket fort. I felt safer in here than I did out of it, even though I knew it was a false sense of security.

"I prefer bunny," I said and leaned over to kiss her cheek. "Everything is going to be fine."

"Do you really believe that?"

I didn't answer. I tried to tell her I did, but the words wouldn't come. Keri knew me too well. She'd know immediately I was lying. The truth was far scarier, and far more sinister than I cared to think about. I shivered involuntarily, and Keri inched even closer to me. I wondered briefly what we might look like on camera right now. Would people find this amusing? Two grown adults hiding out in bed as if it were Fort Knox. Or would they pity us? Worse, what if one day the footage got out into the world, and people got to see us dying? Was that what this show was really about? Some sick and twisted way to watch people wither away and die? Had we signed up for the cruellest reality show in the world without knowing? And if that was the case, would people watch it? Of course they would. As reality shows have proven over and over again, people like drama because it makes them feel better about their own miserable little lives. The question remained though, how much longer did we have in here? Thanks to my greed over the past two weeks, we now only had two more food boxes left, and barely one more cup of coffee to share between us. We still had water to keep us going for at least another week, but it wasn't going to take us long to run out of sustenance completely. My body already felt as if was shutting down, and I had never seen Keri look so weak. This was it. We were dying. Every minute that went by was another minute taken from our lives. Like reality really, only in here we were a lot more aware of it.

"Should we have some food?" she asked.

"Soon," I said.

She squeezed my hand under the cover. "Okay."

I had already heard the rumbling of her stomach, and I was doing my best to ignore the gnawing sensation in my own. We were starving, but we were both scared of what would happen when we finished that last meal, even though neither of us wanted to admit it. Just having that one meal left made me feel like there was still hope, but I wasn't sure how much longer I could hold out without it. I had a million regrets now. I thought back to everything I had done since being in this pod, and how selfish I had been. I'd devoured the food without once thinking of the consequences. But even during my worst moments in here, I never once thought of *the worst thing that could happen.* I never thought we would be forgotten, or left here to die.

Dying wasn't something I thought about often. I could still recall the time one of my clients told me about how he'd had a near-death experience, and how his life had flashed before his eyes. I told him I didn't believe him, because it seemed so 'Hollywood' to me, but he assured me that at the time of dying—or, at least, thinking he would die—the only thing his mind conjured up were things that mattered to him most. He said in the short few minutes his car was flipping, he thought of his ex-girlfriend despite the fact he was with someone new. He survived, and months later he had broken up with the new girl, and had proposed to the old one. I wasn't dying now, at least not in the same way someone in a car crash was, but if nobody came for me then I wasn't sure how much longer I would survive in here. The sudden time limit on my life made me think about things in a way I had never thought about them before. That client had known wholeheartedly his ex-girlfriend was the woman for him. Was Keri the one for me? I wasn't sure. Yet the moment I thought of being without her, or with her being with someone else, I felt sick. What was wrong with me? I'd treated her like a jerk since being in here. No, I'd treated her like a jerk for a very long time. I'd always prepared myself for the one day she would leave me. I had always thought she was too good for me. It was what her family thought of me anyway, and what many other people have said to me too. Instead of breaking up with her, I assumed she'd one day break up with me. I never really believed Keri and I would be together forever. There was always a better guy waiting around the corner, and the idea that we weren't going to stay together had always made me push her away. I turned to her now, shocked at how small she suddenly seemed to me. Had I really been telling her she'd put on weight?

"I don't deserve you."

She turned to me in surprise. "What do you mean?"

"You're the better half out of the two of us. Your family pegged that one a long time ago."

"My family? They're just looking out for me. They don't see what I see. They—

"They don't see what you see because you're too kind to me, and I've given them no reason to like me. In fact, I took pleasure in them not liking me. I have no idea why, I—" I couldn't get the next word out. I wasn't someone who cried. I was ten years old when I had my last big cry, and I only remembered it because my father walked in while I was mid sob and told me big boys don't cry. Apparently losing a dog was not reason enough to shed tears. He told me to stop 'acting like a pussy'. I used that word a lot now, and I only just remembered I'd first heard it from him. Despite promising myself I would never grow up to be like him, it was exactly what had ended up happening. Disappointment washed over me, and even though I knew it was okay to cry, I couldn't help but feel like less of a man because of it. Old thoughts were hard to shrug off, and I inhaled deeply as I tried to steady my emotions.

"It's okay to cry," Keri said quietly as she hugged me into her. A sticky stench was coming off her, but I didn't care. I was sure I smelled the same, as did our pillows and sheets. I tried not to think about the pile of wet clothes in the bathroom and how little clothes we now had left to wear. Clothes were the least of our worries.

"I don't want to," I said, but I lay down and turned to face the wall anyway, and allowed the tears to come. I hadn't expected the force of them to be so strong, and as I cried my body shook uncontrollably. I couldn't stop thinking about everything I had done wrong in my life, and how much I had become my father. As I lay there, I thought of everything. Of the stupid things I'd said to Keri, the comments I'd made to friends, the disrespectful way I always spoke to my mother and how much she didn't deserve it. I even thought about poor Ryan and the way I constantly belittled him. I knew the real reason I did it was because I had always been jealous of him. He was such a nice guy and people loved him for that. I also knew he had no idea I thought this way about him. I knew, most of all, that I was crying not for all the things I had done wrong, but because it was too late to change all of it. We should've been out by now. I cried for all the things I never got to say.

"It's going to be fine," Keri said in a tone I knew meant she didn't believe it herself. "I have an idea. I'm going to make us coffee. Then we're going to figure out how the hell we can get out of this place."

She sounded so confident I almost believed her, but as she got up to make the coffee, I heard her sniffle quietly to herself. She was crying, too. Neither us believed we were going to make it out of here alive. I was the one who had convinced her to come on this stupid show. I was the one who had promised her we'd walk out winners. I was the one who had messed everything up. I deserved to die, not Keri.

34

Keri

The coffee was finished. I'd scooped up the last of it to make enough for one more cup for the two of us, and even then it wasn't strong. I wanted to shout at Jon for having had so much while he was here, but what was the point? The coffee wasn't going to save us. The only way we could get out of here was by someone opening the door. I couldn't muster the energy to complain to Jon anyway, not when he looked so fragile. I hadn't seen him like that before. I didn't like seeing him so weak. He'd always been so sure of himself, and while a lot of that had been cockiness, I would've liked some of his confidence to come through now. It wasn't that I needed a big strong man to come in and save me. I'd never been that sort of woman. I just wanted someone to tell me everything was going to be okay. Seeing Jon cry was something I would never forget. In all the years we'd been together, this was the first time I'd seen him cry. I'd even joked about it with him once, told him he was made of steel. I'd thought he was incapable of feeling anything too deeply, and I'd always wanted to see the more vulnerable side to him. I had even tried to get him to cry a few times – the odd sad movie, a few deep conversations, but he had never shed a tear. I couldn't help but feel a little bad about doing that now. I wasn't prepared for how horrible I would feel to see him break down. The coffee had done little to appease me. In fact, it had only made me feel worse, and as I approached the door I had to stop and steady myself. I wasn't sure when Jon and I had last eaten, because we were both scared about the food coming to an end. The moment we took that last bite was when things would really start to unravel in here. I had no idea what I was doing, or how I was going to get us out of this place, but I had to at least try. I got to the door, which took a surprisingly long time considering it was only a few steps away from the bed, and reached out to touch it. I ran my finger around the edge, trying to see if there was a way to pry it open. I was no longer convinced someone would come for us. We'd hit the buzzer and screamed into the cameras enough times for them to know we were ready to get out. The only reason nobody had come was because there was nobody watching us. Either that, or this show was meant to be sick and twisted. That's what Jon thought it was at least, and I hoped he wasn't right. He was convinced they were out there watching us die, or that they would pull us out just before – a little test to see how long we'd last. I shivered as I thought of Larry watching us with his mysterious crew of merry madmen. I had liked Larry when we'd met, but the longer I stayed in here with Jon, the more he convinced me I had been wrong. I had seen him as a sweet but anxious man, but that nervous energy now morphed into something more sinister. Was this the sort of show he had planned for all along? Why had neither of us done our research before coming in here? Why had we taken it for granted that everything was above board? It had all seemed so exciting.

"Hello!" I screamed. "Hello! Can anybody hear me?"
I banged on the door over and over again, so hard that my hand hurt. I stopped, turned around, and looked at Jon. We had this pet guinea pig once when I was young. He was a skittish little thing and even though his eyes would widen at the sniff of any potential danger, he never ran away. He always froze on the spot, as if he was hoping he'd turn invisible. Jon reminded me of him now, his eyes like saucers, his body stiff. I had never seen that look on his face before.
"Jon, we have to get out of here." I wanted him out of the bed, shouting and screaming with me, but what was the point? The small

burst of energy left me exhausted, and I was both emotionally and physically drained. I couldn't even cry. That would require too much effort. I stood there, staring at Jon while he stared at me from the bed. I had never felt more lost in my life. "Why hasn't anyone come for us?" I whispered. Jon didn't reply.

I needed to pee, but I'd been putting off going into the bathroom for a while. I didn't want to see the mound of clothing in the shower. If I could go back in time and change anything I'd done since being in here, it would be that. Then again, if I could go back in time I wouldn't have come here in the first place. I slowly made my way to the bathroom, and tried not to gag at the smell. The clothes were still wet, a layer of slimy shampoo sitting on it, and the smell was an odd one. Part sweet, part musky. It smelt a little like I imagined the men's bathroom in the gym to smell like, only amplified.

It was strange being back in the bathroom, and while I felt better after finally going to the toilet, I didn't feel the same level of comfort I usually felt after crossing the sanity line. For the first time since being in here, I didn't enjoy the feeling of being alone. I hope the others had gotten out, because nobody should have to go through this alone. I hurried out and breathed a sigh of relief when I saw Jon was there and not some figment of my imagination.

"Jon, we have to get out of here."

"How?"

"I don't know, but we have to try."

"I think we have to face facts, Keri. Nobody is coming for us. They would've come by now."

I stared down at him, wishing he would snap out of it and become the overbearing authoritarian I had always known him to be. At the gym he could whip anyone into shape, and I had never known him to back down from a challenge. I needed him now more than ever.

"I'm making us some food. We need the energy. After that, we're putting our heads together and we're coming up with a plan.

We're not giving up this easily, Jon. You hear me? We're not."

"It's our last meal, Ke."

"No, it's our last meal in *here*," I said with a determination I didn't really feel.

<u>35</u>

Melanie

When I was a child, I loved anything yellow. I used to dream that one day I'd have a yellow door, and whenever I came across one, which wasn't often, I'd be convinced that the place might become my home. It couldn't be any yellow. It had to be so bright it made you stop and look twice. Doors like that were hard to come by, and I had only come across two in my life. I often wondered who was living inside, and I'd lie awake at night and dream of the lives of the families. Surely only happy people had yellow doors? I didn't go back to check, because the fear I was wrong about them made me resort to my imagination instead. My mind had always conjured up the most incredible tales. I wasn't sure where the love of yellow came from, but it punctuated my life in distinct ways. There was the bright yellow smiley face plush toy that sat loud and proud on my bed as a child, brighter than everything else and the first thing you saw when you went in. I had to get rid of it eventually because over years of being the prettiest thing in my room, it slowly turned to a dull mustard version of its former glory. I didn't replace it with another toy, but instead got the more sensible teenage version of a bright yellow scatter cushion. As a child my life was filled with bright objects, and I strongly believed in surrounding myself with things that made me happy. I thought of my own house now, the one outside of this pod. I had always thought it to be my safe place, my little home I was proud to finally call my own, but it was nothing like my childhood room. It was more like this place, I thought as I looked around. Dull and monotone.

In here everything looked the same. I thought I'd benefit from wearing similar clothes day in and day out, but I now longed for something more interesting. I had packed only tones of black, grey, and white, and everything felt flat. I'd chosen these clothes on purpose, in a bid to keep me as calm and peaceful as possible. Now I felt like I had stepped inside a black-and-white movie, and I wished for a bit of colour in my life again.

I sat cross-legged on the bed, drinking coffee while I contemplated what was going on. The coffee kept me sane, but it didn't last, just as the coffee itself wouldn't last much longer. There were two possibilities why I was still here, and while neither of them was nice, one was worse than the other. The first, and best scenario, was that my time was not up, and I'd gotten my timings all wrong in here. Perhaps one day had felt like two and I was now only reaching my full two weeks rather than edging my way to three weeks. This idea didn't entirely work out, because even if I hadn't reached the two weeks, someone should've opened up when I pressed that buzzer. Maybe, just maybe, that was their plan all along. To make us stay the full two weeks and to prove to us that we had it in us to last the full term.

But that would be against the rules, wouldn't it? We could surely sue them for something like that. Or did they think we'd be too proud of ourselves to do anything about it? Maybe there was a bigger cash reward because of it, or maybe we'd signed a form without knowing the full ins and outs. I'd read those forms carefully, but there could've been something I had missed. This was all possible, but unlikely. Deep down I was sure they wouldn't have put us through this torture. Even if we had unknowingly agreed to it, it still seemed unethical. Which led me to the only other option I could think of, and one that made me feel sick to my stomach.

I closed my eyes and tried desperately to meditate again. I wanted to get out of this place, even if only for a little while, but no matter how many times I tried, I couldn't concentrate enough to make it work. My eyes flew open, and I felt the same thing I had been feeling for the past few days. Pure panic. I had spent the past year trying to ease my anxieties, and I thought I'd actually done it. I had truly believed I had turned my life around, one deep inhalation at a time. I glanced at the makeshift window I had created on the wall and imagined all those anxieties flying out. I missed Todd, despite him not existing. He'd felt real to me in here, and he'd made me feel less alone. I thought I knew what it was to feel alone, I'd felt it many times in the outside world, but there was something different about feeling alone out there, compared to what it was like in here. At least the world had offered me enough distractions for me to pretend I wasn't lonely. In here, the solitary wrapped around me. It had seemed so comforting at first, but now was choking me. I stood, and splashed water on my face. My hands were trembling, but they only matched the unsteadiness of my legs. A few years ago I had gotten very ill, and every part of my body had ached. This was worse, because this was not going to go away. If I didn't get out of here soon, my body was going to shut down. The big water cooler was almost empty, but I still had a water source from the taps and the shower, which meant I could survive for some time even once the food was over. I knew that. It was what we had learnt at school all those years ago. The body was capable of a lot more than we thought, but it wasn't my body I was worried about. It was my mind. I paced the room, just for something to do. I was scared to sit down, for fear I might never be able to get back up. As I paced, all I could think about was the second scenario, the one closest to what I thought was the truth. We weren't here to be on some reality TV show. We weren't here to amuse viewers. We were here to die.

I wasn't sure what was worse, knowing I was going to die, or knowing I had never truly lived.

36

Ryan

I was not a good flyer. I couldn't understand people who found it exciting. What was so thrilling about being up in the air with only a thin layer between you and the sky? It made no sense to me. The man next to me didn't think the same way. He was reading his book, flipping the pages with one hand while shoving chocolate into his mouth with the other. He seemed to take a bite with every flip and ate as noisily as if he were eating soup. I couldn't see what he was reading—not for lack of trying—but whatever it was made him laugh at least every few minutes, sometimes a short chortle while other times a great big guffaw that was surprising for his small stature. I wished I could be as unaware of my environment as he was. People like him always fascinated me, and I was always left feeling jealous. Even if I was in the middle of a real shit storm, I'd still look around and wonder how I was coming across to everyone. I picked up the magazine in the pocket of the chair in front of me, and tried to find something to read, but the moment I settled on an article the plane rattled, and my stomach lurched. I put down the magazine, and closed my eyes, happy that the flight wasn't too long.

Going back to Brisbane had never been a part of my plan. In a whirlwind of excitement, I'd remembered the café Sarah worked at, and tried to call her. She wasn't at work that day, or the day after, and her boss refused to give me her phone number. He got a little angry with me when I asked him where she stayed. When I asked him about Larry, he told me I had the wrong place. After that, he told me to stop harassing him. I had Sarah's first name and place of work, but it wasn't enough to bring back much from an internet search. I was left with only dead ends and frustration. It had been disheartening to feel so close to figuring something out and coming out with nothing. It was my mother who had suggested I hop on a plane and visit the café myself. By now Jon's mother had heard about the whole TV show, and she was going out of her mind with worry. Unfortunately, as nice as she was, Jon's mother was not the sort of person who could keep anything to herself. I knew it wouldn't take long for everyone to know what was going on. It had taken a lot of convincing to her that I went to Brisbane alone, under the pretence that she should be home in case Jon turned up. Really, I just couldn't stand to have her with me. I was already nervous on my own, and she'd only make things worse.

"You okay, mate?"

I opened my eyes and turned to the guy beside me who was now staring at me rather than his book. The concern on his face was obvious, and I noticed I was gripping the magazine on my lap so tightly I had scrunched up the cover.

I released my grip. "Uh huh. Just not a fan of flying."

"Really? You know there are more accidents on the road from cars than from planes. You're probably safer up here than you are down there."

I nodded. "I know. The statistics don't help the way my stomach feels, though."

"Don't worry. We'll be there in no time. You from Brisbane?"

"Sydney," I said. "You?"

"Brissie born and bred, mate. You going on holiday?"

"Uh, not quite. Business, I guess."

The last thing I was going to do was get into a discussion about *The Void* and Larry and the missing guys with a stranger. My tone must've come across because he shrugged, wished me luck, and carried on reading. I inhaled deeply, closed my eyes again, and waited for this trip to be over. I wasn't sure what I was more nervous about: the flight, or finally figuring out where my friends were.

When the plane finally landed, I made my out to get a taxi. The guy who had been sitting next to me was also waiting for one, and I noticed the small smile on his face as he got in the car before me. I imagined him telling the driver all about the weird guy he sat next to. I didn't have time to dwell on it, as a car pulled up in front of me, and I climbed in. I gave the guy the address, and he punched it into his navigation system and drove off without a word. I leaned back in my seat, relieved the guy wasn't a talker. I watched as the landscape changed, and felt a familiar twinge the closer we got to Victoria Point. The last time I had been here I had been on my way to the park and excited to embark on an experience of a lifetime. I remembered the thoughts that had gone through my head that day, how nervous I had been, and how unsure I was about whether I was doing the right thing. There'd been a niggling sensation to turn around and go back home, but I'd put it down to pure nerves. I didn't much believe in signs and coincidences, but perhaps something had been telling me this was all wrong. This time we didn't go to the park, and the driver dropped me off right at the café. I thanked him, and got out, inhaling the warm air. Was Brisbane always this humid?

Walking into the café was strange. The last time I had been there I'd been a bit of a mess, wallowing in self-pity after my exit of shame from the pod. The smell of coffee had been welcoming, and Sarah's smile had momentarily made me forget my problems. I looked around for her now, but didn't see her. A young man approached me, and the small bounce in his step made me wonder if everyone who worked here turned into a Winnie the Pooh character.

"Table for one?" he asked with a broad smile.

"Actually, I'm looking for Sarah. Is she here today?"

"Oh, she's off this week," he said.

"Ah damn. Uh, you don't by any chance know how I can get hold of her do you?"

"Sure, let me get you her phone number," he said and whipped out his phone. I prayed the boss wouldn't come in and catch us. This young guy had no issue with handing out Sarah's phone number to a complete stranger, but his boss wouldn't be so kind. I punched in her number, ordered a coffee to go, and headed off down the road to give her a call.

Sarah answered within seconds, her voice as sweet and bright as I remember it being, as if she was right out of a cartoon. Even though she was distinctly Australian, if she told me she'd spent time in the U.S, I wouldn't be surprised. She had that charming southern drawl to her tone.

"Uh, hi," I said, the opposite of charming. Where was I supposed to begin? "This is Ryan. I, uh, I met you about two weeks ago. A bit less. You convinced me to take two brownies, and…" Shit, this was awkward.

"Ryan?"

"Oh, I was one of the guys you saw at the park with Larry."

"Oh yes, Ryan. Of course. I remember ya. Wow, this is a surprise. Wait, is everything okay? Is Larry okay? Did he give ya my number?"

"I was wondering if we could meet. I have a few questions. It's a little weird to ask you this over the phone."

"Well sure. Now?"

"Now would be perfect. Want to meet at the café?"

"It's my day off, how about we meet at Steamers?"

"Steamers? Uh, I'm actually not from around here. I don't know this area at all. Can I walk? I'm standing near your café now." I looked around but couldn't see any other café.

"Mentioned it the last time, didn't ya? The Sydney boy. I remember thinking you would suit Brissie, but I can't remember why now. So, if you're at my work, just carry on down the road, toward the roundabout, then turn left. It's on that road, so you won't miss it. I'll be there in, say, ten minutes?"

"Perfect. I appreciate it."

Steamers was a little more like cafés I was used to hanging out in, and a part of me was disappointed. I liked the old-fashioned style of the café Sarah worked in, and the way it made me feel as if nobody was taking any notice of me. This place seemed a little too pretentious, so I scanned the room for the most secluded table and took a seat.

"Uh, a coffee please," I asked the young man dressed entirely in black.

"What kind?"

"Just a coffee." What had happened to me?

He pointed to the menu where the coffee list was as long as the lunch list. "We've got quite a range."

I grimaced as he told me about their new turmeric coffee, and I shook my head. "Just a coffee."

"Tall black?"

"Sure. With some milk please."

I had thought of ordering for Sarah but I didn't know her well enough, and she arrived just as the waiter came back with my order.

"One of those, please," she said to him, and then smiled as I stood up awkwardly to greet her. I was about to hold out my hand when she wrapped her arms around me and pulled me in for a hug. I wasn't used to people like her, and I liked it. "Ryan, it's good to see ya again. Wow, are you on a diet or something?"

"Diet? No?"

"You're so skinny. We should order cake, too."

"Uh, before we do, I really need to talk to you."

She sat down, her eyes wide as she tried to read my face. "What's going on? Ya seem nervous. Y'alright?"

"What exactly do you know about Larry?"

"Larry? Somethin's happened to him, hasn't it? Oh no, what's wrong? Is he okay?" Sarah's pale face had turned even whiter, but as I was about to explain the waiter came over with her coffee.

"Can I get you anything else?" he asked in the same sort of cheery way Sarah had once asked me.

"No!" we both said curtly at the same time, and the poor guy hurried off as if we'd stung him. I looked after him with regret but then turned my attention back to Sarah. There were more important things to worry about right now.

"Is Larry okay?" she asked.

I sighed. "I'm not sure, but I need to know how to find him."

She narrowed her eyes at me. "Why? What do you want with him? What's going on?"

I told Sarah the whole story, keeping it as truncated as possible while still finding a way to get all the details out. Telling the story to her felt different to when I had told my parents, because I no longer cared about my role in it. Who cared that I hadn't lasted the full two weeks when my friends were missing? The waiter came by once, and Sarah waved him away, and even though our coffees were now cold we didn't ask for more.

"And," I concluded, "that's why I came to see you. Because you're the only link to Larry I can think of. And I need your help. Is there any way he could've done something bad?"

"I... No... I mean... I don't know. I'd like to think I knew him well. He came to the café every day without fail. He ordered the same thing every time. He was so rigid in his order, and so... Well... Sweet. A nice man...

"But how well did you know him?"

Her eyes clouded over at the question. "I guess I didn't know him at all. But…this doesn't make sense. If he was a bad guy he wouldn't have let you and that Elton guy go."

"That's the part I don't understand either. So, you haven't seen him lately?"

She shook her head. "No, I haven't seen him since that day with you." She took a sip of her coffee, then grimaced and put it down. "What if something happened to him? What if that's the reason you can't get hold of him?"

"That's what I thought too, but it still doesn't make sense. What about the rest of the crew. Why didn't *they* let Jon and Keri out?"

"That's true. That doesn't seem right either. Shit, Ryan…" I got the impression by the way she said the word that she didn't swear easily. "What are we going to do?"

"I don't know." I was grateful she'd said *we* and not *you*. I didn't want to do this on my own. "I was hoping you'd know where he was. Do you know where he lives?"

"He lives in the area, but I'm not sure exactly where. He walked to the café every day so it can't be far. Should we just go knocking on all the doors? I don't even know what street he's on. What about the pods you were in? Where was that?"

"I wish I knew. Going in we went straight through the garage, and leaving I didn't take any notice of where I was. Maybe I'd know it if I saw it, but I'm honestly not sure if I would."

"And that Elton guy? Doesn't he know?"

"He doesn't know, but he also doesn't care." I had considered contacting him again, but it didn't seem worth it.

"Charming." She grimaced. "Come on, let's go." She stood up, and scraped her chair back loudly.

"Where?"

"To the police."

"Trust me, they don't care. I already called them." Although it had been a few days since my last phone call with them, I wondered if they would take me seriously now.

"Then you haven't spoken to the right person." She turned to me and I was surprised by the look of steely determination on her face. "My uncle works in the police force. He'll help us."

Relief washed over me, and I hurried out to follow her. The moment we stepped outside, she ran back in, and I stood there looking after her in confusion. Was I meant to follow her?

"We forgot to pay the waiter," she said when she returned.

"You paid? I'm so sorry. Hang on, let me get some cash."

"Don't worry." She waved away my wallet. "It's fine. We'll have to come back here sometime and make it up to the guy. He must've hated us. I think I'm just sensitive because I do the same thing he does, and I hate people like us. Now I know to cut them some slack. You never know what's going on in someone's life. Anyway, enough about that, we have more important things to think about. The police office is down the road. Let's hope he's there. If not, it's an hour's drive to his house."

"Thanks for helping, Sarah," I said as we hurried off.

"We're going to find your friends," Sarah said with conviction. Her words floated toward me and wrapped around me like a security blanket.

"Thank you." I had no idea what was going to happen, or where Jon and Keri could be, but it felt good to finally be doing something about it.

"We're here," Sarah said. I might not believe in destiny, but if I did then meeting her would've definitely fallen into that realm of magic.

<u>37</u>

Jon

Keri and I moved between being awake and asleep, as if we were riding the ocean's waves. When we dipped, we slept; when we rose, we woke. We seemed to move seamlessly from one to the next, and everything felt more and more like a dream. A dream we never woke from. After another sleep of who knows how long, the first person I thought of when my eyes opened was Ryan. A strange sound escaped me, as if I'd swallowed a frog. It was a half choke, half cry that was so odd it woke Keri. She sat up quickly.

"What happened?" she said as she reached for my hand. Her gaze moved fast from one point of the room to another, and I squeezed her hand to tell her everything was okay.

"Nothing happened. I just made a funny sound. I'm sorry I woke you."

"Did you have a bad dream?" She frowned, then reached out to wipe a rogue tear that was falling down my face. So much for trying to stay in control. Ever since I'd cried the other day (yesterday, three days ago, a week), I had found myself more and more emotional. It was as if I was making up for years of not crying.

"I can't stop thinking about Ryan."

"Ryan? What about him?"

"He's all alone in his pod. I know things haven't been easy for us, but at least we've had each other. We've *still* got each other. He's been alone from the beginning. What must he be thinking now? He must be so scared. I was so horrible to him." I was shivering now, even though it wasn't cold. *Not too hot, not too cold, just perfect.* The words I'd first uttered came back to haunt me. There was nothing perfect about this scenario. Keri wrapped the duvet over me, and curled up against me. The warmth of her body against mine seemed to help, but also reminded me of how lucky I was not to be alone in all this.

"You weren't horrible to him," she said. "You were just being you. He was just being him. It's how the two of you are with one another. Don't beat yourself up about it. He knows you care about him."

"No, I was horrible to him. Do you want to know why I told him about this whole show?"

"So there'd be more of a chance of us walking out with the money? So I could finally get that camera I've wanted for so long?" I could tell by the way she was saying the words that she was urging me to go along with what she was saying. Those were the reasons I had given her, and she wanted to believe I was a good person, even if she knew I'd only be fooling myself.

"No, I told him about it because I didn't think he would make the full two weeks. I wanted him to fail so I would feel better about myself."

"That's not true, Jon. I know that's not true."

"You *do* know it's true. Thank you for trying to believe otherwise, but you know as well as I do I'm not a nice guy. Ryan *is* though. He's one of the best out there, and because of me he's going to die alone." My body was no longer shaking. It was vibrating.

"He's not going to die! Neither are we. Stop saying that."

"Do you remember meeting Ryan for the first time?" I asked.

"It was at that restaurant by the beach, wasn't it? We met him for breakfast."

"That's right. Do you remember what he said to you that day?"

She frowned. "He said a lot of things. I'm not sure which part you mean?"

"He said he was happy to see his best friend so happy."

"That's nice," Keri said. "Sounds like the kind of thing he'd say."

"Do you know what I said?"

"I don't remember. It doesn't matter, Jon. All of this doesn't matter."

"I said he wasn't my best friend. I laughed at him, and made a joke. You thought I was just messing around. You assumed that's the sort of relationship the two of us had, but it wasn't. It isn't. I clearly remember the look of hurt on his face that day. Do you know why I've always treated him like that?"

"It doesn't matter," she said again.

It did matter. It mattered very much. "Because I've always been jealous of him." There, I finally said it out loud. It was amazing the things that came out when your life was hanging by a flimsy thread. Suddenly all the lies and pretence seemed pointless. "I've always been jealous of him. For no other reason than he's a better person than me, and I hated that he made me so aware of it."

"You're not a bad person, Jon. I wouldn't have chosen to be with you if you were."

I turned to look at her then. She'd lost the extra weight lately, but at the same time there was a puffiness to her skin I'd never seen before. I reached out and ran my hand down her cheek, wondering when last I'd done something so intimate. She'd cried a lot in here, and her cheeks were stained from the constant stream. Was it possible to stain your own skin?

"I honestly have no idea why you'd be with someone like me. I made you take kettlebells into this damn place."

She tried to laugh, but without the energy it came out sounding like a cough. "You've always been stubborn. The kettlebells were a good idea, you know. I mean, if we actually used them. I'm pretty sure we would've ignored whatever we bought in here. This place..." She gazed around, her head moving so slowly I wondered if her gaze would ever return to me. When it did, I had to look away. She was too raw right now, and every time I looked into her eyes I felt as if I was looking into a mirror. "This place is not like home," she finally said. "You know what sucks?"

"All of this?"

A faint smile. "All of this, but not just that. The fact that you and I are getting on so well now. We should've been getting on like this at the start."

"It's my fault," I told her. "I've been an idiot. In this pod, and at home. I guess I took you for granted, Ke. I'm sorry. I'm sorry for bringing you into this place even though you didn't want to come. I'm sorry for making it all about me. I'm sorry for every stupid thing I've ever said and done. I'm just so sorry." Sorry wasn't enough. I wanted to tell her I would make it up to her when we got out of here, but I no longer thought we were going to leave. Nobody was coming. This was it. This was how it ended for us. I would die knowing I had willingly taken down the woman of my dreams, and my best friend.

"Don't be sorry," Keri said.

"I am. I'm so damn sorry. Ryan's not my best friend, you know. You are. He's my good friend, though. My oldest friend. I never got the chance to tell him that."

The more I thought about Ryan all alone in his pod, the worse I felt. He didn't deserve to die alone. If it wasn't for me, he'd be back at home, taking those harmless selfies his fans loved so much. I'd given him such a hard time about those photos and videos, but only because of the attention he always got for it. Who were they hurting? Why had I made such a big deal of it? Why couldn't I ever let people be who they wanted to be? I was about to ask Keri when she suddenly moved over to sit on my lap. I wrapped my arms around her, and rested my head on her shoulder. I wished there was something more I could do. Keri kept telling me that this wasn't the end, but the more she said it, the less conviction she spoke with.

"Do you really think someone is coming for us?" My face was still squashed against her, and my voice came out muffled and unclear. I hoped she hadn't heard. The moment the words were out I knew I didn't want an answer.

She inhaled so deeply it felt as if I was on a rollercoaster, her body heaving up and plummeting down. She'd heard me. "I don't know."

38

Melanie

Was *The Shawshank Redemption* based on a true story? I'd seen the movie and read the book, but I now couldn't remember. The only thing I *could* recall was that the guy had gotten out of his jail cell by slowly digging a hole through the wall. Something like that anyway. I moved around the small space, trailing my finger over the door, the wall, the pretend window I'd drawn. There had to be a way out of this place. The small vent at the top corner was out of reach. I'd already tried to reach it numerous times, and after plummeting down my makeshift ladder and almost dislocating my shoulder, I decided it wasn't the way to go. I examined the bathroom, but it had been built inside the pod, so getting through it would only lead me to the same wall that already surrounded me. If I was going to chip my way out of this room, it was going to have to be inside the main area. But where? The walls to each side only led to the pod on the other side. The thought of someone else going through what I was going through didn't comfort me, but filled me with a deep sense of anxiety. What if they had finished their food a long time ago? What if they were lying unconscious on the floor? I needed to find a way out. Not just for me, but for them.

I walked the perimeter of the room a few times, until I eventually settled on the fake window I had made in my first week. Why had I chosen that exact spot to draw it? What if it had been a sign all along of a way out for me? I tried to feel if it was different to the rest of the wall, but I couldn't be sure. My mind was not the most trusted thing at the moment. Still, it was worth a try. I couldn't just sit around and wait to die. I already knew nobody was coming to get me, and there was no way this was the end for me. I had too many plans. Too much living to do out there. The only thing left to do was figure out how to get through the wall, and what to use to help me do it. The utensils in here were all plastic, which I was sure had been done on purpose. Was this the test? Did they want to see how we would find a way out? Could we have gotten out all along? I gazed around the room, searching for clues. Perhaps this was a game. Had the others already figured it out? Had I been too deep trying to still my mind and focus on myself to see what had been in front of me? My thoughts whirred with a million possibilities, each one both outrageous and plausible the more thought I gave it. Could that have been the challenge all along? I could no longer distinguish facts from theories, and the idea of this as one giant puzzle made me feel better.

I scooped my pens out of my bag. I hadn't drawn in a while, thanks to the lack of energy and desire. Using the tip of the pen, I began scraping the paint off the 'window', bit by bit. If I had to do this one layer at a time, I would. As bits of paint fell to the floor, I thought about how different I had felt coming into this place compared to how I felt now. Thinking I was just going to die, everything I did seemed to be devoid of meaning, and every action had seemed pointless. Yet what was so different between dying in here and dying in the outside world? There was a time limit out there too, the only difference was that we didn't know when it was. It was a sobering thought, and a strange new energy soared through me as I picked at the paint. At one point the pen slipped from my hand, and after going to retrieve it I took a moment to examine my handiwork. Disappointment ran through me as my gaze settled on the dark brown patch that now sat in the corner of the 'window'. If this was a puzzle then surely I'd have seen something else. Maybe a little latch, a switch, a marking of sorts. Or was I expecting too much, too soon? I moved back to it, and continued to scrape at the surface, this time with more vigour and anger than before. The truth was obvious. I wasn't in the middle of some well thought out riddle. This wasn't like one of those escape room games where one clue would lead to another and lead to another, and eventually lead me to freedom. The only hope I had was that somehow only the first layer of this room was secure, and that after that it would all come crumbling down. It seemed impossible, but what else did I have to go on? I had to at least try. I was no longer willing to give up on my life. Not when I'd come so close to regaining it.

How long had I been doing this? I tried to count as I worked, just to get an idea of whether I was still in tune with the time as I had been before I came here, but it didn't take me long to lose track. I went from counting to fifty-nine out loud to thinking about waffles. My mind moved from serious thoughts to frivolous ones, just as my moods changed from calm to manic. Manic was the one I returned to most frequently, the pendulum no longer swinging but stuck. I took a step back, my hands burning from the constant scrubbing, and my pencil looking as worn and weathered as I probably did. The only thing I'd managed to do was scrape off some paint. I shut my eyes, and inhaled. I was desperate to breathe some calmness and clarity back into my life, but nothing seemed to be working. Were the others as desperate as I was? Were they hitting that buzzer over and over again hoping that someone would come? Or was I the only one who had been left behind? It was hard to imagine that beyond these walls lay a living, breathing, pulsating world, a world where people walked and talked, and laughed and cried. A world where nobody knew how lucky they were simply to be alive. I had to find a way out. I couldn't give up so quickly. My gaze fell on the little fridge, which still held five boxes of food. I'd be hungry, but if I had one box a day, I would at least have a little energy to see me through. The water situation wasn't great either, but there was still water from the bathroom if I needed. If the water continued to flow, I would be okay in here. How long could you survive on water alone? I used to know these things, and I was sure I had it all figured out just the other day, but I didn't trust my brain at the moment. A week? Two weeks? Less, more, I didn't know. All I knew was that with only five days of food left, I needed to use that energy wisely. Could I really chip my way out of here with a pen? The idea seemed ludicrous, but I wouldn't sit and wait for my death to come. I fished my notepad out of my bag again, and as I flipped through I watched as my drawings came to life. It felt as if someone else had done these, a serene version of the crazed woman I had become. Tears streamed down my face as I looked at my little companion. I had to get out of here. Not just for me, but for little Todd, wherever he was.

"I'm going to make it." My finger trailed along the lines of his body.

My life hadn't always been this way. Pre-Andy, of course. When had I turned into the sort of woman who let someone else define her? I could blame Andy all I wanted, but I was the one who had let him get away with it. Dying in here was like letting him win. I wrote HELP ME on a piece of paper, then tried to get it under the door. What if people were walking by without even knowing we were inside? There was a thin layer before the floor and the door, but my paper kept getting stuck on something half way out, and when I pulled it back in it was all crumpled. I tried again, going slower this time, trying to move over any obstacles that might be in the way. It took me almost ten tries, but I finally got it out. The feeling of something finally going my way was so overwhelming I cried. I imagined someone walking by and seeing my note, and the hope that coursed through my body made me tremble. I pictured them reading the words and opening the door, but... I groaned. Why had

I only written HELP ME on the paper? Why had I not explained that the door was locked, and I was dying? What if someone picked that paper up and simply walked off and threw it in the trash? I was an idiot. I tore off another piece of paper, this time explaining who I was, and why I needed someone to get me out of here. This time, probably because of the first sheet, the paper wouldn't go through. I tried over and over again, each time getting more and more frustrated. I gave up with the paper not even a quarter through. I glanced up at the patch on the wall and laughed at my feeble attempt of escape. I threw the pen across the room. I didn't have the energy to throw it as hard as I wanted, but I shut my eyes and imagined it shattering into pieces. I didn't want to give up, but I didn't know what to do.

Moments later, just as I was about to attempt to stand up again, the world went dark, then light again, and I thought I had fainted. I stood up, holding onto the wall for support.

"Hello? Hello? Can you hear me?" I called.

The light flickered on and off again, and I glanced up at the light bulb with fear.

"No! Please don't go. Please stay on." I didn't have many days left, but I'd have even less without any electricity. Could I eat those meals without heating them up? What if I got sick? What if—

The lights flickered once more. Then died.

39

Keri

Jon and I were curled up on the bed, clinging to each other like caged animals with no one else to turn to. We never slept like this at home. There we had a big bed, and we each stuck to our sides of it. Even with outstretched hands we could only just touch, although sometimes I found myself crawling closer to the middle and kicking out my leg so that the edge of my big toe could touch his. We liked our space, which was why being in here had been so hard at first. Now we clung to each other, not wanting to be alone with our thoughts. The air felt damp. Despite our constant flushing of the toilet, the smell of urine remained. It mingled with the shampoo and mould-infested clothes that still lay in a heap on the shower floor. It seeped across our sanity line and into the room, and mixed with our own sweat and tears. If the lack of food didn't kill us, this would. I thought I'd imagined the flickering of a light, but I hadn't said anything. Jon was still asleep, his breathing so rapid I was sure he was right in the middle of a nightmare. The lights flickered again, and my body jerked in reaction. This time I was sure I hadn't imagined it, only I couldn't figure out if this was a good thing yet. I listened, waiting for someone to open the door, but nothing happened. Then, just as Jon stirred beside me, the lights went off.

"Jon!"

Jon jerked up in fright. "What? What's going—" I felt him sitting up next to me, his hands clamouring for mine. "What happened?"

"I don't know. The lights went off. Oh my god, Jon, what are we going to do? It's so dark."

The darkness was overwhelming. I'd been desperate for the lights to go off during our first few days, but I'd adjusted and barely thought of it anymore. Now that the lights were out, all I wanted was for them to come back on. Without a window the room was so dark I couldn't see my hand in front of my face. I turned to Jon, but all I saw was black. I squeezed his hand.

"It's going to come back on," he said. We seemed to take turns in being the positive one, and I was glad he had taken on the role now. He didn't really believe it would come back on, and we both knew it, but pretending was easier.

"I'm scared."

"Don't be. This is a good sign. It means something is going on out there. It means nobody has forgotten us."

We stayed where we were, neither of us saying a word, and both of us hoping to hear the door open. How long had we been here now? I assumed it wasn't as long as it felt, but it was hard to separate reality from my perceptions. Based on the state of my mind and body, I would say we'd been in here almost a month. Knowing we had run out of food only a day to three days ago, meant we had probably only been in here just over two weeks. There was no comfort in that thought. Time had lost meaning a while ago, and the only thing I had left to go on was the way I felt in each moment. I slept when I was tired and drank water when I was thirsty. The only thing stronger than my desire to get out of here at the moment was the need for food, and the thought of eating was becoming more and more all-encompassing. I had never known hunger like this before, no matter how many of those stupid diets I'd done in the past. What had I been thinking? I wanted to go back in time and slap my younger self. My stomach made a weird sound, which seemed louder in the dark with nothing else to focus on.

"Sorry."

"It's okay." Jon's hand was still clasped firmly in mine and I didn't want him to let go. It wasn't like he could go far in here, but I couldn't be alone.

"We're…" I couldn't bring myself to finish the sentence. We were going to die in here, in the dark. Who would go first? I didn't want to leave Jon alone in here, but I also didn't want to be in here without him. How long did we have? "Jon, how long can people survive without food?"

"We're not going to die!" This time he seemed almost angry at me, as if needed me to pretend along with him.

"Okay," I whispered.

A strong desire to pee came over me, and I suddenly couldn't remember the last time I'd been to the toilet. I'd been avoiding it, mostly because I didn't want to see the pile of clothes and be reminded of my stupidity again. It was dark now, so at least I wouldn't see it, but there was no chance I was going in there alone.

"Please come to the toilet with me." I sounded like a small child who was trying to be independent but who still needed her mother. "Of course," he said, and I breathed a sigh of relief that he would be with me.

For the first time I was glad the place was small. It was easy to navigate from the bedroom to the bathroom without worrying about what we would trip on. The smell that greeted us was not pleasant, but I tried to ignore it. We took turns, Jon suddenly needed to go at the sound of me going. Then we slowly made our way back to the bed. All plans of trying to escape had left me. What could we do in the dark? If I hadn't come up with a way out in the light, I was definitely not going to find a way out without sight. My body trembled, and Jon wrapped the duvet back around us. We weren't talking much anymore, because all conversations led back to our inevitable fate, and Jon seemed unable to muster much strength for pretence.

"I don't want us to be broken up," Jon said suddenly.

"What?" What a weird thing to say in this moment. Was this one of those life-flashing-before-your-eyes moments? That part before death where you think of regrets?

"I love you, bunny. I've always loved you."

There was a sea of emotions inside me now, colliding in the storm of my mind. Regret, sadness, disappointment, anger. Why had we come here? Why couldn't we be at home, complaining about things we had no reason to be upset about?

"I love you too, funny. I love you so much."

"I'm sorry for bringing us in here."

We were sitting flush against one another, but I pushed myself even closer to him. "Don't be sorry. At least we're together."

After weeks of living with the light on, my eyes still had not adjusted to the dark, and the title of the show had never seemed more appropriate. With nothing to rest my gaze on, I simply closed my eyes.

"Should we do some exercise? I hear there's a great kettlebell class around here," I said as images danced in front of me. At least with my eyes closed I could pretend we weren't in here.

Jon laughed a little, and the noise comforted me. The sound was like stepping into your best pair of slippers after a long day at work.

"When I get out of here, I'm going to take you out for the most incredible meal, and I'm going to stop doing stupid things."

"Where's the fun in that?" I said gently. I didn't want Jon to change. Why had it taken this experience for me to see that?

"I need to see more of Ryan, too." His voice went a little high on the 'too'.

"You will." Just like that it was my turn to be the supportive one. My turn to pretend. "We're going to have the best life together."

<u>40</u>

Ryan

Everything was taking so much longer than I anticipated, and what had started off as me thinking that maybe Jon and Keri had skipped away to elope somewhere had turned into full-blown panic. It was now the afternoon of the fifth day after the challenge was meant to end. If they were still in there, I shuddered to think how they must be feeling. If the first few days had felt so long for me, how would three weeks feel?

"They might not even still be inside," Sarah said to me, reaching for my hand.

The sudden gesture was strangely intimate for someone who didn't know me, but I gained the impression this was the sort of thing Sarah did. I barely knew her, but I could already tell she was a naturally open and tactile person. She was everything I wanted to be. I let her hold my hand, but I didn't respond. I wasn't sure if them being out of the pod was a positive thing. In a way it was worse if they were out and hadn't contacted anyone.

"There he is!" Sarah said and bounced off her chair.

Relief washed over me at the sight of her uncle in the distance. He hadn't been there when we arrived, and Sarah had insisted we wait for him rather than talk to anyone else. His meeting had gone on long, and we had waited almost two hours. What if something had happened to them in those two hours?

"Sarah, this is a surprise. What—" He noticed me standing next to his niece and frowned. "Is everything okay?"

"We need to talk to you. This is Ryan, and his friends are missing."

"Missing? How long…actually, come on, let's sit in my office. Ryan, I'm Brent." He gave me a firm handshake before heading off to his office with us in tow.

Brent was a tall man, with broad shoulders and an impressive beard. He was the sort of man who took up a lot of space, his personality as large as he was. He sat behind his desk and gestured for us to take a seat. He locked eyes with me, and told me to tell him everything. Despite his obvious 'maleness' – a trait I usually didn't like – I took an immediate liking to him. Was Sarah's whole family this likeable?

I explained the whole situation to Brent, wondering why it felt like I was talking about someone else. The story sounded so bizarre now that it didn't feel as if I'd ever been in that pod. I half expected to discover I'd made it all up. Brent listened intently, and I was glad we had waited for him.

"It's been five days?" he asked.

I nodded. "Yeah, I think so. Or was it four?" I frowned, trying to do the math.

"Doesn't matter. That's still too long. So, you already phoned the police and they wouldn't help?"

"Yeah, they said it seemed more than likely that they were just away on holiday or wanting to be left alone. Apparently kids these days do that all the time," I mimicked the officer I had spoken to.

"They do, but that doesn't mean we shouldn't investigate. Give me the name of the person you spoke to. I want a word with them. For now though, let's not worry about that. Let's concentrate on finding your friends. You said the experiment was taking place in this area?"

"Yes. We got taken to a park, and then he drove us to the place."

Brent shook his head. "Bizarre. I don't know much about TV shows, but this doesn't sound right to me. You only met one guy in this whole process?"

I nodded. "Larry. Well, and the other contestants, of course, but I already knew two of them."

"And the others?"

"A woman named Melanie, and a comedian named Elton Rigby."

"Elton Rigby." Brent sounded the name slowly, as if trying to place him.

"Real name Bob Store. I looked him up."

"And they're still in there?"

"Elton isn't. I called him. Twice. He's…well, he's not very helpful. I can give you his number if you like."

Brent bit his lower lip which was barely visible with his beard. "The other one? Melanie?"

"I have no idea. I don't know her second name." I was annoyed at myself for having such little information for him. "I'm sorry. The whole thing is a bit of a blur, to be honest. I…at the time…well, I guess I didn't think anything strange was going on."

"There was no reason for you to, but you might have more information than you think. Tell me what happened, from the time you went in, to the time you came out."

Brent made me go into more detail than I was prepared for, but the scrutiny made me remember things I hadn't thought about. The direction of the car from the park, at least the beginning of it, to the way the room looked before we went into pods. He made me log onto his computer and forward him all the email correspondence I'd had with Larry, along with any thoughts and feelings I had toward the guy.

"He had a car!" I said with excitement as I remembered the way we'd all stopped to admire it on the way in. "It was a…" I tried to remember what he'd told us. "A Chevrolet Impala. 1956. No, 1958. Blue. Like slightly brighter than light blue." Not the greatest description of such a beautiful car, but I was still pleased I had finally come up with something noteworthy. I could tell by the way Brent was scribbling furiously into his notepad that he thought so too.

"Good, good. There aren't many of those around."

"I don't think Larry drives it around, though," Sarah said. "Every time I've seen him he's been walking. He told me once that walking clears his mind."

"That's okay," Brent said. "I don't think he'd drive a car like that around anyway." He picked up his phone and began making calls, and I knew for the first time that we were onto something. "We're going to find your friends," he said to me. "You did well by coming here."

I hadn't done well. I should've come to him a long time ago. I shouldn't have given up after one policeman told me they couldn't help. I'd simply spoken to someone who wasn't in the mood to do their job that day, and I'd stopped trying.

"Sarah," Brent interrupted my thoughts and I snapped out of it. "This Larry guy. Did he seem like a bad guy?"

Sarah shook her head. I knew she had a soft spot for the guy. "No, definitely not. He's one of the sweetest guys in the world. He seemed harmless."

Brent sighed. "They always do."

41

Elton

Life continued. That was just how it went, wasn't it? It didn't matter who you were, or what you were going through, life didn't simply stop for you. It had been several weeks since I'd walked out of that pod. Every time I turned on the telly, I expected to see me sitting on the floor, ripping my joke book to shreds. It was silly, of course. It would take a long time for the show to see the light of day. There would be editing, promoting, and whatever the hell they did before *The Void* was aired. Still, I thought I'd have at least heard something from Larry or one of the producers by now. Hadn't Larry said something about an interview? Or did they already have enough footage of me making a fool of myself? I tried not to think about it too much, but the thoughts had a way of getting into my head anyway. I'd gone in there with an agenda, but things hadn't turned out the way I'd hoped. Since coming out, it had been hard to see the funny side of life. I hadn't expected to be confronted with my own reality so much. I thought being alone would be fun. I thought I would be hilarious. I thought my little one-man show would send me to stardom. The whole idea seemed so pathetic to me now. I needed another gig. I needed money.

Anyone coming to my house would assume I was doing well for myself. I made sure they thought that. A four-bedroom house, a hot tub, a bloody chandelier. I'd created a reality steeped in lies. What nobody knew about me was that every month I simply got further and further into debt. They didn't know nobody had slept in the other three bedrooms in years. They had no idea that my phone's contact list was filled with people who never called me. Only my mum called me without fail, every Monday at four. She used to call at four-thirty, giving her exactly thirty minutes to talk to me before her soapie came on. That changed when I tried to lengthen the phone call for as long as possible to make her miss the first few minutes. I would take great pleasure in hearing her squirm, trying to hurry on the conversation.

"Why are you in such a hurry?" I'd ask her. "Don't you want to speak to me?"

"Of course I want to talk to you."

"Is there somewhere you'd rather be?"

"No. Of course not."

She'd moved the call half an hour earlier, and I had never bothered with the sabotage again. Trying to find conversation for over an hour was not something that seemed worth it to me. Especially when all she really did was ask me questions I didn't want to answer. I glanced at the clock. It was quarter to four. She'd be calling any moment now. The phone rang, and I jumped. My mother always insisted on calling me on my home phone, and the loud shrill echoed in the far too large living room. Quarter to? Was there some new show she wanted to watch? Or was she hoping for a long conversation this time? She'd be foolish in thinking so, because right now I wasn't even sure if I had enough for five minutes of talk.

"Hi, Mum," I said as I always did when I picked up the phone. She always got upset with this, asking me how I could answer the phone like that without knowing who was on the other side. She clearly thought my social life was a lot bigger than it really was. I was constantly telling her about all the parties I went to, the gigs I worked at, the people I met, even if most of the time they were lies, or at least exaggerated versions of my reality.

"Is that Elton Rigby?"

I frowned. The voice on the other side was definitely not my mother's this time.

"Uh, yes. Who is this? Is my mother okay?" If this wasn't my mum, then maybe something had happened to her. Guilt tugged at my heart. I'd been particular bitter with her during our last conversation.

"Mr. Rigby. This is Officer Brent Stephenson. Do you have a minute to talk?"

42

Melanie

The door was opening.
The door was opening.
The door was opening.

I had thought of this moment for what felt like forever, and I was almost certain it wasn't really happening. As the door opened, light began to flood into the room. I was lying on the floor, unsure of how I had even gotten there, and I shut my eyes in case I was hallucinating. This wasn't real. None of this was real. I was going to wake up and be disappointed from yet another all too realistic dream.

"Melanie? Melanie, are you okay?"

A voice. A real voice.

I opened my eyes. Above me were three faces. Two men I had never seen before, and Ryan. I sat up, then held onto the floor for support as the room began to spin. No wonder I had been lying on the floor. I was too dizzy to do anything. Ryan got to his knees, and took my hand.

"Ryan," I whispered his name. "Ryan. Is that really you?"

"It's me. You're safe now."

"What? How? I…" I couldn't seem to find my voice. My mind filled with a hundred questions, but I didn't know which one to answer first. I was still too worried all of this was a dream, even though his hand felt so real in mine. "Are you real?" I finally asked.

"I'm real," he said. "You're safe. Come on, let's get you out of this room."

"Melanie, everything is going to be fine." The voice came from a man with a beard. A cop. I could tell by what he was wearing. He introduced me to his partner, but their names disappeared in my head the moment he spoke them.

They helped me up, and the sudden movement made me double over and heave. Nothing came out. I'd already thrown up the last of my meal some time ago.

"I'm sorry."

"Don't be sorry. You're fine," Ryan said. I was glad he wasn't letting go of my hand.

I noticed the cops taking in the room, and I followed their gaze. It was strange seeing the room again after being in the dark for some time. It seemed different to me now that the door was open. Less threatening. The room was a mess, as if a wild animal had been let loose inside. I saw the marks from where I'd tried to inch my way out with my pencils. Had I really thought that would work?

"Come on," Ryan said gently. "Let's get you out of this place."

I noticed how good he looked. How clean he smelled. He didn't seem like he had been trapped in a room for weeks. Was it only me then? I followed him out, blinking rapidly as we walked, my eyes still adjusting to the sudden light. It was then that I noticed the room, the one where we'd sat just before going into the pods for the first time, and I saw two familiar faces. A choke escaped me as I took them in. Keri and Jon. They looked like I felt, their faces pale, their hair damp, and bewilderment in their eyes. Our gazes met, and Keri burst out crying. I went up to them, and was surprised when Jon stood up to embrace me. Jon without the H. He seemed different to me now. Keri hugged me too, and I grimaced slightly at the smell of her hair. I didn't say anything because there was a big chance I was only smelling myself.

"What happened?" I asked them both.

"We don't know yet," she said. "They were—

She didn't finish her sentence, because one of the cops walked in with a steaming cup of tea and buttered bread rolls for all of us.

"I'm sorry. It's all I could get."

Neither of us minded what we ate, as long as we were getting something. I'd had many dreams of food while being in that pod, but this buttered bread roll was far better than anything I could've conjured up. The tea, much sweeter than I usually had it, was like drinking nectar from the gods. I almost wept as it trickled down my throat. It should be too hot to drink, but I didn't care. The burn reminded me I was alive.

<u>43</u>

Ryan

Six months later

I was fully absorbed by my bean bag, and so relaxed I was certain I had morphed into it. I cradled a beer while watching a documentary on bees. It wasn't what I wanted to watch, but the show I was enjoying had ended and I was far too lazy (or stuck) to get the remote. My phone buzzed in my pocket, mimicking the bees on the screen, which made me laugh as I answered it.

"Do you always answer the phone with a laugh?"

I smiled. There was nothing better than the sound of Sarah's voice, which now greeted me every morning and night.

"Hey, Tigger. I'm just happy to hear from you. Also, I was watching a documentary on bees."

"And, as we all know, bees are known for their comedy," she said.

"What book do bees love to read?"

"What?"

"The Great Gats-*bee*."

Sarah laughed. "That was terrible."

"You're laughing," I pointed out.

"Out of politeness," she said. Then she laughed again. "The Great Gats-*bee*! Okay, I loved it."

"It pleases me greatly that you find me funny."

"It pleases me, too. So, I've got something to tell ya."

"Should I guess?" I asked.

"Probably, but I'm too excited to wait. I've booked my tickets. I'll be there next week Wednesday."

"For…for good?" The words stuck in my throat.

"For good."

Was there such a thing as too much happiness? I had never felt this happy before, as if I was so filled with joy it was overflowing. No wonder my body felt akin to the beanbag. Happiness had made me soft. "You're really moving in with me?"

"If you'll have me."

"Oh, I'll have you."

For the past six months we'd spoken every day and met up once when she'd surprised me with a visit. Ever since that visit we'd talked about moving in together, and I'd waited for her to officially make the move. My apartment was tiny, but we didn't mind. We'd make it work. It had taken a few days in a small room alone to show me that life wasn't about where you were, but who you were with. We spoke for over an hour now, discussing the big move and making plans.

"I can't wait to spend lazy Sunday afternoons watchin' bee documentaries with you," she said.

I glanced up at the telly now, which had become background noise to me since talking to Sarah. It was then that I noticed the show had changed, and I gasped when I saw what was on.

"Sarah. I have to go. Check the telly. We're on the news."

I wiggled out of the beanbag with difficulty, and fetched the remote. With the volume on full, I sat close to the TV, feeling oddly disconnected to the story I was listening to. It wasn't the first time we'd been on the news, and for a moment I held my breath as I waited for something new to be revealed they hadn't discovered the first time around. The segment was over within minutes, followed by a more recent news story, and I finally allowed myself to relax. A photo of me had popped up on the screen when the reporter had been talking, along with the others. We'd been referred to as 'The Forgotten' even though both Elton and me had left at our own will. Instead of climbing back into the beanbag, I scooted over to lean against the sofa, reaching for the beer I'd placed on the floor.

For a while we'd all been big news, with every channel broadcasting what had happened. We'd been called in for interviews, and the story had shifted and changed depending on who was telling it. After everything had finally come out, I'd gone into hiding to get away from it all. As it turned out, I wasn't as keen for the limelight as I always thought I was. I'd stayed with Sarah, who, in such a short space of time, bounced straight into my heart. She'd taken the whole thing quite hard too, not because she knew Larry, or any of the others, but because that was the sort of person she was. It was why I had fallen in love with her.

"I miss Larry," she'd said to me the other day during one of our daily conversations.

"What do you miss about him?" I'd asked, and I could picture her smiling as she recounted what she knew about him.

"He reminded me of a child. Maybe that's why I connected with him so much. I'm like a child too sometimes, ya know? He was sweet, and caring, and…excitable. It was like he couldn't hold all his energy inside, so it came out in other ways. He had this funny little twitch sometimes, which he always got when he was excited about something."

"You don't think what he did was wrong?" I'd asked. It was a question I had asked myself since it happened.

"I think he went after his dream," she'd said, then sighed. "Maybe it was a bit wrong. It's hard for me to think that way. I mean, if it wasn't for him, I wouldn't have met ya."

That was true. It was hard to get upset about something that ended with such a good outcome. Still, that didn't make it right.

Larry Arnold Dreyton was a sixty-nine-year-old retired science and psychology teacher. He lived alone and had carved out a somewhat monotonous life for himself. He had a critical mind and a watchful eye, and if the police hadn't discovered years' worth of diaries at his home, we might never have known the full truth. Thankfully, Larry Dreyton wrote everything down, leaving no detail spared. He rose every day at 7.04, showered, and walked twenty minutes to Sarah's café. Every day he ordered two boiled eggs, white toast, and coffee. That is, of course, until the day he ordered two coffees. The day that signified the start of it all. The day my life changed. While most of his diary remained in the hands of the police, two pages had circulated through the media. Two diary entries, almost two years apart.

1 April 2016

I'm sorry I haven't written for a while. I've been too angry. My meeting with the local TV station didn't go according to plan. Nobody would even talk to me. Apparently, I needed an agent, a creative elevator pitch, followed by proof—as if that was possible—that the show would work, as well as a whole string of ridiculous things I was not prepared to go through. They also had the audacity to tell me the chance of my idea being successful was rather slim.

"It's a tough business to crack for an unknown," some gum-chewing woman had said to me when I'd phoned to follow-up the meeting. I hadn't met this woman, but she seemed the gum-chewing type.

Maybe I should've forgotten the whole thing. Maybe I should've moved on. Maybe. Maybe. Maybe. However, I'm not someone who can let things go.

I just flipped through my diary. Somehow, with all the excitement (and frustration) going on, I forgot to tell you about my plan. My big plan. The one the TV people seemed to think was a bad idea. Or, at least, a bad idea for an unknown like me.

I've been interested in solitary confinement ever since I saw a documentary about a group of guys in prison. I found the whole process so fascinating. Did we need people? Did we need distractions? What happened when we took all of that away? Would some of us cope better than others? Watching the prison show, I'd been sure I could do it. I was used to living alone. I'd never married, I didn't have a pet, and spent most of my time living in my own head. I didn't need anyone. Or so I thought. I set myself a personal challenge of one week – no phone, no internet, no books, nothing. I'd be fine, wouldn't I? Apparently even a quiet guy like me could only last two days. Despite me living alone, my days were filled with things that kept me busy, and while I loved digging into the minds of others, I didn't like it when the tables had turned to focus on me. Too much introspection had unhinged me, and I'd walked away from the experience a little unsure of my life decisions. I failed at something I thought I was good at, but the experiment stayed with me. How would others do? Could I create my own little documentary on this? The idea grew and grew and grew, until it was all I could think about. Then, one day, I knew what I wanted to do. A TV show, with a seemingly simple premise: Last two weeks and win some money. Sounds easy, right? With no clocks, and no way of telling time, it might not be as easy as they think. Come on, who wouldn't want to run a show like that? If the stations weren't willing to take this on, I'd do it all myself. I had the money. I always believed in going after what I wanted. I better go, I have some pods to build, and some contestants to find.

***

15 March 2018

It took me twenty minutes to get to the café today, five minutes shorter than usual. Even though my legs were long, my gait was slow, so it must've been my excitement propelling me faster. As usual, I was greeted by the fresh-faced Sarah. She was young, talkative, and just the right amount of crazy. Almost the way I pictured myself to be fifty years ago. I shuddered at the thought. Was I really fifty years her senior? Sarah didn't need coffee. She was bubbly enough without it. She bounced back moments later with my cup, and as usual she got it just right. When I'd first moved to Victoria Point, just over five years ago,

I'd worried I wouldn't have a regular coffee spot like I did when I lived on the Gold Coast. I was pleasantly surprised to find such a nice little place situated under one of the big gum trees that lined the street. It was in walking distance to my house, the staff were friendly, and the coffee was served just as I liked it. Sarah was busy that morning, and I wondered why the place was so much busier than usual. For a moment, I thought perhaps some of my contestants had arrived early to scout out the area—something I would've done in their position—but as I glanced around I didn't identify any of the new faces. Not that I'd met them, of course, but I'd studied their features long enough through their application forms to feel like I already knew them. The café was like that, though. One day it could just be me and the house cat for the first hour of the day, while other times the place was buzzing with people. I'd tried to identify the reason, by keeping a daily diary for six months, but I gave up after I was unable to come to a conclusion. Some things, I was starting to understand, simply could not be measured. The trip to the café that morning had been a good one, the extra coffee a break in my routine, and a symbol that my life was about to change forever. I'm in my office now, and it's taking me forever to write this out. I keep glancing up at the screens, making sure the contestants are okay. It's day one, and my heart will not stop pounding. I haven't had this much excitement since I'd stood up in front of a podium for the first time. Goes to show, if you want something badly enough, you should just go out and get it. I was proud of myself. This is what I had wanted to do for a very long time. There was nothing more intriguing than the human mind, especially when it came to discerning how far someone could be pushed. Other than the location and their sworn documents toward secrecy, I'd been very forthcoming with all of their questions. An open book, really. Well, except for one thing. I hadn't quite gotten around to telling them there was no TV show yet. I didn't see the point, really. I was sure the show would get snapped up. If not, I'd give them the money myself. What could go wrong?

***

What could go wrong? I'd seen and heard those words so many times since the diary entries had gone out. It had played in my head on a loop. As it turned out, a lot could go wrong. Larry had been sick for a long time, as his doctor's reports had shown. Maybe it was this steady decline of health which had caused him to put his dream into motion without the go-ahead from the TV station. Perhaps he wanted to leave his mark before he left the earth. How could I blame him? It made me wonder what I would do if I knew my time was almost up. Although didn't we all have a time limit? Sarah and I had discussed this at length, which was probably why we'd ended up together. Why waste time when you knew something was right?

If Larry wanted to leave this world with a legacy, he had done it. Who could forget the story about the man who had died while three people remained locked up inside self-made pods? No wonder the story was still making headlines. Of course, *The Void* never got aired, although small clips had somehow seeped out. Thankfully, there'd been none of me. At least, not yet. I'd been open about my breakdown, and I didn't mind telling people what had happened. I always thought the experience was going to change me, I just never knew how much. I called Jon.

"Did you see the news? We were on again," I told him.

"Nah, I didn't see it. Not surprised, though. I think we're on it more than we know."

"Bet you love being famous," I teased. "Hey, what's going on? Sounds like you're in a war zone," I asked as a loud bang sounded in the background.

"We're moving. Keri tried to pull a box down, and it almost fell on her head. Hey, Ke, careful, you might mess up your hair!" he yelled out.

"She's showing you the finger now, isn't she?"

"You know her well."

"Wow, so you're actually moving. I didn't think you'd go ahead with it. That place close to my parents?"

"No, didn't I tell you? Shit, sorry, I've been so busy I forgot. We found a place down the road. Literally down the road."

"Really? I thought Ke wanted to move out of the city."

"She did, until she saw this place. Hey, any chance you want to come help us pack?"

I laughed. "It's on the top of my list for things I want to do today."

"You can't blame a guy for trying."

"Just kidding. I'll be there. Ten minutes? That's if I ever get out of this bean bag."

"Mate, you're amazing. Thank you. I'll supply the beer."

"You've got a deal."

I squirmed out of the bean bag. Just thinking about Keri and Jon packing made me laugh. The two of them had gone through a rough patch after coming out of the pod, and I was sure they were going to break up. Keri had even moved in with her mum for a few weeks. Now they were inseparable and closer than ever. Which, in their case, meant most of their days was them teasing one another. Jon had celebrated his birthday a week ago, and Keri had bought him a new set of kettlebells which had made Jon laugh harder than I'd ever seen him laugh before. My gift had been tickets to a comedy show – featuring a few up-and-coming comedians, and a headlining act from Bob Store.

I grabbed my jacket and my car keys, and was about to make my way out when I noticed I had mail. It wasn't often I received anything with handwriting on it, so the envelope caught my eye. I stared at it, wondering who would take the time to write to me, then opened it. Inside lay a photo that made me smile. *So, that's where you've been.* The photo was of Melanie standing in front of the Eiffel Tower. She looked different to what I recalled of her, and from the small video clips I'd seen of her in her pod. I always thought of her as calm, and subdued, although Jon had used the word 'sad' to describe her. She didn't seem sad at all in this photo, her broad smile transforming her face and her arms up in one of those typical tourist poses. I turned the photo over to find a small note written on the other side.

Dear Ryan,

I'm sorry I haven't been in touch. I've been avoiding the media for my own personal reasons, as I'm sure you understand. I'm sorry to hear what happened to Larry, and even though what he did to us was not right, it's hard to stay angry at him. I've moved to Paris, and life is treating me well. I want you to know how much I appreciate all you did for us. I liked you from the moment I saw you, and I've always believed I was a good judge of character. Stay true to yourself, and keep happy. Life, as we all know now, is very short. I better go, I have places to explore, and a hungry cat to feed.
Lots of love,
Melanie, and Todd.

The End

Acknowledgements

I loved writing this book. At the time of writing it, I lived in South Africa, but the editing and publishing was all done in Australia. And, with a baby on his way, I'm excited for this new journey.

I want to thank my favourite human, Warren, who has supported me throughout my writing career and who always takes the time to listen to my 'grand ideas'. Thank you for always making me laugh and for always bringing me snacks.

Thank you to my family - Mom, Papa, and Pascal, for always supporting me. It is my constant goal to make you all proud. Thank you also to my friends – you know who you are. You're all crazy and I love you for it. Also, an extra big thank you to a very special alpama, who has been a constant support system this year.

A big thank you to my editor, Nerine Dorman. Your honesty is refreshing, and your feedback invaluable. I cannot thank you enough.

I cannot end off without giving thanks to my online support group – The Dragon Writers. Everyone needs a group like this.

And a special thank you to the guinea pigs. Actual guinea pigs. For general all around fluffiness.

About the Author

Christine Bernard has an obsession for good coffee, books and guinea pigs. She enjoys writing stories seeped in the psychological, no matter what the genre. She also writes children's novels under the name Chris Bee. When she's not writing, she's illustrating. When she's not writing or illustrating, she's probably at a café.

If you want to know when Christine's next book will come out, please visit her website on www.christinebernard.com and sign up to her newsletter.

Also by Christine Bernard:
Unravel
Will
Mute
Haze
Crackerjack

www.ingramcontent.com/pod-product-compliance
Lightning Source LLC
Chambersburg PA
CBHW021244060726
47590CB00005B/1894